CAPTAIN'S TREASURE

CAPTAIN'S TREASURE

NOAH SERIES
BOOK 1

JORDYN KROSS

Published by Scarlet Parlor Press, LLC

Editors: Dayna Hart, Jenny Sims

Cover: Brandi Doane McCann

Publisher's Cataloging-in-Publication
(Provided by Cassidy Cataloguing Services, Inc.).

Names: Kross, Jordyn, author.
Title: Captain's treasure / Jordyn Kross.
Description: [Albuquerque, New Mexico] : Scarlet Parlor Press, LLC, [2024] | Series: NOAH series ; book 1
Identifiers: ISBN: 978-1-959691-11-2 (paperback) | 978-1-959691-10-5 (ebook)
Subjects: LCSH: Pilots and pilotage--Fiction. | Space ships--Fiction. | Extraterrestrial beings--Fiction. | Love--Fiction. | Cargo handling--Fiction. | LCGFT: Romance fiction. | Science fiction. | Erotic fiction. | BISAC: FICTION / Romance / Science Fiction. | FICTION / Romance / Erotic.
Classification: LCC: PS3611.R776 C36 2024 | DDC: 813/.6--dc23

Library of Congress Control Number: 2024909307

For "the ladies" who always support me and whose friendship means the world to me.

GLOSSARY

Buzz - Caffeinated beverage similar to coffee mixed with an energy drink.

Cycle - Equates to approximately an old Earth day without relying on sunrise or sunset.

EMF rods - Specialized fuel that allows spaceships to cover vast distances efficiently.

ER bridges - Einstein-Rosen quantum bridges or wormholes.

GID - Galactic identification microchip.

G-year - Galactic year. Approximately 360 old Earth days. Also g-months and g-weeks.

CHAPTER 1

1017 A. N., Planet Baxianous, somewhere between the Gliese and Hedron Solar Systems

"You've been so good to me, Dezmuhnd Cuocua—so honorable —I will set you free upon my death." The old man's weary voice rattled like dried leaves on a forest floor.

Dez paused, resting the rake on the weed-free path and wiping the sweat from his bald head. He glanced back at his owner. "You are too kind, sir. But I prefer you alive."

"Ha. As do I, but we both know my time is coming." His frail hands gripped the arms of the chair Dez had placed on the paved circle in the center greenhouse. Age was winning the fight for the old man's life in the past months.

Dez shifted the rake and resumed his work. The labor helped him smother the glimmer of hope deep in his chest, where its presence wouldn't fester into dreams. No matter what his owner promised, Dez had long given up on the idea of freedom, finding his fated mate, or ever seeing the paradise where he was raised again. At least among the tall, leafy plants, Dez had the illusion of being outside. He preferred to spend as much time working with the plants as possible, but it would never compare to his lush home planet of Din' Gale. The Baxianous atmosphere, while sufficient for life, remained risky to those susceptible to ultraviolet radiation.

The bell chimed, announcing a visitor.

"Dez," his owner called, "come with me."

Dez rushed to the old man's side and carried his owner into the cool, dim foyer, gently placing him on his feet. The old man clutched Dez's arm. The once vibrant scales on his master's fingers had faded to nearly the same shade of gray as Dez's natural coloring.

A stranger in opulent, hand-embroidered robes cleared his throat. He had a satchel clutched in his bony hands.

Dez's owner addressed the housekeeper, who lingered in the shadows. "Bring drinks to my office." He tugged on Dez's arm. "Dez, you will join us."

The last time Dez had been in the office was the day he'd arrived to honor his contract. It wasn't a room he sought to enter again. After getting the old man into his chair at his desk, Dez took a step back, straightened his gray tunic, and clasped his hands in front of him, waiting for instruction.

The visitor extracted a data scroll and unfurled it on the desk. "As we discussed, the changes to your Last Will and Testament are highlighted." The visitor pointed to a glowing paragraph on the scroll. "Specifically, the release of the indentured servant, Dezmuhnd Cuocoa, and his gift of a travel stipend, the annuity for your housekeeper, and the dispersal of the remaining funds to the designated charity."

Was his owner cutting his children out of his will? Dez had only met the two sons once in all his years of living on Baxianous. It was the only time he'd been treated as property instead of a person. Perhaps his owner had realized the folly of spoiling such entitled brats.

"You can still change your mind. They are your sons—"

"No." Dez's owner waved a hand, cutting off the advocate, and picked up his stylus with the other hand.

The old man's signature on the scroll brought a lightness to Dez's chest. A chance to see his parents again. To hug his sister and finally celebrate her marriage. To be together as a family for the holidays once again. He could envision the joy on their faces as if he'd already been freed. The unreal possibility of a different future than the one he'd committed to as a lifetime of servitude was almost too big to contain inside himself.

He withheld the smile from his lips at the thought of returning home someday. He couldn't take pleasure in the thought of his master dying, even if it would mean his freedom. There was no honor in celebrating such an event, especially before it happened. But he couldn't help the images of his beautiful, lush planet that flashed through his mind or the memory of the clean air. He would have the freedom to travel where and when he wished. Perhaps, after he'd seen the planets, he would start his own farm if there were enough funds to secure a small plot of land.

The visitor rolled the scroll, shook the old man's hand, and turned. Dez caught the man's eye, and the furious coldness he found speared worry through Dez's gut. The urge to warn his master stuck behind his teeth as he clenched his jaw. There were no adequate words to convey his vague misgivings. Besides, it wasn't his place to share his *concerns* with his master.

Three short planetary months later, Dez stood in the kitchen next to the housekeeper, who was also dressed head-to-toe in black, seven days into mourning their owner. His sons had finally arrived from the far side of the large planet, but Dez's owner had already been cremated and the ashes, contained in a polished metal urn, sat on a round table in the entry. The boys, or really men, though they didn't act like it, had barely glanced at the memorial space. Shortly after their arrival, the same man who had updated the will rushed in and joined the sons in their father's office. When Dez attempted to enter the space, the eldest son dismissed him and told him to wait in the kitchen.

Dez fidgeted. Soon. He would be gone from this hellish planet soon. Released to the paradise of his true home. The announcement couldn't come quickly enough.

"You two, come to the office," the older son barked through the door he'd opened. Dez followed the housekeeper and mirrored her pose of submission, waiting for the big announcement.

The visitor rolled up the data scroll that had been open on the desk. His condescending smirk was Dez's only warning that his gut had been correct months ago—the lawyer had been in collusion with the sons.

"My father's estate has been settled. As expected, he left everything to us, his cherished sons." The older son's gaze darted from Dez to the housekeeper, watching for an argument.

Dez froze. The hope that he'd been wrong about the advocate drained from him, leaving an ice-cold anger in its wake. The lawyer had betrayed his owner, taken his credits, and likely the sons' too. For what? More credits? Honorless bastards, the lot of them.

"...disposing of the assets." His master's son had been speaking, but Dez had lost focus. "As part of that effort, your contracts will be sold at auction tomorrow. You will continue to perform your duties until your contracts are transferred. We will tolerate no slacking, no disobedience, no resistance." He crossed his arms and glared at Dez.

Dez could likely kill the weakling with his bare hands—such a coddled, useless excuse for a male—but that would only earn Dez a swift death and dishonor his family. He'd sold himself willingly and provided the funds to his sister. He had no regrets. The promise of freedom had only been a brief illusion. There was no way to prove his owner's intent to free him.

Perhaps his next owner would be as kind and easy to work for. Or maybe they might actually free him at some point.

Dez shook off the drugging thought. Hope was a wicked tool that would only invoke pain in the heart of the hopeless. He clenched his jaw and forced the fire of betrayal down before he was inspired to dispense retribution to these spoiled, conniving sons of bitches. Better to find peace with his reality and release all thoughts of seeing his family or living as a free man again.

The advocate addressed Dez and the housekeeper. "Finish your duties for the day, then wash and dress. The auction is this evening."

Dez swallowed down the urge to run from the unknown. The housekeeper shivered. Tears streaked down her face, but she too said nothing. He'd gladly speak if he could say something to comfort her, but there wasn't.

The auctioneer led Dez onto a makeshift stage in a large warehouse that evening. Bright lights blocked his view of the crowd.

"Dezmushnd Cuocua. Native of Din' Gale. Note the natural physique designed for hard labor. The contract is for life and is a voluntary state," the auctioneer bragged.

Dez held his head high, proud he wasn't a prisoner. It only meant more money for the heirs and the auction house, but at least he had his honor. The attendant had Dez spin. The form-fitting shorts they'd allowed him to wear when he refused to appear naked provided only the illusion of modesty. They were the exact gray tone of his natural skin but without his stripes. Still, his soft cock was on prominent display. At least he couldn't be sold to a breeder. Din' Gale males couldn't perform for anyone other than their mate.

He was destined for a long, celibate life of servitude, but his sister was happy and bonded to her mate. That was all that mattered. The bidding rattled on and on. Dez ignored the number as it rose higher and higher. None of the credits would go to him or his family, and there was no indication of who the bidders represented. He was just a product, and the sooner the auction concluded, the sooner he could get off the stage.

Finally, the bidding wound down. The auctioneer was pleased with the result based on his giddy tone when he said, "Sold to the Kolben Mining Company."

Dez's legs weakened. The Kolben Mines were a death sentence. If a mining accident didn't get Dez first, the wicked cold would finish him off before they ever got their investment back.

Cyra Maejzur pressed herself against a tiny bare spot at the back of the docking bay. Captain Auvi barked orders to the team bringing on the new cargo. Four handlers kept control with stiff leads attached to his wrists, neck, and waist. The captain and Varik had argued bitterly before they'd set a course for this planet to accept the contract. It was the disagreement that had her sneaking into the bay. But the lack of drama disappointed. She'd expected a raging criminal or a feral beast. Granted, the male was tall and muscular, wore a shock collar, and was guarded like a deadly threat, but he didn't make a fuss. He calmly walked on board *The Treasure*, his muscles relaxed and his face impassive.

Doc Maretine used a med-scanner on the...prisoner? Passenger? Cargo. The male's bald head turned in her direction, and his dark yellow eyes narrowed, pinning her in place. His gaze left her exposed, and her gills fluttered as fear rushed through her veins. No, not fear—it was closer to anticipation, similar to the feeling she'd had when she'd run away all those years ago and boarded Captain Auvi's ship for the first time. Anticipation of the unknown and recognition that the events might put her at risk. But the pull to this male was something else, something more dangerous than running away. Her heart sped, and her skin tingled. She warred between boldly stepping forward to confront the possible threat and wisely pressing deeper into the shadows.

The fact she shouldn't be in the docking bay at all kept her in place. Captain would be pissed if she exposed herself after his warning about unsafe cargo. They already had a load of deadly spiders, and, supposedly, this male was just as big a threat. Doc finished his assessment and pronounced the male disease-free. The crew led him deeper into the ship to confine him to a cell in the cargo hold. Captain Auvi turned for the deck. Cyra held her breath.

Varik passed her and paused. "I see you. Should I tell Auvi his precious princess defied his order?"

Cyra bit her tongue. What could she say? Varik would tell or not. Either way, she had no defense.

His brief chuckle held no mirth. "You don't fool me with this innocent good girl act. I know you for the siren you are, and soon, Auvi will see it too."

His parting footsteps echoed through the empty bay like a death drum.

Cyra rushed back to her quarters. Several minutes later, the shaking stopped. Before she could really calm herself down, Captain Auvi summoned her to the bridge.

The crew of *The Treasure* scurried to their positions in preparation for launch. Appendages flew across the digital panels to control the ship. Comms came in from the hangar crew authorizing the ship to leave the facility. The ship glided out onto an available launchpad. Captain Auvi stood in the center behind the thrust console and barked orders. "Set a course for Cassan."

"Aye, Captain," the navigator replied.

"Engineer Varik," Captain barked. "All systems ready?"

"Everything but the boost to leave the atmosphere, Captain." Didn't Captain Auvi hear the sneer in Varik's voice?

"Cyra, to me." Captain Auvi sat behind a U-shaped panel of controls.

She hustled over, and he pulled her onto his lap with a single tentacle as soon as she was within reach. "Ready?"

"Yes, Captain," she said with as much respect as she could to make up for Varik's slight to his authority.

Engines hummed. Crew confirmed settings, preparing to launch back into space.

"Countdown to launch." Captain Auvi's tentacles wrapped around Cyra's thighs. He pulled her legs apart, causing her gauzy dress to ride up her legs. His turquoise and sand circular markings contrasted with her ocean blue skin, reminding her of her home planet. Other tentacles held her arms and caressed her breasts under the thin fabric. She leaned her head back against his cool flesh and closed her eyes, shutting out the other crew members, especially Varik. Even before she'd become the captain's latest launch assistant, Varik had gone out of his way to make her life miserable in every petty way possible. Somehow, he'd convinced the rest of the crew that she shouldn't be on the ship at all. That she was useless.

But Varik's eyes were always on her, even when she wasn't helping Captain Auvi launch the ship. Varik's gaze overflowed with lust and jealousy, envy and betrayal as if he hadn't been the one to use her and toss her away. His hatred was never so intense as when her captain's flexible appendages wrapped around her to drive her to orgasm.

Screw him.

He deserved the chance to experience the desperate despair of being discarded by a lover. One more reason she allowed the captain to use her to power *The Treasure* into space.

Energy thrummed through her—core quivering, thighs squeezing, even her fingertips tingled. The engines of the ship revved to full power, the vibrations transferring through her body. The ship lifted from the pad, gaining altitude. Auvi continued to tease and stroke her. Occasionally, a sucker latched onto her clit, giving her a tugging kiss. An image of the gray man between her thighs flashed before her eyes. She shook, holding back her cries of approval, gripping the arms of the captain's chair to hold herself together as he took her apart. Auvi was always so careful never to penetrate her. A fact her core regretted and her brain appreciated.

"Ready for exit, Captain," a pilot called.

Her body went rigid with pleasure.

"Now, Cyra," the captain spoke in a low voice, for her ears only. "Place your hands now."

Cyra tilted forward and slapped her palms onto the two red circles of the control panel just as her orgasm hit. The circles illuminated, and a sensation of being sucked into the console traveled up her arms. The ship lurched up, fire erupting from the engines. Captain Auvi continued to rub his sex organ against her until she burst. Energy exploded through her body and out her hands, providing the boost required to break the atmosphere around the planet.

He held her in place as the gravitational forces pressed her into his rubbery flesh. The pressure made her pleasure more intense than anything she could create in the privacy of her quarters. She clenched her jaw to hold back the scream her body naturally tried to release. She might be fine with being an exhibitionist, like Captain Auvi, but she doubted the rest of the crew enjoyed being forced voyeurs. If she kept quiet, they could concentrate on their jobs and pretend two beings weren't having sex behind them.

He soothed her as she floated down, petting her hair and

stroking her skin until her gills quit flapping and she relaxed completely. "Perfect," he whispered in her ear before letting her go.

"Varik," the captain snapped at the engineer who continued to stare at Cyra. "Go check the cargo."

"Is that really the best use of my time, Captain? Shouldn't your med crew or your transport crew be in charge of your creepy-crawly cargo?"

Cyra shivered, both at Varik's snide tone and the thought of the poisonous spiders running around the ship. Technically, they were confined to the cargo hold designed for live transport, but she still recoiled at the idea of having such dangerous creatures on board. They weren't the only threatening beings on the ship. The captain could be just as deadly as the spider's bite if he was in the wrong mood to put up with an impudent crew member. Something Varik should keep in mind.

"I gave you an order." Auvi released her, and she rushed from the deck to avoid the brewing fight. The wet room would provide the relief she sought after a successful launch. On any other ship, she would struggle to stay healthy, coating her skin in saltwater washes as many times a day as she could. Captain Auvi, also from Chalcanth, had fitted the ship with its own special tank filled with salt water chemically altered to remain in gel form until it warmed with body heat. He was kind enough to allow her to use it freely. But she only did so when Varik was on duty. She dreaded ever running into him in the closed rooms.

In the wet room, she removed her dress, closed the water-tight interior door, and slipped through the seal into the tank. The gel liquefied around her, allowing her to swim underwater without ever encountering a solid spot. Captain Auvi often complained that the medium didn't liquefy sufficiently, but she still found him in the chamber more often than not. Would he stay on deck or join her?

She preferred solo swims, using the private time to think and imagine—like she'd imagined the gray bald head at her pussy. A shiver ran up her spine, and she pushed away the fact that the gray man had interrupted the launch sequence.

The familiar dream of what her life might be like when *she* was a transport ship captain wiped him away completely. She focused on logistics over random lust. How would she deal with crew in-fighting? How would she run the ship? What changes would she make? She'd decided that she would have a water chamber on her ship, no matter the cost.

What would have happened to her if Captain Auvi hadn't taken in the ragged runaway five galactic years ago? She owed him her life. He'd taught her everything about running a ship, from maintenance to navigation. Only recently had she become his launch assistant. The first time he'd wrapped his tentacles around her and explained what he would do, she'd nearly come just from his description.

"Take off your panties, Cyra. Don't wear them on deck again. Now, I will wrap you in my arms and stroke every bit of your skin, covering you in my oil. It will excite you, lighting up every nerve ending until my touch won't be enough, and you'll beg me to touch you more intimately. Beg me to fuck you. I won't, but I'll make you come like you've never experienced. And all of that energy will be transferred directly to the ship's launch engines. You will power us into space."

Since then, she'd been eager to help the captain every chance she had. She loved him, not romantically despite their interactions, but in a hero, savior kind of way. It was messy and not entirely healthy, but she'd left her planet to avoid having a mate. Captain Auvi provided the perfect excuse to hold herself aloof from the crew, and she still had her needs met. It was a perfectly imperfect compromise.

Cyra roused herself to exit the water chamber. In the antechamber, she dried off, dropped her dress over her head, and reached for the door. A sharp pain razored through her, taking her to her knees. She ran her hands over her clothes, panting to release the terrifying pain, searching for a source. Nothing was physically wrong with her. But she'd been stabbed in the brain and the heart simultaneously. As quickly as it hit her, the pain passed. An empty ache remained that made no sense. Silent tears fell from her eyes. The urge to curl into a ball on the floor was nearly overwhelming. But the risk of being discovered in a weakened state by Varik motivated her to drag herself to her quarters.

CHAPTER 3

"Captain, a word?" Varik's seductive voice echoed up the tubular hallway that connected the bridge to the rest of the ship.

Auvi swiveled his upper torso to face his former lover. The male was still as captivating as the first moment Auvi had seen him. Tall, lean, pale blue skin, with eyes and hair so dark Auvi would've sworn they were black instead of the deepest shade of green. But his aching, racing-heart reaction to the Chalcanthian male had been replaced with the sick, swirling bile of betrayal. The only reason he kept him on the crew was because no better engineer existed in the galaxy.

No, that was a lie.

In truth, he couldn't quite give up his attachment to the love of his life. Even if Varik's presence made Auvi murderous, sending him away would be unrecoverable. He was the only being who'd ever tied Auvi's tentacles in knots.

Auvi sighed, longing for a future that didn't exist. "Make it quick. I'm meeting Cyra."

"We need to talk about her and her place on this ship." Varik closed the distance between them.

Auvi resisted the urge to step back or to clutch the male to his chest, both of which warred within him. "Why would her role on *my* ship be any of your business?"

"There was a time you trusted my opinion." Varik's voice took on a coaxing quality, and Auvi shifted away.

"I think we both know why that ship sailed."

"You got it all wrong." Varik shook his head. "But I'm not here to talk about us."

Another lie. Auvi glanced down the hall, longing for the privacy of his quarters.

"What do you really know about this girl? A vagabond you picked up because of some sob story. And now, she's like your first mate in all senses of the word."

So Varik believed Cyra was Auvi's lover? That explained some of his angst and gave Auvi a perverse pleasure.

"In a short time she's gone from being an underfoot intern who could barely run a comms unit to launch assistant?" Varik crossed his arms. "What's next? Engineering?"

Auvi would never put Cyra under Varik's authority. "I'm the captain. I place people where they are best suited." Except Varik was best suited to be shot out an airlock, but Auvi couldn't bring himself to murder the treasonous bastard. Or even kick him off *The Treasure* at the next port as he should have done when he'd first discovered Varik's double-crossing plans. If only he knew why, but even if he asked, Varik would lie. Their conversation had dragged on too long as it was.

"I know what I did was wrong. But it was one lapse. I've been loyal to you for years. I'm still loyal." Varik grazed his fingers down one of Auvi's tentacles. "You have to miss us as much as I do."

Auvi shuddered internally. His former lover's touch still ignited him, but the involuntary reaction disgusted him. There was no future with the betrayer.

"I'm going to prove myself to you again, get back what we

had. And if my efforts expose that female for the fraud she is, so be it."

"Anything else? I'm late." Auvi made his tone purposely cold. Varik could turn any argument. His power of persuasion kept them together far longer than Auvi should have allowed. The signs had been there all along.

Silently, Auvi resumed his trek down the corridor. The prospect of searching for a new engineer daunted him, but he could no longer avoid the task. Varik had obviously decided Cyra was the only reason they weren't back together. Auvi blamed himself for that. And by perpetuating the deception, he'd put Cyra in danger.

"I will get you back," Varik called out behind him.

Not a chance.

The temptation to go to the wet room was strong, but Cyra was likely there and preferred her privacy. He'd gone earlier that cycle to prepare for the ER bridge crossing. Traveling the wormhole while dehydrated was an experience he preferred never to repeat. He returned to his cabin and locked the door. After taking care of some urgent correspondence, he checked the listings for engineers looking for work. Perhaps he could pick up a new hire on Cassan station to complete the delivery leg of this transport.

A yellow light flashed, and an announcement that the ER bridge crossing was one galactic hour away echoed through the ship.

There—that listing looked promising. A female. Exceptional training. Former captain of her own ship. There was a story there. Auvi would like to hear it. He typed a quick message to send after the crossing. A scratching sound dragged his attention from the video screen. Odd.

Scritch. Scritch, scritch.

Of all the noises the ship made, he'd never heard that before.

Auvi stood, scanning his room. The noise came from above.

He shifted his gaze, catching movement as the creature dropped.

Eight pointed legs dug into his soft head.

CHAPTER 4

AN INCESSANT CHIME reverberated through Cyra's quarters, demanding she wake up. Confused and groggy from the sleep aid she'd taken to deal with the bridge crossing, she had no idea what time it was. Had she overslept?

"What?" Cyra asked as the door slid open.

"Cyr." Her best friend, Veda, peered up at her with puffy eyes. "It's terrible." Veda *never* cried. She nurtured in a stoic, calm manner fit for a physician.

"What's happened?" Cyra crouched down to Veda's level.

"It's the captain." Veda choked on a sob.

The phantom agony Cyra experienced in the wet room came flooding back. She lurched up. Wide awake, the pain made sense—Captain Auvi. She'd had episodes in the past, when she was much younger, where she'd felt another's pain, like when her mother gave birth to her siblings. It had only happened with those she was very close to. "Is he going to be okay?"

"Doc'll be here to explain everything as soon as he can." Veda took Cyra's hand and guided her back into the room, closing the door and setting the lock. "I'll stay with you."

Cyra moved, but it was as if she was watching herself from

above. She shuffled across the floor as if she were floating. The gravity emulator could have been turned off for all she was aware of what was happening. It was too soon to lose Captain Auvi. No one else cared for her the way he did. Her captain had to survive.

Veda pointed at a chair, and Cyra sat, unaware of how much time had passed until Doc gripped her hands, sending warmth through her icy fingers. "I'm so sorry, dear."

Cyra saw the truth in his eyes. She heard it in his voice, soft and hesitant. The truth she'd held in since Veda had come to her door—Captain Auvi was dead. Her heart cracked into pieces. "How?"

"It appears to be sudden system failure. He was fine after the launch. He left the deck and returned to his quarters, according to several crewmembers, but he didn't come to the galley for last-meal as expected after we crossed the bridge. I had to override his door—" The doctor took a deep breath. His face morphed into a mask of resignation and regret. "There was nothing I could do."

Tears ran down her face for Captain Auvi and for herself. His death terminated her future. The amount she'd saved wasn't near enough for her own ship. No way she could remain on *The Treasure* with Varik as captain—him demanding she help him with the launch.

She shuddered.

Never.

"Cyra. Listen to me," Doc commanded.

She sucked in a breath and lifted her chin.

"Captain Auvi spoke with me a few g-months ago. He made changes to the title of the ship. Changes no one else knows about. Varik will assume the interim captaincy until we reach the Cassan Space Station. He believes he'll only need to notify the authorities of the captain's death, and he'll be given title to the ship. That's not the case." The doctor paused, and his gaze drilled into her.

She nodded.

"I don't have any way to prove this death was anything other than natural causes. The Hapolochians decay so rapidly after death that it would be impossible for me to tell if something or someone had a hand in his demise. Nothing suggests Auvi didn't seal his quarters himself. No one else is recorded as being in the room. So we have to act as if what appears to be true is true. Do you understand?"

Cyra twisted her fingers together, considering Doc's words. There was a possibility that someone had killed the captain? That someone was still on the ship? If they felt threatened... She nodded, her gaze locked on his watery brown eyes.

"Good. Now, Captain Varik asked that you join him on deck, but I'll give you a sedative instead because you're so over-wrought." Doc paused until she gave a slight nod of understanding. "I'll explain you're unable to join him for the foreseeable future. Veda will stay with you to make sure you don't have an adverse reaction to the injection."

Cyra stood and impulsively hugged the doctor. "Thank you, Doc."

"I may be retiring, but I have some time left to help set things right."

It was a kind sentiment, but with Captain Auvi gone, nothing would ever be right again.

***

"I'm going." Cyra combed her hair, fighting the fatigue of carrying so much sorrow. "It's the least I can do."

Veda tugged on her robes, plucking the seams. "If Varik sees you—"

"It will only confirm what you and Doc have told him—how distraught and unable to function I am." Cyra dropped her comb into the vanity drawer and closed it. "Captain Auvi would attend if the situation were reversed, no matter the risk."

The door chimed. Veda admitted Doc.

"Are you sure about this?" he asked.

Cyra stepped around him. "I don't want to be late."

Flanked by Veda and Doc, she proceeded through *The Treasure*. The large metal-clad corridors filled with more and more crew members, their feet pounding like death drums, the closer they got to the lower, port-side deck. Varik stood at the front, puffed up like an ice bird of Kolben—deadly as one too. Cyra ducked her head, unable to tolerate the sight of Varik assuming the role of leader. The last thing Captain Auvi would want is to have his betrayer lead his funeral ceremony. But the dead had no say in what happened after they were gone, no matter what they'd planned while they were alive.

Fortunately, Varik's words were swift if not heartfelt. A bag on a metal gurney was rolled close to the airlock. With a shudder, Cyra recognized the biohazard label and what it meant. She whipped her gaze to Doc.

"His remains liquefied. We had to scrape together what we could."

Her stomach churned. For as strong and regal as her captain had been, to be ejected in a waste bag into space was the ultimate indignity. The portal sealed. The outside vent opened, and the bag whisked out the tube into the endless darkness. Cyra's legs went weak. She clung to Doc.

"Quite a show you're putting on." Varik's dark tone oozed over her.

Veda grabbed Cyra's arm. Doc and Veda guided her away. Doc called back, "I'm returning her to her quarters. She shouldn't have attended. It was too much."

The phantom itch between her shoulder blades demanded she glance back, but she refused to meet Varik's eyes again. He could glare at her all he wanted because she'd be off his ship as soon as they docked.

Back in her cabin, she curled into a ball on her bed and wept.

Veda continued to bring her food at regular intervals. Most of it went untouched.

"Cyr, you have to get up." Veda tugged her from her bunk. "It's the pre-dock meal." Captain Auvi's tradition dictated all available crew gather for a parting as a way to build unity.

Cyra let Veda bully her through the motions of cleaning up and putting on a fresh uniform.

A line of folding tables ran along the corridor outside the standard mess area, which was too small to hold the entire crew all at once. Cyra retrieved the special tray Captain Auvi had purchased for her from a lower storage cabinet in the galley. It held her food divided so different things wouldn't touch. She choked on her grief, clutching the tray to her chest. She missed him so much.

From the buffet line, she filled the wells with tiny bits of food with Veda's help. They sat at one of the emptier tables, and Varik placed his piled plate across from them. Cyra's stomach rose in her throat.

"Cyra, so good of you to join us. You appear much recovered." Varik's smarmy voice was as disgusting as his plate.

"Thank you," she said softly, thankful to be seated between Doc and Veda.

"We'll be docking at Cassan in a cycle."

Cyra didn't respond. Stopping at the space station was standard, and he hadn't asked a question. Where was he going with the comment?

"I'll be informing the authorities that Auvi Thenal has died."

"You mean *Captain* Auvi?"

"I'm the captain now. I will inform them of the death so that his assets can be transferred as he instructed. It would be best if you remain on the ship since you've been so ill."

"No." She shook her head.

"No?" He jerked his gaze from his food to her.

"I have some things to take care of. I'll be off the ship for several hours."

Varik sputtered, his face purpled with rage. Why was he so angry? If anything, she expected him to kick her off as soon as they docked. His hatred of her wasn't a secret.

"Captain Varik, she respectfully declined your request." Doc's voice was calm and controlled. "At this time, you are the interim captain. Once you become the official captain, you can, of course, set any rules you want for your crew. I suspect you will need to re-sign the existing crew as their contracts technically expired when Captain Thenal died."

Varik glanced around. The nearby crew watched the show. He tugged his uniform and picked up his fork. "Right, of course. If you feel that Cyra can travel off the ship without ill effects to her health, then, by all means, she should go."

The meal continued in uneasy silence. Right before everyone rose to leave, Varik spoke. "Doc? Is it still your intention to retire after we land at Cassan?" He tried to sound casual. "I just ask so that I know how many contracts I need to have drafted."

"This is my last trip on *The Treasure*. I'll miss the ship and the crew, but I'll enjoy spending my remaining time relaxing in paradise. But please let me know if I can be of assistance before we arrive."

"A status report on our living cargo. I need to know that my

—*our* investment is healthy and this detour, necessary as it is, won't impact the quality of our goods."

"Yes, Captain." Doc rose and gestured politely for Cyra and Veda to leave first, then followed them closely.

Cyra glanced back and caught the calculating scowl on Varik's face before he smoothed it and turned away. A cold chill shifted up her neck, leaving her with a headache and a gut full of worry.

CHAPTER 5

CYRA PACED IN HER QUARTERS. Doc's plan required too much waiting and too little certainty, but she didn't have a better one. Finally, the Cassan station master cleared the ship to dock. Cassan was a huge manmade station—a city without a planet. The docks were cavernous, multitiered structures with the ability to store spaceships stacked and packed like protein bars in a box. Hangars opened and encapsulated the space-crafts, creating airtight seals around each one. Decontamination units automatically deployed. The ships and crews were cleared of radiation and foreign bodies before access was granted to the rest of the station. *The Treasure's* hazardous, live cargo caused the approval to take longer than usual.

As soon as they entered the hangar—freed from the protective bubble—Doc arrived at Cyra's quarters and escorted her to the lower-level loading dock.

Varik, dressed in a pristine flight suit, practically vibrated as he stared at the dock's door as if he could open it by will alone.

Cyra hung back, partially hidden by Doc. A beep sounded twice, and the loading bay ramp lock clicked, releasing the wide metal panel to lower and slowly reveal the inside of their sealed hangar through the gap. Gray metal panels, as big as a quarter of the ship, were welded together to form the giant cell of the bay. Beings in white hazmat suits waited to guide them to the decon units.

Varik took the first steps down the ramp before it had settled on the floor. He spoke over his shoulder to the gathered crew members. "I expect you to be here in two hours when I return, at which time we will complete the new contracts."

None of the crew members made eye contact or even nodded in acknowledgment to Cyra or Doc on their way down the ramp. Their avoidance didn't bode well.

Doc called out to Varik, "I believe you will need me to record the death and its cause as the captain's physician."

"What?" Varik whipped around midway down the ramp.

"You'll need me to sign off on the cause of death and certify there was no external influence." Doc slowly descended toward Varik.

Varik grunted. "Come with me."

"Cyra, you should come with us as well." Doc held out his hand toward her.

"Why would you think *she* needs to be there?" Varik asked. His narrowed eyes burned into her.

"They may want another witness. Cyra was closest to him, spent time with him prior to his passing, and she may have been the last one to see him alive." Doc's voice was level and a bit condescending.

"Whatever. I don't have time to argue. Those spiders have to get delivered on time, or I'll lose a fortune."

"I've asked Veda to stay on board. Keep an eye on all the cargo." Doc held Cyra by the elbow, guiding her down the rough ramp.

"The station has assigned us additional security," Varik said over his shoulder.

"They're required to remain *outside* the ship." Doc's voice carried over the mechanical hum of the bay.

Varik huffed and entered a decontamination tube. Doc and Cyra followed. Finally cleared, they shuffled into the chaos that was the station. Although not her first visit, the massive number of beings and businesses within Cassan once again overwhelmed and awed Cyra. There were med centers that specialized in particular species as well as general medical facilities. Every product in the galaxy was available for purchase. Restaurants and bars and live shows. Sex workers and playgrounds. Cinemas and sports competitions—both Old Earth and anti-grav. Cassan accommodated everyone and everything.

There could be anywhere from one to five million sentient beings inhabiting or traveling through the station at any one time. She loved that she could buy the things she wanted, but the sheer number of bodies made her want to curl up in a ball and rock back and forth until the nightmare ended. That was her inner child. Her grown-up self trailed Doc and kept her eyes focused down and just in front of her to block out all the flashing lights, moving bodies, and interior transport vehicles. Although she'd never had a reason to visit the official galaxy offices and wasn't sure how far they had to go, she could do this. Doc wanted her there for some reason that he had not disclosed. Something to do with *The Treasure*. So she'd face her fear of crowds for him and for Captain Auvi.

Cyra shifted on the bench in the records office, waiting for their number to be called. Her ass was numb, and she was bored out of her mind in the bland, once-white-turned-gray room. The only distraction was a station feed into a video display mounted at ceiling level, delivering a nonstop stream of advertising. The ads for species-specific restaurants, clothing for unique body shapes, and questionable entertainment were already repeating.

Finally, they were called. She stood just to get her blood moving through her legs again. Varik was already at the video screen addressing the records clerk, who was somewhere deeper in the locked-off part of the offices.

"I need to report a death," Varik told the bored-looking Nelite. The species often occupied customer service jobs as their egg-shaped bodies and lack of emotion worked to their advantage.

"Credentials? Certificate?"

Doc stepped forward, forcing Varik to back up. "I was the attending physician, Doctor Alfred Maretine," he said, holding his arm to the scanner to present his galaxy identification.

"Name of the deceased?"

"Auvi Thenal."

"Do you have his recovered GID?"

"Here." Doc slid a clear bag containing the chip that had been embedded in Captain Auvi's primary right tentacle through a slot below the screen.

"Cause of death?"

"Unspecified natural causes."

"Date of death?"

The questions went on from there in a rote manner. The more clinical questions the records representative asked, the more twisted Cyra's guts became. Was this all there was when so great a being passed? There should be rending of clothes and stoppage of work. The heavens should weep, and the stars should go dark. How could his life matter so little now? She was disheartened and humbled because her passing would be met with even less concern.

"I have an updated property transfer record." The display

shifted from the representative to a full-screen view of the document. It was clear enough that Cyra could read it over Doc's shoulder. Captain Auvi had left his ship to her.

Her legs weakened, and she braced against the counter.

"Is there any other document of record to be recorded?" the clerk asked.

"No," Doc answered firmly.

"The death record is finalized. The titles of any and all solely owned property are now in the name of Cyra Meajzur, GID number 380943.8905468.78900001.AQUDelta998. Is there anything else that you require?"

"No." Doc turned to Cyra. "Where's Varik?"

"Huh?" Cyra asked, startled out of her disbelief. She turned to where Varik had been last, but he was gone. "He was just here."

"Let's go. The credit union. Now." Doc grabbed her hand and started dragging her through the crowds at a much faster pace than they had used to get to the records office. "The credit accounts—"

Doc's comm rang with a shrill tone. He stopped. Cyra jerked to a halt to keep from plowing into him. "Veda. What's wrong?"

Veda's distressed voice carried through the speakers. "Don't come back. The spiders are loose. I've sealed the cargo bay."

Cyra's heart skipped. The deadly spiders were loose on *The Treasure*? What about the male that had been brought on board? If he was locked in with them—

"I'll get Dez out —"

"Get off that ship. I'll alert the station."

Doc ended the transmission and punched more buttons on his comm.

"We have to get back to her." Cyra grabbed Doc's sleeve, tugging him toward the dock.

"If I know Varik, he's already on the way to empty the accounts. If we don't stop him, you'll have nothing."

"You can't know that's where he went. And this is Veda." Her dearest and only friend.

"She's capable of getting to safety."

Cyra shook her head. The spiders could be anywhere on that enormous ship. One bite and her friend would be dead. But if Doc was right and Varik was taking all the funds to run *The Treasure*, she'd have no way to keep the ship. Wouldn't even be able to pay the docking fees to leave Cassan. Besides, Doc was being a pessimist. Varik wouldn't be able to do anything without a death certificate, and Auvi's instructions left everything to her.

"It's your call, Captain."

Cyra snapped her gaze to Doc. "What?"

"As of a few moments ago, you're the captain of *The Trea-sure*. You're in command." A passerby bumped into Cyra's shoulder, causing her to wobble. She grabbed Doc's arm.

Credits? Or Veda?

"We're going back to the ship. Now." The bodies filling the thoroughfares of the station parted like the sea for her. She wasn't thick or broad, but she was very tall, and she could move. The fear for her friend and her own future warred within her. If she was wrong, and Varik got the accounts—no. She'd deal with that possibility later. Her friend's safety came first.

CHAPTER 6

"We have to get out. Now." A short, curvy, brown-skinned female threw open the door to Dez's cell. She wore a white suit that bagged on her short frame and carried a helmet under her arm.

He stood but didn't move so as not to frighten her, although she already appeared agitated—her wide-eyed gaze darted around his cell and back over her shoulder. "What's wrong?"

"The spiders—they're deadly. One bite—" A large black blob scurried across the ceiling not three meters away from the panicked female. She tossed a bag at him. "Put this suit on. We have to get out of here."

Dez tugged the top open, and the contents expanded. The material was light but thick, unlike any he'd encountered before. He slipped a leg into one hole, forcing his boot into the foot space. The fabric stretched, but it was still a tight squeeze.

"Hurry." The female put the helmet over her head.

Once he had the coverall over his lower half, he had to tug the suit over his shoulders. The female reached for the suit's closure. He stepped out of her reach and sealed himself in. She pointed at the helmet, and he fitted it over his head, grateful that it, at least, was roomy.

"Follow me." The voice came through a speaker in the helmet.

Dez nodded.

She scouted their exit and darted forward. A black blob dropped behind her. Dez booted it out of the path, wrapped one suited arm around the female's middle, and ran for the deck where he'd first entered the ship.

She squeaked. The noise came through some audio device in the helmet. "Put me down."

But Dez had no intention of waiting for her short legs to cover the distance they had to travel. He'd deal with the consequences after they were safe. With the suit on, the customs of his world were respected, at least in principle. They reached the loading bay in moments, and the ramp was already down. He set his cargo at the edge. "Call the station security for help."

She started down the gangplank, comms already in her hands.

He called out to her, "Which way to the galley?"

She turned, her brow wrinkled. "It's back at that Y. Take the leg that doesn't lead to the cargo area. But you need to—"

Her feet cleared the ramp. He pressed the button to his left, and the ramp lifted to close. The female squawked again. He spun and ran, praying he'd find what he required. The galley turned out to be spacious, with a single large table bolted to the floor. He grabbed a chair back for leverage as he raced toward the cupboards and nearly landed on his ass when the seat spun. Fancy but not helpful.

He ripped open doors, not bothering to close them. On the lower left side, tucked in a corner, he hit pure gold. Concentrated capsaicin oil. He tugged the container free from where it had adhered to the shelf. Apparently, the ship's crew wasn't much for spicy food. That explained the crap he'd been eating since he'd come aboard. Edible but bland.

In another cabinet, he found a cleanser in a spray bottle. He poured out half the contents, added the oil, and tested the mist. Too direct. He adjusted the nozzle so a wide, fine spray burst out with every squeeze. Perfect. Time to hunt some creepy-crawlies.

In the corridor, he scanned the ceiling. Nothing...yet. He turned right, toward the cargo bay. His gut warred with his feet, arguing that he should run away from, not toward, the threat. But if the deadly spiders escaped onto Cassan, who knew how many people could be hurt. Better to contain the threat, only risking himself.

Cyra raced through the aisles between the berths. The docking area of Cassan had never been so impossibly big. Air heaved in her lungs, her gills flapping so fast they vibrated. She'd lost Doc somewhere in the central commerce area, and he'd told her to leave him. She'd hated to do it, but he was a grown man and not facing killer critters like her best friend. Hell, her only friend.

Finally, she got to *The Treasure's* berth. The docking crew was absent. Veda must have notified them about the breach. She cleared the isolation entrance and finally made it into her bay. Her eyes watered, burning from the air. She sneezed.

A small being in a hazmat suit approached her. Veda's face peered at her through the clear visor. Cyra took the respirator mask in Veda's hand and placed it over her face. The audio connection synced, and Veda's voice came through. "They're venting the room. It should only be a few minutes before we can take this off. You're lucky you didn't get here sooner. You wouldn't have made it three steps in."

"What happened?"

"The guy in cargo?"

The large, muscular man appeared as if he'd heard them talking about him. His maskless face was void of emotion, and the air didn't seem to affect him. Cyra couldn't take her eyes off him as he came down *The Treasure's* ramp, squeezed into a hazmat suit that fit him like a second skin. His muscles rippled with each movement—a confident conqueror returning from battle.

"He was amazing," Veda continued.

Cyra couldn't argue.

"I freed him from his cargo cell. And then he got me off the ship and went back in. He made chile oil spray to corral the spiders back to the safety of their container. But it was so strong on the ship that the support crew couldn't breathe. They vented it out here."

The man stalked her, his yellow gaze heating her. Cyra's fluttery anticipation returned. What was it about this male that made her insides giddy? It was a ridiculous reaction. She was the captain; she couldn't be acting like a schoolgirl with a crush.

"The security crew is closing the container." His low voice vibrated Cyra's insides in a completely different way—lower, deeper. "They're asking for a manifest to verify the count. Make sure none are still loose." He spoke to Veda, but his gaze never left Cyra.

"How?" The word escaped with her breath.

"I have the documentation for the shipment," Veda replied. "Is it safe for me to go to the lab?"

The man's head pivoted between them. "I see your lips moving behind the shield, but I can't hear you."

Cyra removed her respirator. The air was much less caustic. "She said she can get the paperwork if it's safe to go back on board."

His powerful shoulders lifted and dropped. "Assuming we have them all back in the box, yes."

Cyra nodded at Veda, who shuffled off in the voluminous folds of her hazmat suit.

Alone. Cyra was alone with the big gray male, and the intimacy weighed on her chest, as if he was pressed against her instead of standing half a meter away. She shivered and steeled her spine. "Thank you for saving Veda—Dr. Artz. And for your help with containing the cargo."

He shifted slightly closer. "It is my honor to help. Where is your captain? Thenal? He should be here to oversee this." His brow wrinkled. "Or the maintenance crew? I found no one else on the ship."

"Captain Auvi died." Tears pricked at Cyra's eyes. "I'm the captain of *The Treasure* now."

Her comm pinged with a group text sound. She glanced at the screen. Varik sent the entire crew a message. Had he heard about the spiders? How could he? Cyra tapped her device to read the shared memo. The comm slipped from her hands. The gray man caught it before it shattered on the dock floor.

The absolute gall of that bastard to lie to the entire crew. Cyra shook, and the image of Varik's taunting face grinning over his win filled her vision, blocking out the reality of the cavernous dock and hero of a male in front of her. She balled her hands and forced the threat of angry tears back down. How much more was she expected to take?

"I assume you received bad news?" The male's voice petted her.

Cyra took a deep, steadying breath. "You could say that. The first engineer just sent a message to the entire crew that I'm the new captain but that I have no money to pay them and they should contact him because he has a line on new jobs for all of them. I can't fly—" She flung her arm in the direction of the huge transport ship. "Without a crew."

Cyra swiped at the tear that had escaped. Varik's unflattering terms for her had been perfectly aimed to damage her reputation and confidence. The temptation to lean into the large gray man before her, a stranger—cargo—was difficult to resist. She would give anything to have someone take the burden from her. But just because her dream of being a captain wasn't emerging from a ray of sparkly sunshine didn't mean she was ready to give up. She didn't need some random male with his arms crossed, muscles bulging, and forehead wrinkled in a scowl to provide comfort. Besides, he didn't appear interested in providing any.

"All clear," Veda called from the top of the loading ramp, carrying the helmet of her hazmat suit under one arm. "Your chile spray idea saved us a huge fine, Dezmuhnd."

Dezmuhnd? She glanced at the impressive male by her side.

"Dezmuhnd Cuocua. But please, call me Dez."

"Thank you, Dez." What was she supposed to do with him? Put him back in cargo? Did it matter since she had no crew?

"You are Captain—" The lift in his voice requested she supply her name.

But what name should she give him? "I'm Captain Maejzur." The words were like a mouth full of seashells. "Cyra."

Dez tilted his head in a shallow nod. "Captain Cyra."

Doc's cry from the far side of the dock freed Cyra from her awkward introduction. Doc was breathless and half shuffling, half running toward her.

She held up her hand to slow the older man down, worried for his safety. "We're alright. The spiders are back in the cage. All of them."

Veda rushed to her mentor and took his elbow. "The

Cassan docking crew says it appears someone tampered with the container. They're making a safety fix to it now."

Cyra groaned. The charge for the fix would be added to her docking fees. "I have to go to the bank." Varik's lies had poisoned her and probably the crew, but the frugal Captain Auvi would have plenty of credits in his accounts. "Veda, Doc, can you handle things here?"

"Veda will see to the ship. I'll go with you." Doc's tone allowed for no dissent. "I have the proof of death you'll need to transfer the accounts."

What she needed to do was get a new crew, but addressing the credits and accounts first made sense. "Let's go."

CHAPTER 7

"Nothing left," Cyra repeated for the third time since the credit agency manager had explained the accounts were closed. Her knees weakened, and she sank to a bench outside the facility. She'd hoped Varik was lying until the very nice but very useless man confirmed the truth. "Why did Auvi have Varik's name on all those accounts?"

Doc grimaced. "He loved Varik once. Maybe he still did on some level. They'd both lost faith in each other some time ago. But Auvi hated dealing with the mundane. He brought up changing his property inheritance months ago, and I jumped on changing it because I knew he would procrastinate. I had no idea the credit accounts were held in both their names." Doc sat next to her and tried to put his arm around her shoulders. She was much taller than Doc, so it was more like around her back, but it was still comforting.

"Varik knew about the accounts but not the change in the plans for *The Treasure.*" Cyra blinked hard and shook herself as she stood. "We have to get back. He could have been the one who tampered with the spider container. Who knows what else he's up to?"

Cyra hurried back to the hangar with Doc in tow.

The security staff had the area cordoned off. Cyra held out her arm to allow access to her GID. After scanning the chip, they allowed her to enter.

"Veda?" she hollered through the empty vessel. "Veda, where are you?" She moved to the cargo hold.

"I'm here," Veda said, emerging from the lower level. Her confusion was written all over her face. "Why are you screaming? And why are you back so soon? I thought you'd be another hour at least."

"I need to change the authorizations for the ship's systems immediately. Make sure Varik can't get back on board or into the systems remotely."

Cyra deleted all of Varik's authority—including several back doors he'd created in multiple subsystems, the sneaky bastard. She finally understood why Captain Auvi made her study so much. She had more knowledge about the ship than most engineers and captains combined. If it was possible to be in multiple places at once, she could run *The Treasure* from top to bottom solo.

Next hurdle: crew.

If she didn't find at least a skeleton crew willing to work for the promise of payment after they delivered the spiders and Dez, her time as captain would be short-lived. Her stomach soured. Dez had saved Veda and possibly Cassan. He should be treated as a hero, but he was still cargo, and she had to honor the contracts to deliver all the goods on the ship. If she could.

She dropped into the captain's chair and gazed unseeing out at the bleak metal hangar through the unshielded windows on the bridge.

When a few wayward crewmates entered the hangar, she shifted from slumped to alert. They must not have received Varik's message. She had to tell them something that would make them stay, but she couldn't make herself rise to share all her bad news.

Moments later, Doc called from the door to the bridge, "Cyra, the crew is waiting outside the lower deck. You need to speak to them."

She stood with a sigh. "And tell them what? I have a ship with a partially completed contract and no money to pay them for the work they've already done?"

He moved briskly down the corridor. "Why don't you let me speak to them?"

It might be weak, but she jumped at the chance to hand that conversation over.

Doc stepped forward and held up his hands. "Listen."

"Where's our pay?" someone in the crowd of over fifty called out.

"I can explain everything. You may not like what you hear, but I'll tell you the truth, unlike what you may have already heard."

"Varik said—"

"Captain Auvi was a good captain and kept this ship on an even keel for a very long time. I've worked with some of you longer than I can remember. The captain entrusted this ship to Cyra." Doc gestured back to where Cyra was planted. The crew fidgeted and gave each other knowing looks. "And while Captain Cyra has been on this ship for several galactic years, you may not know her as I do. She's trustworthy, reliable, and incredibly intelligent. She's a planner, and if anyone can figure out how to keep this ship profitable while taking exceptional care of its crew, it's her. Auvi invested his time training her to be his replacement. She knows how to run this ship, but she needs you. Auvi gave her his loyalty. If you trusted Auvi, you can trust his judgment now."

"Trust doesn't pay my bills," a voice called from the crowd.

Several crew members were already tramping down the corridor.

"Look, Doc." Jarem, the navigator, stepped forward. He was burly and had scales covering his shoulders and small curved horns. It made him look more fearsome than he was. "It's not that we don't trust Captain Auvi, but we work for a living. Even if we deliver this cargo, the first half of the money is gone. Varik told us it was already spent. It takes fuel, food, and lots of fees to fly this behemoth. We might have enough fuel and food to make the delivery, but what then? There are docking fees on Morgual. And with no contract, how are we supposed to get all the way to Kolben to make the second delivery?"

The remaining crew murmured in agreement.

Jarem gestured to his coworkers. "We have no desire to be stuck on a shithole planet like Morgual or, worse, Kolben. Sorry, Doc. I don't care how smart Captain Auvi's sugar-butt is. I'm not willing to bet my life on her." He turned, and the few crew who hadn't already wandered off followed him.

Cyra stared down the empty hallway. The sting of the sexual nickname reverberated through her, leaving a stain of self-doubt. Maybe the crew had a point. Perhaps she could sell the ship and—

No.

Auvi gifted her the dream of her lifetime. She'd be damned if she'd cave in before she'd at least tried to make it work.

"What are we going to do?" Veda asked.

"I don't know." Cyra crossed her arms. "But I'm not ready to give up. Captain left me this ship. It's way too soon and I'm not really prepared, but *now* is when I have to do this. I don't have the luxury to wait until I'm ready."

"I can help you secure a new crew," Doc offered.

"I don't have any credits beyond my meager personal

account." Cyra pursed her lips, holding back the small number she'd confirmed earlier.

"Credits aren't everything," Doc mumbled to himself, deep in problem-solving contemplation. "All we need is a couple of professionals who know how to do things."

"I know enough about how the ship works that I could get by with an engineer and a navigator. At least for the short term. If Veda will take on the duties of monitoring the cargo?" She tilted her head at her friend. It was a huge ask.

"For you, Cyr, yes. For us. Besides, where else am I going to find a ship where I will be the Chief Medical Officer and be working for my best friend?"

"So I can pay you with a fancy title?"

"Seems like a surer thing than a big raise." Veda chuckled and nudged Cyra gently.

Speaking of managing the cargo... "Where's Dez?"

Veda glanced back toward the crew quarters. "I asked him to move out of the cargo bay and into one of the smaller sleeping berths. I was lucky to get him out with neither of us getting killed. Until we deliver those damn spiders, I don't want anyone in there with them."

"Good call." Doc smiled his approval at his protégé.

"Great. Now, how are we going to get *The Treasure* to Morgual to deliver the damn things?" Cyra brushed her hair back from her gills, wishing she could hide in the wet room. An extended swim called to her, but she couldn't avoid her problems. She was the captain.

"We should split up and hit the favorite gathering spots of the space crews. See if we can talk some of them into coming back, one-on-one, and if not, ask around for good and available engineers and navigators," Doc replied.

"Is it safe to leave the spiders?" Veda asked, betraying the fact that she was not looking forward to having to network with drunken sailors.

"I don't want to do this anymore than you. Probably less, in fact." Cyra hugged her best friend, seeking courage more than giving any. "But you're right. Varik could do anything while we're gone."

"I can remain on the ship and provide security." Dez's voice startled Cyra, and she spun to find him lingering in the shadows of the intersection of corridors.

It was a terrible idea. And perfect. She shouldn't. Veda's and Doc's gazes were locked on her, drowning her in expectation. Veda shifted her eyes in Dez's direction with a lift of her eyebrows.

Cyra sighed. She was terrible at this captain stuff. "If you're sure?"

"It would be my honor to help you."

His honor? "Thank you. Doc, can you get him a comms unit so he can call if anything happens?" She shifted her focus back to the attractive male who should be in a cargo hold and not in her awareness at all. "Don't be a hero. I mean, you've already saved us once, but don't put yourself at risk. If there's a problem, contact the dock security and then call me."

"Yes, Captain."

There it was again, that fluttery feeling, but this time between her legs. Time to get some distance. "I'll let the station master know we're leaving Dez on the ship to monitor. Meet you at security."

Veda and Doc appeared as Cyra left the skeptical official's office. Having already had a biohazard emergency, the man was anxious to get *The Treasure* away from Cassan. The good news was he'd agreed to extend her credit so she could leave. But only if she left in the next three cycles.

No crew. No credits. And no other options.

Cyra pinned her dark green hair up, making sure it still covered her gills. "We need a plan."

"You and Veda should park yourselves at the Rusty Bucket." Doc pointed down a crowded corridor where every other door was a bar. "Varik's banned from there after our last stopover. I'm going to roam some lesser-known transport haunts and listen for any gossip. I may be able to find someone to send to you for approval."

"We just need two, an engineer and a navigator," Cyra repeated as if that made the task easier.

"My shuttle doesn't depart for two cycles. I'm sure we can find the required crew members by then." Doc's reassuring smile said more about how difficult this task would be than if he hadn't tried to convince her. Too bad they didn't have more than a few cycles. Doc patted her arm. "No time to waste."

"It's going to work. You'll see, Cyr. Everyone loves Doc. He'll find the crew we need." Veda tugged her forward.

Spaceship personnel packed the dive bar—a menagerie of different humanoid species from all the various solar systems that relied on Cassan as a travel waypoint. Wall panels aged with a faux-rust patina gave the place its name. Although it was difficult to tell exactly what color they were in the sparsely lit space. The long bar was made to look like concrete. Probably some plastic polymer. Cyra only saw concrete in use on planets, not in the station. Veda tugged her past the packed bar seating and through the tall tables.

Cyra didn't bother to try to be inconspicuous as she moved through the crowd. It would be helpful if everyone knew her whereabouts just in case someone actually wanted to contact her about a job.

The service at the Bucket was marginal, but she wasn't there to drink. They found an empty table at the back. Maybe they would find a crew quickly and they could both go back to the comfort of *The Treasure*. Cyra didn't bother to make conversation. There was nothing to say—either they found a crew or they didn't. And they knew better than to discuss their concerns with so many ears tuned for gossip. It was better to remain silent and let others wonder about them. Maybe Doc would get lucky. She hoped so, because at this point, luck was all she had and it hadn't been on her side so far.

CHAPTER 8

Varik held up his glass to the few former crew members who remained at the table with him. "Can you believe it? She thinks she's going to be captain of *The Treasure* and keep me—the best engineer in the fucking galaxy—on her crew when her only claim to fame is being a fucking tentacle slut?"

The crew laughed, but his stomach twinged at the possibility it was *at* him. He'd been Auvi's tentacle slut once and loved it. Maybe he shouldn't have taken Auvi for granted. Perhaps he should have tried harder to apologize. Maybe he shouldn't have cheated on someone he loved.

A pinprick of pain arced through his heart. But if Auvi had loved him half as much, the temptation never would have risen. Auvi practically ignored him between launches. And after what Varik assumed was an argument, Auvi had abandoned him—for Cyra. Varik had done everything but beg, and Auvi still fucked him over. One lapse in judgment—a single mistake—and Auvi treated him like irredeemable garbage. Tossed him away. Took everything and gave it to *her*.

The shot of liquor burned down his throat, but pain was simply a reminder he was still alive. He'd find a way to recover. That infiltrating bitch may have stolen his ship, but she'd have no money to run it. No crew either, since he'd told them the truth: she was broke.

If he exposed her for the failure she was bound to be, he might be able to reclaim the ship—his ship. No sane being would agree to crew with her. To rocket into deep space with zero financial resources and a cargo full of deadly spiders was a death wish—especially since the deadly spiders may or may not have been properly contained. And the male they'd been transporting to Kolben was likely dead as a result. Too bad really. A bystander in the war with the usurper.

She'd fail. It was only a matter of time.

And he'd be waiting to repossess his future.

"Another round. On me," Varik called out, celebrating his decision not to let Auvi's backstabbing little whore take him down. He'd use Auvi's—no, *his*—money to buy the crew's loyalty until he found another ship in the next cycle or two. Load up the people loyal to him and then do what he did best— endear himself to the new captain and make himself indispensable, using the ship as if it were his while he bided his time.

Besides, if Cyra couldn't find a crew, she'd be looking to get rid of *The Treasure*. As it was, the dock fees would rack up the longer she was on Cassan. If he could delay her leaving—

"To Varik." The crew raised half-empty glasses in his honor.

Varik cheered along with them, getting louder the more he drank.

"You didn't want that old hunk of junk anyway," one of the systems crew slurred out. "Now we can sign on to one of those fancy tourist ships." The guy waggled his eyebrows. "Fuck the rich tourists out of some credits. Am I right?"

Varik forced a smile because the idiot had no clue what a gem *The Treasure* was. When he selected a new ship to commandeer temporarily, he wouldn't be looking for a cruise liner. Really, he shouldn't have to be thinking about finding another ship at all. Varik clinked his glass against the guy's tumbler. Had the guy's comment hinted at what they thought of Varik? That he was the captain's toy—had fucked the captain for his money. They wouldn't say it directly to his face, but they implied it.

Fucking tourists for tips?

Seriously?

The best engineer in the galaxy?

They'd show him some respect if they had any idea about his vision for the future or where he'd come from. He'd clawed his way to the top, studying in every spare moment, taking every shit assignment, until finally he'd been on the best live cargo ship. *The Treasure* wasn't a piece of crap. Nothing could beat her for the cargo life-systems, the energy efficiency—some of which he was responsible for—or the comfortable quarters. Other ships might be faster or fancier, but those guys hadn't seen the crew living quarters—racking in with strangers like canned goods on a shelf. When the ship's income was tied to the tourist accommodations, the crew got shafted.

He'd personally attended to every system on *The Treasure*, making sure it was in the best condition and the most efficient state as if the ship were his because it was supposed to be. He'd spent so much time and effort caring for her, seducing Auvi, and going along with every little whim of his captain so he could be the captain. He'd trusted Auvi, and the man had ripped away everything to leave Varik with nothing.

The unfairness settled like a poisonous fog deep inside, coating every bit of him with revenge and bitterness. Auvi truly had fucked him in the end. And that smirking bitch, Cyra, had helped him do it. Varik couldn't afford to let her win. He'd built his entire future on the idea he would one day be captain of *The Treasure*. He had to expose her for the fraud she was. "She won't find anyone to fly with her. Then, when she's crying and broken, I'll do her the kindness of buying that hauler from her just to save her from starvation."

He spoke to no one.

They weren't listening to him, just drinking their fill on his credits.

Varik quieted as the server came over with another round. He took the opportunity to grope the female's chest, earning himself a slap. He laughed, raised his glass, and hollered, "To stupid bitches who think they can rule us by riding our cocks."

"Stupid bitches!" the bar cheered him.

Except for a female with dark hair who slinked out of the bar. Something about her was familiar, but he couldn't recall the details. Probably just some past easy lay. He turned back to the crew, plans whirling through his alcohol-washed brain. No matter how far down he was, he'd been lower. He'd pulled himself up then, and he would do it again.

CHAPTER 9

Cyra stifled a yawn. They'd been sitting at the Bucket for hours without conversation beyond a few males trying to hit on them. As soon as she tried to talk to them about a job on her ship, they laughed and walked away. She pushed her chair back and stood. A pale, almost translucent female dressed all in black with waves of red hair caught Cyra's eye. The woman darted between tables, eyes locked on Cyra, mouth frozen in a determined line. Cyra sat down again, wide awake.

"Captain Maejzur? I'm Blaize Dreheer. Doc Maretine sent me."

Oh wow. It was the first time a stranger addressed Cyra as captain, and it was like she'd drunk three Rings of Saturn cocktails. But the caffeinated alcoholic rush of that beverage had nothing on being called captain. She barely kept a huge grin at bay. "Have a seat."

Blaize dropped into the empty chair and introduce herself to Veda.

"So what do you do, and why are you looking for a job?" Cyra didn't feel like wasting any more time.

"For the past few g-years, I've been contracting as an engineer. Between jobs, I pick up environmental systems maintenance work on the station. Not the most glamorous work, but it keeps me in food and shelter."

"Why short-term contracts?"

"At first, I thought I might captain my own ship again. Short-term contracts pay pretty well, and I saved as much as I could. But there are long periods between." Blaize brushed her deep red hair back over her shoulder. "I thought I would earn credits faster and build a network of crew members who would want to work with me. That didn't exactly go as planned either."

Cyra stiffened. Why would a talented engineer who had been a captain want a job on *The Treasure* with an inexperienced commander? Did Blaize plan to grab the ship out from under her? "You were a captain?"

"Right out of a ninety-cycle boot camp. I had a small inheritance and spent it on a shiny new ship for me and the person I thought was my mate. It was a crazy plan. I didn't even know enough to know better. He convinced me we could be successful. I hired some other classmates and somehow got a commission to provide transportation for the Galaxy Exploration Division. But they didn't renew."

Cyra's biggest fear was her story would end like Blaize's. To taste her dream and then lose everything would be worse than never being a captain, assuming she could even get a crew and get off the station. She'd get every detail she could get from Blaize so she wouldn't repeat the woman's mistakes.

"My lover was a complete lying bastard. He hated I was a better engineer than him. He sabotaged things and told lies about me to the crew. It's possible he's still sabotaging me."

Cyra set her jaw to keep from interrupting. Why did some males have to be so deceptive and competitive? Doc wasn't like that. Captain hadn't been either, at least not maliciously.

"He thought if he made it look like I wasn't doing a good

job, he could take over. He fucked me over literally and figuratively. Then I found out he was fucking his best friend, the communications officer, too, the rotten asshole."

Cyra nodded, encouraging Blaize to continue.

"I ended up putting a lien on my ship to pay the crew. When I didn't get another contract, I lost it."

Veda winced audibly.

Blaize glanced at Veda and nodded. Then she turned back to Cyra. "The man who fucked me over? I think you may know him."

"Me?" Cyra flinched. She hardly knew anyone who wasn't a member, well, former member, of *The Treasure's* crew.

"Varik?" Blaize asked hesitantly.

"Varik." Cyra's outburst betrayed her shock that it could be the same person attacking them both. Was this a setup? "Your lover was Varik *Pectori?*"

Blaize grimaced with a slight shrug.

What a complete asshole. It hadn't been Cyra's relationship with Captain Auvi that made Varik act out. If what Blaize said was true, he'd ruined her life too.

"I'd heard he had hooked up with the infamous Captain Auvi Thenal and was acting as the 'launch assistant' in addition to being the engineer."

Cyra nodded, her cheeks heating and her stomach souring. She never was an official crew member. She'd never been on a ship before Captain Auvi rescued her. She hadn't known he was infamous, or that strangers looked down on what she did for him, or that anyone knew what it took to launch *The Treasure* beyond the immediate crew.

"I want to join your crew. I have experience on all kinds of ships and systems of all ages."

Blaize would be a dream come true if Varik didn't send her. "I can't pay you. Varik emptied the accounts."

Veda chimed in, "She means we can't pay you right away. Our credits are tied up in the current shipment."

"I don't care. I want Varik to suffer. Making sure he doesn't get his hands on your ship is a start. Making sure we all make a fortune would be even better. I want to be a partner."

"A partner?" Cyra's gills flapped under her hair. She took a slow breath and searched Blaize for signs of deception like tics or nervous movements. But the woman met Cyra's gaze directly.

"I have credits. Not enough for my own ship but plenty to chip in. Give me a contract for this delivery. If you aren't happy, pay back my credits and drop me back here on the station, and we call it good. If you are happy, I'm an official partner and get a split of the profits once we have profits."

Cyra glanced at Veda, who stared back with wide eyes. Cyra could almost hear Veda screaming, "Do it," in her head.

"Alright, one delivery and we'll renegotiate at the end of that. Meet me at *The Treasure* tomorrow at mid-cycle.

"We're in dock alpha, bay 6801. We'll finalize the terms and put them in writing." In the meantime, Cyra would search for anything she could find to corroborate Blaize's story. If Varik had sent her—

"Got it. I'll see you tomorrow, Captain. Nice to meet you, Veda."

Blaize left the bar, and Veda released a quick squeal.

Cyra wasn't quite ready to celebrate unless Blaize proved to be honest. "Let's get out of here."

"One down. One to go," Veda said as she followed Cyra out of the bar and back onto the ship.

"Captain Cyra, Veda."

Cyra startled. Dez stood statue-still at the top of the entrance ramp. "Dez." She tried to slow her breathing. "Everything okay?"

"Yes, Captain. No issues to report."

That voice and those eyes—not to mention the man himself —were distracting. But she couldn't afford to be unfocused. "Thank you. Uh, Veda, can you, uh, get Dez whatever— I have some work to do. Excuse me."

"Sure," Veda replied, her tone suspicious.

Cyra didn't have any answers or even a bad explanation, but she hadn't lied. There was work to do, so she didn't hesitate to disappear into her quarters and open her data screen.

After hours of research, Cyra confirmed most of what Blaize had shared, so she escaped to the water chamber and stripped. Finally, she could find some relief. Her tears would only add to the contents of the pool. No one would have to see how sad and scared she truly was.

On the upside, they'd possibly found an engineer seemingly committed to making the business work, if for no other reason than to make Varik suffer. But on the downside, Cyra would be responsible for the well-being of another crew member. She didn't know how to take care of herself, much less command a ship.

And she still had to find a navigator, get the ship refueled, pay the dock fees, restock the food stores, and figure out how to get paid for delivering the damn spiders. She hated spiders— particularly big and nasty spiders. Spiders that could kill. And then there was Dez. The man who was destined for Kolben, the frozen mining planet, where lifespans were notably short. Maybe she'd acted rashly when she'd run from being married with babies on her home planet. Being a captain was everything she'd wished for, but the reality was dreadful.

"Why?" she screamed into the liquefied gel. Why did Auvi have to die on her? She wasn't ready. Not only did her heart miss him but her body did too. Tears streamed down her face only to be absorbed by the medium in the tank. She still swiped at them, angry with her weakness. Captain's tears wouldn't pay a crew.

She wallowed in her missteps and cursed the fates that had placed her in the precarious position of having everything while being on the brink of losing it all. Swimming until exhausted, she left the chamber and returned to her cozy quarters to rest before facing another challenging cycle. Every cycle that passed while stuck on Cassan brought her closer to failure.

She lay on her bunk, staring up at the curved ceiling, and forced herself to count her blessings. A habit her mother had instilled in her as a child.

Veda, a trained medic, cared for the spiders without hesitation and would remain on the ship. Her loyalty was unquestionable.

Doc committed his last days on Cassan to helping her find the specialists she needed. Already, she had an engineer who didn't just want a job, she wanted a partnership.

If she could get a navigator and a communications officer, the ship could function. Even just a navigator would get them off the station. But how long would it take to find one?

And Dez? He'd saved them from the spider outbreak. He'd watched over the ship. But he was a complete mystery, and what he did to her body without even trying was dangerous. She didn't need another risk to her leadership.

Cyra, Veda, and Dez sat at the small galley table the next morning eating the meal Doc had prepped. Dez's yellow gaze burned into Cyra every time she glanced up from her tray as if he could see the dirty dreams she'd had about him. Her cheeks heated, and she focused downward, pretending she couldn't feel his eyes on her like a caress. Like his fingers hadn't slid deep into her, coaxing an orgasm from her that left her thighs wet and her body aching. If her door hadn't been locked when she awoke, she would have accused him of entering her room uninvited. Instead, he'd invaded her thoughts, which was so much worse.

An odd noise disrupted Cyra's shame cycle. "Did you hear that?"

Dez stood. "I believe someone is hailing you from outside."

Cyra made her way to the open ramp surrounded by the other three.

Blaize. For a little thing, she had a set of lungs on her.

"What are you doing?" Cyra asked as she lowered the ramp the remaining way to the deck.

"Sorry for the hollering, the stupid security people wouldn't let me call you," Blaize explained somewhat breathlessly as she entered the ship.

"I should have notified them you would be coming, but I didn't expect you until later." Cyra had suspected Blaize would back out after finding Blaize's school records and the deed to her lost ship. The woman was truly brilliant and had been a captain in her own right. She hadn't exaggerated at all.

"I could hardly sleep, thinking about joining you. I hoped for a chance like this. It isn't quite the same as owning my own ship, but in some ways it's better. I'm a more skilled engineer than I ever was a captain. That's why Varik was able to turn my crew against me so easily, you know? If I had bought the ship and then hired a captain, it would have lasted a lot longer. It isn't easy being a leader. But you already know that, don't you? I mean, it seems like you haven't been the leader long, but you already know all the problems that come with being the captain. The finance and the hiring and the other stuff. Oh. I'm talking too much again. Sorry. I talk when I'm nervous." Blaize clamped her jaw shut and tightly crossed her arms.

"How do you do that without breathing?" Cyra could go days without saying more than a few words. Blaize had just blurted a week's worth of words at light speed. "I mean, I have gills, and I still breathe more than you do."

Blaize laughed. "I've worked with all males. I got used to telling them everything really quickly, so I could get it all out before they interrupted."

"I'll learn to listen fast, and I promise not to interrupt." Cyra smiled at Blaize, happy to have her on the crew. Cyra gestured to the man beside her. "Doc's already started editing a standard contract template so it would have a partner clause."

"Excellent. Nice to see you again." Blaize shook Doc's hand.

"You know Veda." Cyra paused as they acknowledged each other with a nod. "She's taking over Doc's position as Chief Medical Officer." Blaize made noises of approval. Cyra hesitated with the next introduction, but it had to be done. "And this is Dezmuhnd Cuocua. He's a...our guest." She couldn't introduce him as cargo but wasn't sure *guest* was the right word either.

Blaize held out her hand. Dez clasped his hands behind him. "You may call me Dez."

"Hi, Dez. Nice to meet you."

"You as well." The smile he gave Blaize should not have prickled in Cyra's chest, but it did.

"I'll take you to the galley." Cyra picked up the pace, trying to out run her odd reaction. "You and Doc can work on the contract there. Add whatever details you want with him. After you're done, Doc's continuing the hunt for a navigator. And I need to see about provisioning the ship for our journey." Which would take a miracle since she only had her tiny savings account.

"I would be happy to accompany you, Captain," Dez said from the back of the group trailing her.

"Veda's going with me. We'll be fine." Cyra planned to get some distance from the man who set her on edge and invaded her dreams.

"Do you mind if I stay here, Captain?" Blaize asked. "I'd like to spend as much time with the ship as possible before we take off."

"That's fine." Did Blaize recognize leaving her on the ship alone, or practically alone, was a test? Would she pass? Or was Cyra being a complete idiot? Better to know before they left the station if Blaize wasn't trustworthy.

"I would be happy to help you," Dez offered.

Cyra clenched her jaw and quickly forced herself to relax. Jealousy? Really?

"I work better alone. No offense, but I'm better with no distractions." Blaize smiled apologetically. "No conversations. Can you add me to the systems so I can look at everything?"

"I'll do that before I go." Cyra paused in the corridor where it split, ignoring the wash of relief that Blaize didn't want Dez to help her. "I can probably answer any questions you have about *The Treasure*. But Varik was the last engineer and, although he thought he would get her, I don't know if he took the best care of everything. Or if he left any surprises behind."

"And what would you have me do, Captain?" Dez asked at the entrance to the galley where Blaize and Doc were already getting settled.

So many things. No, bad Cyra. "Um. Nothing?" She steeled herself against the unwanted attraction. "You're not crew. You're cargo, so I guess just relax until we can take off again."

Dez stepped back as if she'd slapped him.

Crap, that cargo thing hadn't come out right. She opened her mouth to try to fix it.

"Yes, Captain." Dez turned away before she could summon better words.

Shit. He didn't deserve that. He'd dealt with the spiders. Been nothing but helpful and respectful. She'd fix it later because she still had so many urgent tasks ahead of her she couldn't worry about a temporary passenger's emotions. She was having enough trouble dealing with her own.

CHAPTER 10

The fuelers and suppliers of all things that made space travel possible resided in the grimy bowels of the station. Cyra craved her water tank as she tiptoed through the passageways, accosted by the loud machinery used to fabricate engine parts and other ship internals.

Veda held part of her ever-present scarf over the lower half of her face. "That smell is something else."

Cyra heard her clearly over the din and agreed. Burnt chemicals and ozone, along with sweat and other biologicals she didn't care to think about too hard.

Veda pointed at a sign farther up on the right. Gareth's Galaxy Garage. If they didn't get the exotic mass fuel rods there, Cyra wasn't sure where to try next. The clerk at the last stop said this was the only fueler who would offer any kind of credit, but that it would cost them in the long run.

It wasn't like she had a choice. They had to load the ship to capacity with EMF rods if they were going to get to Morgual, deliver the spiders, and make it back to Cassan without using an ER bridge. If they had to jump, there was the potential they would miss the delivery deadline anyway. Despite the work that had been done over hundreds of g-years to stabilize bridge travel, there was always the possibility time would shift.

Cyra entered the shop. A once-blue counter with a thick, protective clear barrier, three tattered chairs, and a beverage maker that burped the occasional wisp of smoke filled the cramped space. Veda lingered near the door, scarf still clutched to her nose and mouth even though the smell wasn't nearly as bad once inside the shop. Cyra cleared her throat and approached the glass barrier between the customer area and a cluttered office space.

A giant of a man rose and stepped forward. Hair covered every visible surface, even his snubbed nose, and his muscles had clusters of muscles layered on top. "Can I help you? Directions?"

His baritone voice was soft, coaxing. Cyra dropped her shoulders and blew out a reluctant breath. Last chance. "I'm not lost. In fact, I was directed here. I need...I need help."

The giant glanced around her, looking for what she didn't know.

"I need fuel for my ship. I was told to ask for Gareth."

"That's me." His brow wrinkled. "You have a ship, but you don't have a fuel supplier?"

"It's a recent acquisition. I'm told you'll work on credit."

He stepped back and crossed his arms. "Maybe."

"That went better than I expected." Veda trotted behind Cyra.

She should slow her steps for her shorter friend, but couldn't suppress her urgency to get back to her ship and as far away from Gareth as possible. Yes, they had fuel. On credit. But only half of what they needed and at twice the price, once the cost of the credit was calculated. At least he hadn't asked for sexual favors like some fuelers had once they found out who she was. Varik had truly gassed the atmosphere around her, and gossip traveled through Cassan faster than light speed. Everyone loved a dirty story, especially if it was at least partially true.

She sighed and slowed her stride. It wasn't Veda's fault she was in this situation. "Hungry?"

"Starved," Veda puffed out between panting breaths.

They'd missed standard meal time, but they should be able to find something on the way back to the ship. Which only highlighted her next problem. Food. Her minimal credits would go a lot farther if she purchased raw, preserved ingredients. But they might starve because their cooking would be inedible. If they bought synth stuff to generate and reheat, they would eat, but not for long. Maybe they could learn to cook or learn not to taste. They stopped at one of the many shopping-district stands—nooks in the wall—for a bowl of noodles.

"I'm buying." Veda pushed Cyra aside with a well-placed hip bump and tapped her embedded GID over the payment scanner.

Cyra closed her eyes and sighed. "Thanks."

"You know, you offered Blaize a partnership, but not me. There something you're not telling me?"

"What?" Cyra gaped at her stiff-backed friend who stared at the food-stall vendor as he slid their portions into biodegradable bowls.

Veda took the food and led them to a narrow bench in a cluster of mostly empty seating. "Are you planning to replace me? I know I've been a junior medic as long as you've known me, but that was because we had Doc. He's been training me all this time." Veda jutted her chin out. "I can do the job."

Cyra touched her friend's shoulder. "I could never—would

never—replace you. It didn't occur to me you wanted to be a partner or even that you weren't. I can't imagine doing this without you."

Veda stared at her for a long moment, then nodded. "Good. Then you'll let me pay for the food for our trip and you'll give me the same contract you're giving Blaize. But without the provision for the single trip. I want our partnership in writing. I don't want anyone to question my position on this ship."

"Done. And you know I would never let anyone get away with questioning your skills or your importance."

Veda pulled the lid from her dish and wrapped the steaming noodles around her chopsticks. "Things happen. I only want it in writing to make sure what happened with you and Captain Auvi doesn't happen to me."

"I'm glad you said something. It was an oversight, an assumption, on my part. I need you. Besides the food, I need you to speak up when I'm making a mistake. I need you to keep being my dearest, most honest friend, as well as my partner on *The Treasure*." Cyra pressed her lips together to keep from gushing about how important Veda was to her. She'd messed up not recognizing that she'd offered Blaize, who was a stranger, something she hadn't offered Veda.

"Of course." Veda nodded and stuffed the bundle of noodles in her mouth as if they hadn't just been on the precipice of a ruined friendship all because Cyra wasn't thinking.

Cyra ate, grateful that she'd kept her friend and at least had fuel to deliver the spiders. And food for the trip. If they could find a navigator in the next cycle, they just might save *The Treasure* and form a working transport business.

Cyra and Veda met Doc on the dock as he was leaving.

"We got provisions. Not that you care much about that," Veda told him in a teasing tone.

"I care. I just won't be joining you for many more meals. You know I'll miss you." Doc patted Veda's shoulder.

"I know." Veda's sadness dripped from her words.

"I'll do my best to take care of you before I go." Doc gave Veda's shoulder a quick squeeze before turning to Cyra. "I think your new engineer will be amazing. She's been in the accelerator for most of the day. She's cursed Varik's name loudly and with great creativity several times."

"I'm not surprised," Cyra told him.

"I'm off to find a navigator. I planted some seeds earlier today and checked in with the bartenders I primed last night. Nothing's dropped yet, but I have every faith the right one is waiting for us."

"I'll go with you." Cyra handed a small bag of foodstuffs to Veda. The rest would be delivered.

"I hope you're right, Doc," Veda said. "Will you be back for last-meal?"

He winced before he could mask it. "Ah, no. I'll—we'll eat out."

"Lucky," Veda huffed and went into the ship.

"Maybe Blaize can cook?" Cyra called over her shoulder as she followed Doc back into the station.

They weren't getting lucky at all. They'd been to two bars, a restaurant, and an exotics strip club Doc had been referred to— an experience Cyra never wanted to repeat. She was convinced there were no navigators on the entire space station. They hadn't shared which ship they were trying to staff. She'd denied being the captain, but word was already out.

They were running out of time. Doc was leaving, fees were racking up, and those spiders would starve before they were delivered if they didn't leave soon. Cyra strengthened her resolve as she entered the next bar. She would find a navigator inside. No matter what. She took a seat at the bar next to Doc, looking over the crowd.

Groups of males hung out in packs, playing various table games and drinking heavily. Same as the last places.

Doc nudged her and tilted his head to the far corner.

Cyra spun a quarter turn and peered into the shadows. A lone female sat at a table in the corner. Head down, she had streaks of stark white in her dark hair.

"If she's from the planet I think she is, we've hit the jackpot."

Cyra frowned, unsure what Doc was talking about.

"Can you see her skin?" Doc squinted.

"To dark."

The woman must have felt their gaze on her. She lifted her chin and locked onto them with vivid pink eyes. Doc picked up his drink, moving faster than he had all night. Cyra grabbed her own glass and followed him over to the woman. Her skin was pale yellow with a golden warmth, and the clingy V-necked magenta top she wore made her pink eyes even more striking.

Doc held out his hand. "I'm Doc."

"What's up, Doc?"

Doc chuckled. "I see you studied ancient media."

She blasted a full-smile up at him. "I'm Rhysa." She turned her gaze to Cyra. "And you are?"

Should she answer Captain Maejzur? No. Even though Rhysa was a female, she might still be judgy. "Cyra."

Rhysa smiled just as big and flirtatiously. "Have a seat." Rhysa pushed two chairs back from the table. "You two are the only people in several attempts to offer even the hope of a decent conversation. Plus, you're both pretty attractive." She waggled her eyebrows at them.

Doc sat, shaking his head. A wry smile teased his lips. "I'm not looking for a date. We're looking for a navigator."

"I've been known to do some navigation on occasion. What's the occasion?" Rhysa leaned forward, put her elbows on the table, and rested her chin on her folded hands. The tip of her tongue grazed her lips and her pink gaze bored into Cyra.

"Our crew's had some turnover," Doc replied. "There's an opening."

"Tell me about the current crew. Are you the captain?"

"No." Doc gestured to Cyra. "She is. I'm the about to be the former medical officer. My protégé, Veda, is taking over my position on *The Treasure*."

"Oh *The Treasure*." Rhysa sat up, the corners of her lips tilted up, and focused on Cyra as if Doc had disappeared. "I've heard of you. Word is you're into tentacle sex."

"Uh?" Cyra had no idea how to respond.

"Tell me." Rhysa closed the space between them, close enough to kiss. "Is it as good as they say? I've never had the chance to find out." She batted her eyes. "But I would be all over trying it." Rhysa glanced under the table. A frown wrinkled her forehead when she rose.

"That was the previous captain," Doc said flatly. "It's a long story. Suffice it to say, *Captain* Maejzur is a good captain. She just needs a crew capable of making the next delivery."

Cyra appreciated Doc defending her, but she would have to learn to address these rumors herself, and quickly.

"So it's short term?" Rhysa asked.

"Not necessarily." Cyra rubbed her hands along her legs. Why was it so much more difficult to deal with Rhysa than Blaize? Probably because Blaize already knew what Varik was capable of and still wanted in. "I'm willing to sign you on a trial basis. See if it works for us."

"Who else is on the ship?"

"The engineer. Blaize Dreheer?" Cyra added a questioning tone to the statement, wondering if Rhysa knew her.

"It's all females?"

"So far, yes."

"Who else are you hiring?"

"Just a navigator. Possibly a communications specialist. For now." If they could find one willing. Their conversation didn't seem promising.

"You're in luck. I'm from Blaque Poll."

Cyra looked at Doc, unsure of the significance. Doc gave a slight nod. Apparently, he'd guessed her origins correctly based on her looks.

"We're only the best navigators in...well...anywhere."

"I've heard that," Doc said. "Are you looking for a job?"

"I've never worked on a ship that didn't have males."

Dez's name sat on the tip of Cyra's tongue. But he wasn't crew. He was cargo. And he was off-limits. "Is that a problem?"

Rhysa grinned at Cyra, heat in her pink eyes. "Might be a benefit in the short term."

"Why aren't you contracted now? You should be in demand." Cyra couldn't figure the female out. If she was the best, why was she talking to them?

"Got kicked off my last ship for initiating an orgy."

Wow. Given a hundred guesses as to why Rhysa was unemployed, Cyra wasn't sure she could've figured it out.

"You like to have sex with your fellow crew members." Doc made the question sound like a statement.

Rhysa shrugged. "I liked it with them. I didn't like the captain. He was pissed I turned him down for a private session."

"That won't be a problem between us. I won't be asking."

Cyra wasn't convinced she should hire Rhysa. There were already enough crazy rumors.

"Don't get offended if I offer. I won't be offended if you decline."

Cyra gaped, then closed her mouth. She took a sip of her drink. There had to be a way to turn the conversation. "I should probably explain our financial situation to you before you agree."

"What's the problem?"

"I can't pay you until we deliver our current cargo."

Rhysa leaned back again and tilted her head. She narrowed her eyes. Cyra would have felt less pressure if she'd been shoved under a microscope in a biology class. Finally Rhysa said, "It's not like I'm going shopping between here and there. I assume you'll be returning to the station after the delivery."

"That's the plan. For now. It depends on if we can pick up another shipment once we deliver the current cargo." She should feel bad about omitting the details of Morgual and the spiders, but she couldn't afford too much conscience. "That would be the goal."

"Just put in my contract that if you terminate my services, you have to keep me until you can drop me back here at Cassan."

"Done."

Rhysa shifted forward and stared at Cyra hard enough to see beneath her blue skin. After a long moment, Rhysa softened, and gave Cyra a slight nod. "So when are we leaving? I have some things I need to bring over."

"Well, that's up to our engineer, Blaize. Also, we're waiting on fuel and food deliveries. But we could leave within ten hours or by the next cycle at the latest." They had to or Cyra might as well jettison the spiders herself and try for a job at the strip club.

"I'll be ready. Have my contract when I get there." Rhysa drained her drink.

"Done." Doc stood. "Rhysa, is there a last name you want on the contract?"

"Yeah, Tanguey."

Cyra stood. She'd either just negotiated the best hire in history or made the worst decision of her life.

CHAPTER 11

CYRA HAD BARELY SLEPT. And what sleep she got was filled with heated yellow eyes and a muscular gray man who wanted to do wicked things to her body. Despite, or maybe because of, the dirty, disjointed dreams, sleep appealed much more than the problems of being captain. But if she'd didn't rise, she'd miss saying goodbye to Doc. She dreaded losing him after he'd provided so much support. He'd filled in the role of mentor Auvi had always had in her life, making the loss of her captain easier to process. But once Doc was gone, there would be no safety net. Every decision she made would matter not only to her but to the women who joined her in this inadvisable endeavor.

No credits.

New captain.

Poisonous spiders. And barely enough fuel to get to the delivery planet. The urge to pull the coverlet over her head was strong.

The door chimed.

She sighed and rose. Veda stood in the corridor, her appearance perfect if Cyra ignored the slope of her shoulders and the sadness in her eyes. "It's time."

"Give me five minutes, and I'll meet you on the lower deck."

Veda nodded and shuffled down the wide corridor alone. Cyra's heart hurt as much for her friend as herself.

The trip to the outgoing transit dock compressed them among beings who seemed resigned to their fate rather than excited about what the cycle would bring. Cyra's own party was the worst of all. Too soon, Doc stood outside the shuttle that would take him to retirement paradise.

Veda shook with silent sobs. "I'm going to miss you so much. I won't know what to do."

"Yes, you will." Doc patted the hand he held in his. "It's time for you to spread your wings, little one. It's time for me to find some pleasure while I still can."

Veda sniffed. "I promised myself I wouldn't cry. I loved spending my days with you, learning from you."

"And I loved teaching you. But you're ready."

Cyra couldn't help but feel like Veda's loss was an echo of her own. At least Veda had the chance to say goodbye to her mentor.

Veda gazed up into the eyes of her mentor. "Will you contact me sometimes?"

"Of course." Doc gave her a reassuring smile. "You know your mother will still ask me how you are even after I remind her I am no longer on the ship. I've taken care of you for so long, she'll expect me to continue. And I will, from afar. Captain Cyra is going to be a good captain." He patted Cyra's arm but stayed focused on Veda. "You'll have so many new adventures. It's your time." He wrapped his arms around the little bronze woman, his own bronze skin only slightly darker. Veda sobbed into his chest, clinging to him.

Cyra wiped away her own tears.

Veda held Doc until the shuttle staff announced the final boarding.

Doc stroked her hair. "Veda, I have to go. I'll send a comm when I get there. Let me know how the spider delivery goes. And take good care of Dez. He has a rough future in front of him."

"I will. I promise." Veda hugged Doc once more and stepped back.

Cyra clutched her friend's hand and waved to Doc as he disappeared into the cruiser. She wanted to cry and be scared like Veda, but she was the captain now. She had to be strong for her crew and be the person they could rely on. There was no one left for her to cry on. No one left to reassure her that everything would be okay because it wouldn't be unless she made it so.

Cyra and Veda made it back to the galley despite blurry, tear-filled eyes. Blaize and Rhysa were in the galley, drinking from steaming cups.

Cyra tried to pull herself together. "Hi, Rhysa. Didn't expect you so early."

"Didn't have anywhere else to be, Captain." She paused. "Sadly. Maybe there will be some action where we're going."

Being called captain still didn't feel right. Cyra poked the food replicator.

"The provisions haven't arrived." Blaize handed her a covered cup. "Rhysa brought buzz."

"Thank you." Cyra clutched the biodegradable container, already slightly soft and drank deeply. The warmth was followed by a sense of clarity that she only got from the caffeinated beverage. "Where's Dez?"

"He came out earlier. Grabbed a protein bar and went back to his quarters. He's kind of weird about touching. I tried to show him where the bars were stored and he jumped about a foot away from me." Blaize lifted a shoulder briefly and then drained her cup.

It was weird, but as long as he was settled and still on the ship, Cyra wouldn't question his quirks. "So where are we going for first meal?"

Blaize cleared her stuff from the table, went to the recycle bin, and tossed her trash. "I'll pass. Had a protein bar and I still have a ton of work to do."

"What do you mean?"

"Varik's idea of keeping the systems well-maintained and mine are radically different. He always thought I fussed over the details too much and that I spent too much time in the engines, turbopump, and thrust mechanisms. But I say a clean system is a well-working system. And since we depend on the ship for our very lives, what is too much time? A tiny issue caught early is a non-issue. But Varik liked it when things went wrong, and he could be the hero saving the day. I think if I'm doing my job, you'll never even know I'm doing it. So yeah, there's a ton of fussy cleanup to do, and I'd really rather get started than spend a whole bunch of time in an eatery." Blaize shrugged.

"You sure?" Guilt settled in Cyra's gut, along with the buzz. She'd didn't know how rough the mechanical systems were.

"I'm good." Blaize flashed a smile and bounded out into the corridor, her red braid bouncing on her back.

Cyra made a note to review everything Blaize had done and to make it a priority to stay on top of all systems in the ship. When Captain Auvi was leading—a twinge of loss hit just thinking his name—she'd followed his lead and let the team do their jobs with little oversight. And while Cyra didn't want to manage oppressively, she should have an accurate view of what was happening on her ship. Captain Auvi had trusted too easily and too much.

They made the quick trek to the Alexo Diner near the dock. Capsule shaped windows broke up the corrugated metal facade. A variety of beings filled the booths, but the three women were seated quickly in a recently vacated space and served more buzz before they had to ask. After deciding on their meals, they punched their orders into the display embedded in the table.

"While we wait for food, I have your contract," Cyra said to Rhysa. The last thing Doc had sent Cyra before he left. She forwarded the document to Rhysa's comm. Cyra bit her tongue to resist babbling to fill the silence at the table. In the background, dishes clanked, and the cook called out orders for pickup. Servers bustled, and diners chatted. But a black hole of weight settled on Cyra's shoulders as she waited for Rhysa to sign off on the terms.

"Where are we headed first?" Rhysa asked after they had ordered, and Cyra had transmitted the contract to her.

"We need to deliver our cargo to Morgual."

"The shit hole at the far end of the Gleise solar system?"

Cyra nodded. "I've calculated the EMF rods needed, and we can make it in one go without using a wormhole."

"That's ridiculous. It will take g-weeks longer." Rhysa scowled.

"It will take longer, but not g-weeks. Blaize has already found enough engine improvements that we won't need to use ER bridges. Besides, I'm not sure what the time impacts might be. I can't be late for this delivery. As it is, we'll be cutting it tight."

"All the more reason to use the bridge. Odds are we'll end up there sooner."

"I'm not willing to bet our only source of any income on odds. We can do this fast, or we can do it right. For this particular delivery, we have to take the more conservative route." And for any future deliveries because crossing bridges was the worst.

"Are you sure Blaize has actually improved the ship's performance?" Rhysa's pink eyes bored into Cyra.

"No, but I'm not considering possible improved performance in my calculations. I expect you can find some efficiencies in our navigation as well." Blaque Poll navigators were supposed to be badass. Let her earn her reputation.

"Of course, I will. But I'll also plan some alternate routes with the available bridges. Just in case things go catastrophic."

Cyra'd had enough of *things* going catastrophic, but she couldn't argue there was a zero probability of more going wrong. She tamped down the churning doubts and attempted to be the confident leader she should be. "I appreciate you considering the possibilities and *respecting* my decision."

"I had to know you had considered all the options." Rhysa grinned at Cyra.

The server delivered their plates at that moment, cutting off any response Cyra might have made. She was tired from the confrontation but felt even more confident in her decision. She trusted the ship, and her faith in Blaize was increasing. If her plan didn't work, she was no worse off than if she hadn't inherited the ship.

"Who are you getting your fuel rods from?" Rhysa asked between tiny bites of her food.

Cyra swallowed her mouthful of seaweed slaw. "Gareth."

"I know him." Rhysa's tone held a load of innuendo, and she grinned. "I'll make a visit, chat with him, and confirm he's not *screwing* you on price. Did you already reload the food and water?"

"Supposed to be delivered soon." Another thing to check on.

"I'll see Gareth after we finish, and I want to check out your nav systems before we take off."

"Once you have our route plotted, can we review it? Our dust shields take extra energy." Navigation wasn't Cyra's strongest subject, but she knew enough to evaluate the courses Rhysa defined.

"No problem. I'll route us around the thickest clouds."

Rhysa finished her grains and berries, leaving Cyra and Veda to finish and pay.

Veda wiped her lips with her napkin and took a deep breath.

Cyra braced herself. Her friend had on her serious face, and Cyra wasn't sure if she could manage any more complications before they left the station.

"Cyr, you need to move into the captain's quarters."

"What?" Why would Veda even suggest such a thing? Captain Auvi's quarters had always been off-limits.

"It doesn't make sense to leave that area of the ship empty. It's closer to the deck."

Kind of a lame argument. "Most of the ship will be empty, and I'm perfectly capable of walking."

"You're the captain." Veda crossed her arms and glanced in the direction Rhysa had gone. "You have to take on the trappings of the office."

"We barely have a crew." And could she really be a captain if they only had two crew members and hadn't flown anywhere? "And I don't want to lord anything over you. You're my partner. Blaize bought in as a partner too."

"This trip will be successful. But only if you take the role

Captain Auvi trusted you with. You're not lording, you're leading. That comes with filling the spaces Auvi left empty."

Like Cyra's chest?

A pang of loss ripped through her, but she blinked back the tears. Veda was right; she had to fill the role, even the parts that made her uncomfortable, like dealing with clashing personalities. "Don't take offense at Rhysa's confrontational ways. Smart people should question authority, especially if they don't know the person." Cyra gave her a pointed look. "And even if they do."

Veda dropped her arms, and a slight smile formed on her lips. "I guess so."

Cyra found Rhysa at the navigation deck hours later. "I didn't know you were back."

Rhysa gazed up at her with those oddly pink eyes, and a smile bloomed across her lips. "Captain, you're going to love my news."

"Yeah?" Cyra braced herself. She didn't know her navigator well enough yet to trust that she actually would like whatever Rhysa might say.

"The fuel rods?"

"Uh-huh?"

"The invoice will have a fifteen percent discount." Rhysa fluttered her eyes.

"That's great."

"And...we're getting twice the number of rods delivered. Blaize said *The Treasure* could hold them. So we should have enough fuel to make it there and back."

Cyra's chest squeezed. "I don't have the funds to pay for double the delivery yet."

Rhysa tilted her head. "You don't understand. Same total price, minus fifteen percent. Double the rods."

"How...?" Cyra sputtered.

"I took care of his rod, and he's taking care of ours." Her voice was giddy, and she gave a little shake of her hips.

"But..." No way should one of her crew have exchanged sexual favors for their travel.

"Don't worry. It was truly my pleasure." Rhysa dragged out the words with a seductive inflection. "And really no different from using your orgasms to launch." She raised a thin eyebrow. "Right?"

Ow. A perfect punch in the gut. And completely accurate. "Right. But I don't want you to think you *have* to do that."

"I don't. But what I do have to do is get an upgrade for the nav system. Stat."

"What's wrong?" Cyra was getting seasick from the emotional swings of the conversation. Had she really dreamed of being a captain one day? It was nothing like she'd imagined.

"Nothing I can't work around, but the maps haven't been updated in forever, and the subscription wasn't renewed. There are so many better options out there. I mean, we could renew. What budget do you have for updates?"

"Nothing. We don't have any budget until we make this delivery. This is essentially an unfunded startup."

"How would you feel about me covering the updates to the systems? With credits, not booty. I wish, but it's difficult to suck a dick through a wireless network connection." Rhysa laughed.

"I won't be able to pay you back for...I don't know how long."

"Can I buy in? Blaize mentioned she's a partner, and I have some funds. If we want maximum efficiency in the route and smart routing around the dust clouds, I need better tools."

"I can offer you the same partner contract I offered Blaize."

"Done."

"I'll edit your contract now." Cyra paused. "Thanks, Rhysa. For the fuel and for…" Cyra blinked back unexpected tears. "For trusting me enough to invest."

"Thank you for letting me get in on what I think will be an amazing business. You've got an incredible ship."

Cyra glanced around the bare metal panels and the dated systems. *The Treasure* was older, but she was a veritable unicorn as one of the few transports that could move a variety of live cargo. If they got the spiders to Morgual, the future was theirs. Big if.

"We need to be ready to launch as soon as the rods arrive," Cyra told herself as much as Rhysa. "The food and other provisions have already been loaded."

"Rods should be here shortly. Just enough time for me to download the new software and update the maps. I'll be ready when you are."

Cyra wasn't ready for any of this. But that wasn't a requirement. The time for overthinking was past. It was time to launch, *Captain*.

CHAPTER 12

AFTER CYCLES of searching and coming up empty, Varik had finally found the perfect target—a gentle captain, Twalley, with a small research ship, the *Harlan Johnson*, in need of an engineer after he disappeared. Varik had warned Twalley's engineer about the special cocktail and the paid pussy. Maybe not as strongly as he should have. The male would likely recover in a few cycles, but Varik would do anything to get on a ship and go after his *Treasure*.

He still couldn't believe that insufferable bitch had robbed him of his rightful inheritance. Auvi loved him, not her. *He* was the engineer capable of captaining the ship. Not some little fish whose claim to fame was quick, powerful orgasms. Hell, he'd been the first to discover her natural talent in that area. Even as a virgin, she hadn't been anything so special he'd hand over his property to her. But somehow, Auvi had. Thank god the accounts still carried his name or he'd be completely fucked. No ship, no money, nowhere to go.

The fact Auvi planned to leave him in such a position was still incomprehensible.

Too bad he'd waited to draw the final line until after Auvi had updated his disposition of assets on death. If Varik had been aware of his captain's plans, he would have acted sooner. Oh well. Space dust through the nebula.

"I'm not sure I can afford you," Captain Twalley told Varik in a voice barely above a whisper, causing Varik to jolt. He'd forgotten the little captain to his side. "My grant for the next phase of research hasn't been credited. It can take cycles."

"I told you. I have plenty of credits." Varik smacked the smaller man's shoulder. "I might want to visit some places along the way, but I'm sure we can come up with a compatible schedule."

"I need to be available *here* to receive the terms of the grant and make sure I have the funding agency's agenda prioritized in our schedule. Without them, my research dies. It's not just money. They hold the publishing key."

"Of course, of course." Varik was frustrated with the soft little man, but it wouldn't do to scare him off. Varik had to get on the ship before he could take over. There was nothing else to do but wait. He'd approached nearly every docked ship on the station that could make the run to Morgual. No other captain would even consider him for an engineer position. Apparently, some of the old crew had spent a lot of time badmouthing him all over the station, pissed that he hadn't kept his promise to employ them all yet.

Selfish, impatient bastards.

New plans took time to implement.

But his reputation hadn't been that stellar even before losing his position on *The Treasure*. The thing with Blaize had been his first time out after the training class, and some people still remembered it.

Fuck.

Heated outrage shot through him. That was why the female in the bar looked familiar. How could he have forgotten the stupidly orange hair and bizarrely pale skin? Shit. What had he said then? The memory was fuzzy. She could be badmouthing him and bringing up old rumors if she was on station. No wonder none of the other transport captains would even entertain taking him on. They'd only heard *her* side of things, and he had no way to correct their impression if they wouldn't even talk to him.

He clenched his jaw. No other choice remained.

He had to keep this little worm of a research scientist on the hook. But what if the previous engineer reappeared? Didn't matter. All that mattered was reacquiring *The Treasure*. In fact, he should check on her. Were the spiders out? He had no intention of delivering the damn things. He'd jettison immediately, especially if he could get his hands on the ship before it left Cassan.

"Listen, Captain. I have some errands to take care of, but you have my comms. I'll stop by the office first thing."

The man made mewling noises of approval as if Varik had to get permission. Whatever. He strode from the cantina and hurried to the dock. One glimpse. He had to see his *Treasure*.

No.

Varik stared through the portal at the empty dock.

The Treasure was gone.

They'd left.

He beat his fists on the thick airlock door. But maybe it wasn't all bad. Perhaps the spiders had done their job. He double-timed it to the dockmaster's office.

"Excuse me." Varik gave his most charming smile and eyed the dockmaster, searching for a clue to the male's weakness. "I was supposed to meet a Captain Meajzur in dock 6801. But there's no ship there. I might have got the number wrong."

The dockmaster lifted his shaggy bearded face and blinked copper eyes at Varik. "*The Treasure?*"

"Yes, that's the one." Varik stepped fully into the office,

expecting the male to explain how the bay had to be vacuumed due to a release of dangerous biological hazards.

"Launched a few hours ago." His copper eyes narrowed. "Who did you say you were?"

"I didn't." Varik spun and left before he took his rage out on the officer. That would only result in being locked up, possibly for a long time. He needed *The Treasure*. As soon as he returned to his rented quarters, he let loose with a long scream of obscenities. Why the fuck couldn't he catch a break?

How had she gotten fuel with no credits?

And how had she taken off with no crew? Even if Blaize had joined her, and that made the most logical sense, she'd still need more crew.

Fucking Auvi.

Varik took a quick shower to calm down. He could try to strong-arm Twalley, but the wishy-washy captain wasn't interested in speeding up his launch. Assuming those bitches were on the way to Morgual, the only way he'd be able to intercept was to launch that cycle. He'd have to route through a bridge too.

With the captain resisting leaving Cassan, there was no way to catch up unless he found another ship. He could watch the docks, but he was better off installing his tracking software on the *Harlan*. He would bet Blaize, or whoever the new engineer was, hadn't discovered the beacon he'd planted months ago on *The Treasure*—just in case. If he could load up his tracker, he would know when they were leaving Morgual and be able to find them anywhere.

Varik called Twalley. "Captain, have you received any updates from the agency?"

"Not yet. These things take time."

"No rush." Varik did his best to sound relaxed and obedient. "I'd like to meet your remaining crew soon and possibly get familiar with the systems. I know you aren't ready to contract, but we can lay some groundwork. No cost to you."

"Of course. I'll see if I can't round up the crew for a meet-and-greet meal sometime in the next few cycles."

It wasn't access to the ship, but it was a start. Varik could identify who on the crew was weak and could be replaced with people loyal to him. He had plenty of time now that he'd missed the first window of opportunity to recapture *The Treasure*.

Remaining pissed about the lost chance wouldn't solve anything. Instead, he'd stay focused on the future. He would add it to the accounting he was going to settle when he finally had that bitch, Cyra, in his grasp. She would pay for taking his captain and taking his ship and taking his dignity by making him grovel to a weakling like Twalley.

CHAPTER 13

"Who's making last-meal tonight?" Cyra asked Veda. "I want to keep up the tradition of at least one shared meal a cycle."

"It's a good tradition, even if the food leaves something to be desired."

Cyra shrugged off the embarrassment. "Captain Auvi instructed me in many areas, but culinary skills wasn't one of them."

Veda wrinkled her face. "I can mix up a treatment to solve the worst Bagwas worms infection, but that doesn't translate to cooking dinner."

"Maybe Blaize or Rhysa could give it a shot tonight. We could rotate if all of us suck equally." Cyra found them on the bridge.

"I don't cook." Rhysa crossed her arms.

"Well, I'm no chef." Blaize whipped her gaze from Rhysa to Veda to Cyra. "I can tune our engine's consumption of mass fuel, but that doesn't mean I'm an expert with other consumption."

"Veda and I have already taken our turns. Shared last-meal

is a tradition on *The Treasure.* One we're not giving up." Cyra puffed out her chest in her best captain's pose.

"Flip for it?" Blaize asked, pulling out a flight token that was probably from her school days. "Faces you cook, ships I will."

Rhysa glared at the disc. "Captain Cyra can flip it."

Blaize handed over the token, and Cyra flipped it a couple of times to make sure it wasn't weighted. "Okay, this is for the kitchen duty."

"Fine, but faces *you* cook," Rhysa said.

Cyra flipped the disc. "Ships."

"Shit." Rhysa glared at Blaize before stomping toward the corridor.

"And Blaize is cooking tomorrow," Cyra called out behind her.

"Shit." Blaize dropped into the engineer's station chair. "Do we have noodles?"

"Is Dez joining us for last-meal?" Cyra asked Veda. He wasn't technically part of the crew, but she'd barely seen him at all. Not that it mattered. It didn't at all. Except that she was the captain.

"I wasn't sure what you wanted. I've been bringing him trays, but I'm a little concerned. He's not eating much." Veda glanced toward the door that led to the crew quarters.

Great. Another problem. "Let me know if he doesn't eat tonight, and I'll deal with it."

"Thanks, Cyr," Veda replied.

Rhysa hadn't lied. She was a terrible cook in a crew of terrible cooks. If she hadn't choked down her own cooking, Cyra would have sworn she'd done a worse job on purpose. With her gut churning, Cyra left the galley and retreated to her water chamber. If she lost the ship, she'd never have the luxury again. Good food would be nice, but the saltwater gel-pool was everything, especially when she had to deal with her only two crew members being completely at odds with each other. But they were amazing at their jobs. Blaize's improvements to the systems cut their drag, and the speed they maintained was phenomenal. Rhysa had routed a super-efficient path, and they would be near Morgual within another cycle. The cycle was nearing the end when she finally pulled herself from the tank. She caught herself heading toward her old quarters before she recalled she occupied the captain's quarters. The ship and the crew and the cargo were her responsibility. But for the first time since Auvi died, Cyra finally slept without waking from a nightmare.

"I've contacted the space port," Cyra announced after arriving on the bridge the next day-cycle. "We should have approval to land by the time we arrive."

"Why are you contacting them so early?" Veda asked. She sat in one of the stations no longer assigned to a crew member. She probably didn't enjoy hanging out alone in the back of the ship closer to the cargo bay. Couldn't fault her for that.

"Biohazard deliveries require advanced notice. Granted, it's for one of the pharmaceutical factories, but we still need additional approvals. I also had to contact the buyer to initiate the process from his end to receive those damn creepy-crawlies. Technically, we are at the outside edge of our delivery date."

"Any chance they won't approve it or the customer won't accept delivery?" Rhysa asked.

"I don't expect any issues." Cyra hadn't considered that the customer might not take delivery. If that happened, they were screwed. She wouldn't have funds to leave Cassan a second time, and she'd have a cargo full of deadly spiders wanting to eat something or someone.

"They have to take delivery. They contracted this shipment. What reason could they possibly have to decline a shipment? Can they even do that?" Blaize asked.

"Until the spiders are off the ship and the credits are in our account, I suppose they can do whatever they want. They didn't negotiate the contract with me. They contracted Captain Auvi. I'm counting on their need for these bugs to make them honor what is arguably a null-and-void contract."

"You could've mentioned that part before we left Cassan," Rhysa said.

The back of Cyra's neck prickled. "I hadn't actually considered it until I started requesting all the authorizations."

"It'll work," Veda said quietly.

Cyra silently thanked her best friend for always believing in her. Next order of business. "Did Dez eat?"

Veda tilted her head. "Not much."

"Do you know where he is?"

Veda supplied the room number he'd selected. Cyra noted it was the smallest crew quarters available. Used in the past for the low-level maintenance crew, it had a double bunk and not much else if she remembered correctly. She'd stayed in one when she'd first come aboard.

"Dez?" Cyra knocked on the door. It slid open, and she took a step back. Shirtless Dez was even more mouthwatering than fully clothed Dez. Cyra blinked away the inappropriate impulses. "Veda says you aren't eating. Are you sick?"

"Surprisingly, no. I should be ill from eating the substances you call food." He crossed his arms, and his muscles bulged. Dark lines traced the edges, making them stand out even more.

Cyra crossed her arms to avoid reaching out to touch him. "You have to eat. The meals are balanced with protein, carbs, all the nutrients."

"Processed in an approved warehouse and machined into packages. I can taste every wrapper, every box the garbage you call food was transported in before it reached this ship and sadly my plate."

Heat lit Cyra's cheeks. "I'm sorry we don't have a chef, your highness, but might I remind you that you're not a passenger. You're cargo. Cargo I have to deliver in some semblance of health. So you will eat, even if I have to put you in a medical coma and put a tube down your throat."

Dez puffed up. His yellow gaze burned into her like lasers, converting the heat of her embarrassment to an achy fire. "Fine, Captain. But may I make use of the remaining capsaicin oil?"

"The what?" Cyra hadn't expected him to use such a calm tone as angry as he clearly was. His control was intoxicating.

"The oil I used to repel the spiders—no one else seems to appreciate it. It will help me swallow the muck you call food."

And there he went, reminding her of how he'd saved her ship. "Of course you can use that if you like it." She swallowed down the swirling sea of lust, shame, and inadequacy. "Can you also please join us in the galley? I'm sorry about the cargo comment. It was uncalled for."

"It was accurate. And yes, I'll join you." Dez relaxed his stance. "Anything else?"

So many things from her dreams came to mind, none of which were appropriate. She blew out a heated breath, seeking something to say. "We'll be landing on Morgual soon."

Dez nodded. An electric silence sparked between them and neither made the move to fully retreat. Cyra opened her mouth to say something to fill the void, inexplicably unable to walk away.

"If there's nothing else?"

Cyra shook her head. If she spoke, she'd say something she shouldn't.

The door swished closed. The frustration of a barrier between them shoved low in her belly. She chided herself all the way back to the deck. Dez was cargo, and she had to eliminate any attraction she might hold for the male. Cargo. If she repeated it often enough to herself, she might remember the next time she saw him.

"We have all the authorizations to land," Cyra told Blaize and Rhysa the next cycle.

"Have we heard from the buyer?" Rhysa asked from her seat on the bridge as she refined the landing plans to route to the assigned dock.

"He's hedging, but we have the spiders." And no way to get rid of them. "It's not like he'll get another shipment anytime soon. We're one of the few transporters that caries biologics in this region. Not many ships are even equipped for live cargo." Acid swirled in Cyra's gut as she repeated all the reasons the customer had to accept the order more to refocus herself than appease the crew. "The environmental systems, lockdowns, redundant life support systems, food delivery systems. Captain Auvi put his investment money there. The ship may not have the latest and greatest in terms of engines and navigation—at least it didn't—but we do have the best cargo support systems."

"What's the plan if the customer doesn't pay?" Rhysa's pink gaze bored into Cyra.

"First, I'll try to wait him out, but we have a brief window for that to work. The spiders will be starving." And Cyra so didn't want to buy spider food or to even know what they ate. "He may be trying to bluff. If that doesn't work, I'll post them for sale and see if we have any other takers on planet."

"Good. If he sees a posting for his cargo, that may be the fire he needs to finish the deal." Rhysa turned back to her screen.

The landing went perfectly. Cyra couldn't have asked for more technically skilled partners—they easily did the work of a crew of ten. *The Treasure* was docked in the high-security area of the port. Veda would stay on the ship with Dez while Cyra met with the buyer. Blaize and Rhysa were tasked with finding more fuel and food.

Cyra arrived at the pharmaceutical company's satellite office. The tang of chemicals and char saturated the air, and the landscaping had a distinct brownish-gray tinge. Cyra couldn't wait to get off the planet, but first, she had to get the contract paid, the spiders delivered, and hopefully another contract secured. No pressure.

She waited in the utilitarian lobby. Pale gray floors, high windows, and bare white walls with framed images of happy beings in sunny locations clearly benefiting from better living through chemistry. And clearly not on this planet.

A hairless male stomped toward her with mottled, greenish skin that had a rubbery appearance. His eyes were bulbous and slightly to the outside of his head. She'd have to ask Veda what planet he was from. Maybe he was a native, but she had seen no one like him at the docks. He didn't greet her; he just came to a stop and stared.

"Habarek? I'm Captain Cyra Maejzur of *The Treasure*. I have your delivery."

"*Captain* Cyra? Where's Captain Auvi or Varik?" The buyer looked over her shoulder as if a male would suddenly appear with whom he could conduct business. As if she hadn't explained the situation prior to their arrival.

"As I explained, Captain Auvi is deceased. I was his designated heir. Your shipment is in perfect condition and ready for delivery. I just need the payment and delivery instructions."

"I'll have to review the contract. It appeared that the

delivery wouldn't arrive, so we dropped our original storage location. And I need to verify our payments to this point."

"Of course. We will be on planet for the next few cycles. If you elect not to receive the shipment in the next twenty hours, we'll post the cargo for sale as our contract allows. There will be no refund of credits paid to this point."

"Are you threatening me, little girl?"

Cyra's knees went weak at his authoritarian tone. She stiffened. "It's *Captain Maejzur*, and no, I'm not threatening you. I've reviewed our contract, and I'm just reminding you of the provisions."

Habarek grunted. "I'll be in touch."

"I look forward to concluding our business." So much. She couldn't get on the other side of that contract fast enough.

Cyra was shaking, but she wouldn't let the bastard see it. He probably knew the contract as well or better than she did, testing to see what he could get away with. She hadn't considered that there may have been more than one partial payment. She would review the records with Veda and send the asshole a final invoice so that if he paid, they'd get all the credits they were owed. And she absolutely had to secure another contract immediately.

Cyra went to the bar near the dock to network. She could check cyber site postings, but Captain Auvi always got his best contracts by word of mouth. Anyone could post a job, but talking to someone in person was much more likely to seal the deal. With any luck, she'd also get some gossip about her client and his likelihood of stiffing her on the payment. What would she do with the damn spiders if he reneged and another buyer couldn't be found?

Let them out in the lobby of that damn building.

Tempting, but the potential for innocents to be hurt would stop her from doing anything so bold.

The tiny bar was squeezed between manufacturing warehouses. The door looked like salvage from an old ship, but she recognized the name from stories Auvi had told. Crain's. If this was the right place. Not like the name was that unique. The inside was dark, and she paused to let her eyes adjust. The occupants varied from workers clearly coming off a shift of gritty labor to lifelong drinkers with a smattering of more sophisticated types engaging in mid-cycle meetings away from their businesses.

Not the only female but still a bit out of place, she sat at the bar and ordered a house cocktail. Auvi had told her that bartenders liked it when you trusted their mixing skills and were willing to pay a little extra for a nicer drink. It also gave her something to break the ice and talk to them about. This bartender was an odd-looking creature with four arms and an ovoid head supporting thick tendrils of not quite orange...hair? She wasn't sure if they were male or female. Didn't matter. This being would be her new friend by the time she finished her drink.

"What do you wish to drink?" The voice told her no more than the appearance. Gray, somewhat oily skin, and large dark eyes.

"Do you have a special house cocktail? Something that I can only get here?" Cyra leaned forward and smiled.

"Do you have any allergies?"

"Um, no, not that I know of." That was an odd question.

A few moments later, the bartender placed a layered drink of purple, iridescent blue, and white foam in front of her.

"Wow. This is beautiful. What's in it?"

"Taste it, and I'll tell you."

Cyra sipped from the special straw with a small hole at each layer resulting in a perfectly mixed mouthful. "Oh my god, that's good." It reminded her of her home planet, tropical and fruity with a hint of an ocean breeze.

"I call it the Auvi. A captain who used to come in here sometimes when he had a shipment. He was an odd specimen, like me. Only he was…"

"A fleshy being with dark blue circles rimmed in brown all over his body. His eyes matched his marking, and he had multiple appendages he could use as arms or legs."

"You know him?" the bartender asked with a gasp.

"I did." A pang of loss ricocheted through her. "He passed away and left me his ship. I'm Cyra, Captain Cyra."

"You're Cyra? He told me about you." Their hand wrapped around hers, cool and smooth. "I am so sorry he's gone. He loved you."

"I loved him too." She sniffed back her tears. "I miss him more than I can say."

"He was very good to me. I feel your loss. But what are you doing on Morgual?"

"Dropping one of the last shipments Captain Auvi contracted."

"If I can help you in any way while you're here, let me know. It would be an honor to help his ward. I'm Gorga, by the way."

"Gorga, it's a pleasure to know you." And it was. She'd dreaded introducing herself to a stranger, but once again, Auvi had taken care of her without even trying. It made the next request much simpler. "There is one thing I could use your help with."

"What's that?"

"I'm looking for another transport job."

"Hmm." Gorga wiped the bar top and moved away, checking on the other customers at the bar. Slowly, they worked their way back. "There's an auction happening today.

One of the big muckity-muck factory owners died. I assume you transport the same things as Auvi."

"I do."

"There are supposed to be some biologics on the block. Not every buyer will be on planet."

Cyra's heart raced. Could it be that easy? "Here's my comm connection." She held out her device for the data transmit. Gorga held theirs up, and a ping signaled success. "I would appreciate anything you could send my way."

"You got it, Cyra. Let me know if you want another one of those." They pointed at the drink before moving away again.

Cyra still didn't know what was in the drink, but she finished it in honor of Auvi.

The next cycle, Cyra's phone chimed at breakfast. The buyer offered to pay less than ten percent of the balance due. A woefully low balance. Auvi had received payments that were more than half of the entire contract. "I can't believe this."

"What?" Veda asked, setting her spoon in her bowl.

Cyra held out her comm. "The buyer is trying to short us big time."

"We barely have any income from this contract as it is." Rhysa had reviewed the documents with the others and been upset.

Not as upset as Blaize when she realized who had the contract money—Varik. "Don't respond. It's the best tactic. At least that's what they taught us in contract negotiation class. I took all the notes but was never very good at that part. But my professor said the best way to get someone to recognize an unreasonable offer is to remain quiet, especially if you have something they want. And we do—the spiders."

Veda chuckled. "You didn't do well during that class?"

Blaize turned bright red. "Just that test. I did better with the written part, but the professor said I gave up too easily. I don't like being greedy."

"It's not greed. At least not on *our* part. We did the damn job, so he should pay us. I'd be happy to talk to him." Rhysa's pink eyes flared almost as red as Blaize's cheeks.

Cyra's phone pinged again. Gorga from the bar. "I think I'll let the buyer wait. Let's see if Blaize's professor was right." Cyra dropped her spoon in the muck that was supposed to be grain cereal and stood. "I have to make a call."

CHAPTER 14

"Hey, Cyra." Gorga's warm greeting was optimistic. "I have a lead on a job for you. How do you feel about thuringies?"

"Thuringies?" Cyra froze mid-step.

"Yeah, a pack of them." Gorga's teasing tone let Cyra's legs move again. "A broker picked them up at the auction. Needs to get them to Kolben over in the Heychsix solar system."

"I'm familiar with Kolben." And headed that way. The contract could be the bit of luck she'd been looking for, but... "What are thuringies?"

"Specialized guard dogs. Well, dog-ish."

"Wow, he came a long way to get pets."

Gorga flashed a warning hand. "These aren't pets. They're big, well-trained, and vicious. But it could be a very lucrative contract between the special handling and the distance."

"Why would anyone auction off specialty guard dogs?"

Gorga chortled. "Not by choice. The owner recently went to prison for fraud, blackmail, and racketeering."

"Nice."

"Almost as nice as his dogs. The authorities had a hell of a time getting them off the property."

Cyra traversed the large dock out to the city streets to get a better comm signal. "Why would anyone want to buy these animals? And from a source so far away?"

"It's rare to find them anywhere other than Morgual. We're about the only planet for light years that has a decent training program."

Cyra wouldn't call anything about Morgual decent. It was a dirty, overcrowded planet with much too much unregulated industry. The sky hadn't always been a sickly yellow. Farther away from the true industry, the factory owners kept spacious homes with extensive air-cleaning devices. It wasn't like they didn't know what they were doing to their planet. It was just too profitable to be motivated to stop.

"So how do I get in touch with this trader?" If she wasn't so desperate and didn't have partners counting on her—but she did.

"I gave him your comm info but told him to wait to contact you. You'll likely hear from him tonight."

"Thanks, Gorga. I owe you."

Cyra made her way back to the ship. She'd never consider taking the contract for a transport all the way to Kolben if she wasn't already going. It would take g-months to get there. Could she manage the dogs on the ship for the entire time? It wasn't like spiders. They'd have to eat, exercise, and evacuate their waste.

Cyra called a meeting in the galley and explained the details of the possible transport.

"We should navigate through wormholes to make sure we're profitable." Rhysa leaned back in her chair, arms crossed.

Cyra cringed at the casual term for a bridge. Traveling through an ER bridge seemed like she was being processed through the guts of a worm. It was too accurate a term, and she refused to use it. No shortening of the trip was worth that experience, in her opinion. She wouldn't use one unless there was no other way. "Plan as if that's not an option."

Rhysa huffed.

"Meet back here for last-meal to discuss the quote."

Cyra spent the hours between digging through Auvi's files and searching the database for any information on previous transports to Kolben. The only contract she found was the existing one for Dez. She examined the details, noting one alarming caveat. She frantically checked the dates again. If she didn't deliver Dez in the next ninety-one cycles, not only would they forfeit the remaining payment but they would also owe the deposit and a hefty breach-of-contract fee.

She should have read the damn thing sooner, but there was no time for regrets. She continued digging until she found the template for live cargo transport contracts and the accompanying quote sheet. There were a lot of blanks, and she only had some of the answers. How dangerous were these dogs? Was there any way to control them? Damn, she should have asked. How big was big? With a shrug, she entered forty-five kilos each and winced at the result. That was a lot of food. Which meant they'd have to stop and load up on the way to Kolben, probably on Cassan. She finished poking at the data, then rushed to the galley.

Her comm buzzed with an incoming call. She glanced at the time. Hours had passed.

"I'm Helfang. I got your number from Gorga." The trader's gravelly voice blasted in her ear. She held the device farther out.

"Yes, um, Helfang. This is Captain Maejzhur of *The Treasure*. How can I help you?"

"I just picked up a thuringy pack at auction. I need them transported to Kolben."

"Will you be traveling with the cargo?" A part of her hoped

he would so he could own the trouble of caring for the animals. On the other hand, she didn't want word to get out about exactly how small *The Treasure* crew was.

"No. I have a few more stops before I head back to Cassan. I don't live on Kolben. I just have a contract to make acquisitions for them. Tell you the truth, I hate the cold."

"When will you be bringing me the cargo?"

"Call off the launch sequence, Captain." Helfang chuckled. "We need to talk price."

"I need more details to quote you a price. Do you have the biologic requirements, food, and environmental needs?"

"There are five in the pack. Don't want them losing muscle on the trip. A high protein diet and some kind of workout provision should keep them in the same prime shape that I purchased them. I'll send you the details."

"What about their attack training? I heard the authorities had trouble retrieving the little darlings from their owner's property."

"Not a problem. Two things. First, you have to know their training commands. I have the key for that. All the commands and their meanings. Second, you need someone confident enough to command them. They have a highly developed vomeronasal organ and can smell fear."

"Great." Cyra gulped down her trepidation. Maybe one of her partners would be comfortable commanding a pack of thuringies. "I'll prepare a quote. We require half the payment at the time the cargo is accepted for transport."

"That's not a problem, as long as we can agree on the price," Helfang said.

"I'll be in touch." The comm screen went dark.

"So what do you think?" Cyra asked after everyone had eaten.

"I think we still need a chef. This food sucks." Blaize frowned and stirred the remnants on her plate with a fork.

"You cooked it."

"I know, I'm poisoning myself."

"I will cook next." The usually silent male's voice surprised Cyra. His deep tones resonated through her, leaving an echo of inappropriate desire.

"Are you sure, Dez? You don't have to." The itch between her shoulder blades warned Cyra that this would be taking advantage of the essentially captive man.

"I cannot do a worse job than the previous two last-meals." He gazed down at his bowl, but Cyra wasn't sure if it was a look of disgust or disappointment.

"Hey," Rhysa barked.

"Are you arguing that you're a better cook than the rest of us?" Cyra asked with a tone of warning that Rhysa could have the job if she wasn't careful.

"Not at all. Go for it, Dez. Captain's right, you can't suck worse than me." Rhysa made an O with her mouth and dragged her fingers down the sides. "Although I've been told I suck quite well."

Time to change the topic.

"About the thuringy contract," Cyra spoke over the rest of the group before they completely lost focus. "What should we charge? I can't find any history that Auvi ever transported a pack of dogs, so beyond Dez's contract..." She glanced at him guiltily. "I don't have any basis."

"I need to consider possible medical needs. How dangerous are these beasts?" Veda asked in a voice barely above a whisper.

"Before we think too hard about getting to Kolben, we need to figure out how we're going to get back to Cassan. We'll need more EMF rods just to make sure we make it back there, and that's if we can even get the ship to launch again. I've never worked with an emotional energy panel. It doesn't have any documentation. The original manufacturer went out of business. Go figure. Not too many people want to have to orgasm on the deck just to get their ship into orbit. I mean, the only ship I can think of where that might be an asset is a pleasure cruiser, and even then, you wouldn't want it on the deck. But besides that, we need more fuel to be safe, and the prices here are ridiculous. Rhysa got us more rods on Cassan, but what we have left is exactly what we need, with no room for error. If anything goes wrong... And with the extra load of...of the cargo and the food to support said cargo— Have we received payment for the damn spiders? I mean, it would be nice to have them off the ship, and then we could prep to take on new cargo. As it is now, I wouldn't be confident that I could keep the spiders contained. Putting additional live cargo in the same area will be a problem." Blaize looked up and took her first breath. The rest of the crew had their eyes glued to her, and their mouths hung open.

"I don't know what to answer or reply to or question first," Cyra said.

"She does go on once she gets started," Veda replied.

"I already heard from the pharmaceutical company." Cyra pulled her hair away from her gills. "I didn't reply to his crappy offer like you all suggested. I got another message just a few moments before last-meal. He wants to talk."

"Let him wait some more. Call him after first-meal," Rhysa told her.

Cyra nodded.

"As for the fuel," Rhysa continued. "Prices here are ridiculous. If we get a few, we should have plenty to make it to Cassan, but there's no way we can make Kolben without taking wormholes. The calculation doesn't work any other way."

"Let's sell the spiders, find out what the requirements are for the new cargo, and see how much deposit we're getting. The deposit may be enough to get us the additional fuel and the food provisions we need." Cyra hoped she wasn't wrong.

Veda tapped Cyra's shoulder. "Don't forget the possible additional medical supplies. Dogs have very different metabolisms from humanoids, and I've only had minimal training with canine-based life-forms. So it could be tricky."

"That reminds me. We have to make a provision for them to exercise. I did some research, and I think if we give them a fairly open space with bedding and then treadmill time—"

"I would be happy to assist with managing the dogs."

Cyra turned to Dez. "I can't ask you to do that."

"I have nothing to occupy my time on this ship. The tedium is almost as bad as the food." He lifted a forkful and let it plop back into his bowl. "*Please*, give me something to do."

Cyra met with the pharmaceutical rep the next cycle. The quiet negotiation tactic had been effective. He transferred the remaining credits owed and had the transportation vehicle and a specialized handling team ready to move the spiders. Tension on the ship dropped noticeably, but Cyra remained concerned about their next contract. Nothing was done until the final contract was approved. And if she didn't close the deal... Not possible. She had to make it happen.

Helfang was waiting at the bar when Cyra got there. "Sorry I kept you waiting. I had to finish up a prior commitment."

"No problem, you can pick up the tab to make it up to me."

Cyra smiled. Sometimes you had to spend credits to make credits. Besides, if Helfang was happy with her work, they might get future contracts. "We've rearranged the cargo bay space to accommodate exercise equipment for the pack while providing appropriate kennel space." She placed the contract on the table. "We have a price in mind. We considered the number of animals, the additional food, medical, and fuel requirements and, of course, the distance."

"How much?"

"Seven hundred fifty thousand. Half up front."

Helfang winced and sucked in a breath. "That's pretty steep."

Cyra had seen that negotiation tactic before. "It's quite fair."

"Will you guarantee delivery?"

"I will guarantee five hundred thousand. The remainder is non-refundable."

"Done." Helfang held out his hand, and Cyra offered him her comm to approve the contract with his thumbprint and embedded GID.

"When do you want to transfer the cargo?"

"Tonight. I can transfer the deposit now if you give me your account data." Helfang picked up his own comm.

Had she underbid the job? They had all added their costs and then doubled the values—twice the fuel, twice the food, additional medical, and the staff time. She had expected him to negotiate more. The fact that he jumped on the price told her she should increase her quotes in the future, but at least she and her partners had a contract.

They were officially in business with the first contract not previously negotiated by Auvi.

After finishing her drink with Helfang, she settled the tab and thanked Gorga. She planned to make an effort to cultivate relationships with locals on each planet they reached. There was no better advertising for her transport business than word of mouth.

Her reputation on Cassan was so tattered, making her performance on this contract and her local planet connections even more critical. She could afford to do nothing to sabotage her fragile position.

Snarling and yapping filled the corridor outside Dez's quarters. He rose from the lower bunk, contemplating how to once again fill the hours between lousy meals on the ship and how he could keep from losing his mind from boredom during the long journey he still had to make. The door slid open, and Veda and the captain trailed five burly men, each with a canine on a leash.

Dez rushed to catch up. "What are you doing?"

Veda didn't slow down. "I have to complete the medical assessment. It's a requirement for live cargo."

Dez recalled the inspection Doc had given him, including a blood draw when he'd first boarded *The Treasure*. "How do you plan to do that? They'll eat you two alive."

"They won't," Captain Cyra said, as if she was trying to will it so. "See their muzzles?"

Dev caught a glimpse of the metal and leather cages strapped to the dogs' faces. "Those will have to come off for them to eat."

"They have a remote release." Captain Cyra marched forward, undeterred by the deadly sounds coming from the beasts.

"And when they need to go back on?" Dez feared for the little doctor and the stunning blue captain. There was no way he'd let anything happen to either of them. But it would hurt his heart if the dogs marred the captain's skin.

"I'll cross that wormhole when I get there." Veda double stepped to catch up to the pack.

Dez followed, determined to provide some protection. The handlers placed the canines in their individual kennels but didn't offer a bit of help to Dr. Veda. He half expected them to sit down and play a game while they waited as unconcerned with the intake as they were. Dez scowled at the useless group and stayed by Veda's side as she scanned each dog and documented their initial health status. The dogs were calmer one-on-one but still big enough to eat her in one bite.

Captain Cyra dragged her finger over her comm, muttering to herself. "There are commands somewhere in this paperwork."

"Can you hold up that front paw so I can get a sample?" Dr. Veda asked with a syringe in one hand.

"Sure." Dez wasn't sure at all. He ran his hand down the flank of the large male who came to Dez's waist. His head was like a bowling ball, and he butted into Dez's thigh, leaning in. A low rumble came from deep in the dog's chest. "That's it. Who's a good boy?" Dez kept petting the beast with one hand and turned the dog's collar with the other. Credit. The name was woven into the collar. "Good boy, Credit." Dez lifted the required paw. "This will be a tiny pinch, boy, but if I can do it, so can you."

Veda parted the long black fur and plunged the needle in.

The purring stopped. Dez petted the dog more firmly, cooing positive words.

"Okay, all done." Veda dispensed the tiny sample into the reader. "No issues." She glanced at the handlers, who were ignoring her and the dogs. "Do you think you can put this one in his cage and bring out the next one?"

"I will kennel Credit." Better to get the crew to see these beasts as individuals and worthy of care as soon as possible.

"Right, I'm sorry. Kennel." She reached out and ran her fingers along the dog's chest. "Good boy, Credit."

They continued to work through the pack: Reaper, Vengeance, Wrath, and finally Dez brought out Queen. The lone female resisted being removed from the cell, then tried to run, nearly pulling Dez off his feet.

"*Prasanta.*" The captain's command filled the cargo bay.

Queen stopped pulling. The lead went slack, and her tongue lolled out.

"Good girl." Dez patted the female's bronze fur but didn't miss the intake of breath from Cyra. He dragged his gaze away from the woman who'd captivated his dreams from the moment he'd boarded the ship when Veda cleared her throat.

"I sent the commands to your comm. I...I have to go." Captain Cyra tapped her screen rapidly as she hurried to the exit, her face a light shade of purple. The handlers parted for the majestic female.

Dez fought the impulse to follow her, to elicit more of her gasps. He blinked. Where had that come from? The dog bumped his leg. He'd forgotten he was holding the lead.

"I'm ready." Veda's tiny smile confirmed she hadn't missed a bit of the tension between the captain and himself. He'd tried hiding, but staying locked in a room with terrible meals brought to him three times a day wasn't a long-term plan. Whatever the captain triggered in him would pass.

Dez led Queen to Veda.

But no command from any of them worked when it came time for the blood draw. The dog would not cooperate at all. Veda finally gave up. "I'll get it later. There's no sign of infection in any of the others, and they've been kenneled together and quarantined for the past g-month."

Dez kenneled the resistant female while Veda showed the handlers off the ship. He made sure each of the dogs was freed from their muzzles and had plenty of water in their drip feeders. Hopefully, it wasn't the first time they'd been transported.

Credit lapped at the metal tube, and Dez relaxed. They would be fine. But maybe he should stay with them to make sure. Anything to avoid the unfamiliar sensations of lust that swept through him every time he was too close to the captain. Somehow, the dogs were safer.

Veda paced behind Dez as he knelt by the kennels. Her worrying audible. "We're working on getting food supplies for the ship. I'm not sure what the protein will be. It's quite expensive on this planet. And the dogs will require so much to maintain their health."

"Veda, would you consider presenting a unique request to Captain Cyra?" Dez glanced over his shoulder, his fingers still buried in Credit's fur.

"What request?"

Dez released the dog and stood, hands clasped together in front of him. "I have not been back to see my family since I entered servitude. It has been five g-years. Kolben is a great distance, and I won't be able to see them again, probably in my lifetime or theirs. I would like to request your captain consider a trade."

"A trade?" The data pad clutched back to her chest.

That didn't bode well, but he had to at least ask, especially if they were planning to buy food on Morgual. His stomach turned, and the words fell out. "If she will supply the trip to my planet, I will supply the food and fuel needed to deliver me to Kolben."

"She won't trust that you will stay."

"My word is my—"

"Life. I remember." Veda paused her pacing. "Can I ask you something?"

"Of course."

"Why did you sell yourself? If you can supply a ship for a trip like this, why would you sell yourself?" The final question was almost accusatory.

"I am not wealthy, nor is my family. My sister fell in love with the prince. He was also in love with her, but it's custom that the female brings a dowry to marry. My family could not supply her the sum that would meet the level required by a prince."

"You sold yourself so that your sister could marry for love." Veda's voice was filled with awe he didn't really deserve. He'd done the right thing. That shouldn't be awe-inspiring.

"Because I did this for her and for him, I feel confident that he will grant my request to provision the ship for the trip."

"But why? Why wouldn't you have him buy your freedom?"

He flinched at the dishonorable suggestion. It would be like requesting his sister's dowry be returned. "I have no need of it. I agreed to servitude, and I honor my commitments."

"What about you and *your* future?"

"I was an adult and hadn't met my mate. I don't expect to meet one now that I do not live on Din' Gale." Although his reaction to the captain concerned him. "I won't be socializing with anyone other than my family while we're there. I'll travel to Kolben either way. If your captain grants my request, we'll both benefit."

"You could ask her yourself."

Dez rubbed the back of his neck, scraping at the desire to ask for much more than a visit home. "She's more likely to listen to you, her best friend."

"I'll talk to her. It's unlikely, Dez. Cyra is a new captain, and this is a high-risk request." The tiny brown doctor had backed completely away.

A wave of inevitability stole through him, taking his energy. He knelt by Queen's kennel, trying to coax the female into allowing him to pet her. "She would not consider it high risk if she knew me better."

CHAPTER 15

Cyra paced the length of the bridge, surrounded by tech decks and display screens. Rhysa had left to work her magic to secure discounts on food and fuel. Blaize was probably buried deep in the bowels of the engines, tweaking every last bit of efficiency she could get. And Veda was with *him*. Dezmuhnd. Dez.

A visual of the huge male, deep gray with dark striped lines that made Cyra's mouth water. Her reaction to his hard body, planes of muscles, and deep, foreboding gaze confounded her. She didn't care for big, burly types. Auvi had been muscular, but it had been hidden underneath his rubbery flesh. And Varik was lean and long like her. Dez was a predator by design. Her insides clenched. Her libido bubbled a willingness to be his prey. She was so lit up, she could probably launch the ship with no additional effort. She dragged a finger across the panel where she and Auvi launched the ship so many times. She'd loved her captain in a respectful way. He'd known her body well enough to use it, but she'd never experienced such a primal reaction to a male before she'd seen Dez enter *The Treasure* with his sinuous stride. How many cycles had it been? Her life had been complete chaos from practically that moment on, but the first time she'd gazed into his piercing yellow eyes was burned into her brain. Every time she'd been around him since, her reaction only got stronger. And when he managed the terrifying thuringies, her core had fluttered. Fluttered, for fuck's sake. She should not be reacting to him.

He was cargo.

She was contracted to deliver him like so much crated goods. Her crew, her ship, and her future all depended on her, keeping her focus on her head and not on her heated pussy.

Water.

She should cool off before the crew met for last-meal. The tank would center her, and she wasn't accomplishing anything by pacing the bridge and imagining Dezmuhnd helping her shoot *The Treasure* into space. With a curse, she spun and raced to the one place she could wash away those crazy feelings of attraction for a beast of a man who likely wasn't attracted to her species anyway.

Hours later, the crew met for last-meal, and the food was unexpectedly edible. She slurped in the noodle with a hint of spice, resentful that it was one more way Dez affected her body.

"This planet sucks." Rhysa dropped her fork onto her half-finished plate. "I can't get anyone to give me a discount on fuel. It's like no one here has ever heard of a fucking blow job. They seem to only get off on money. Sex is an unknown concept."

Blaize and Cyra laughed.

"The food and medical situation is just as bad. This place is expensive," Cyra offered after she quit laughing at Rhysa's antics.

"We might have a way around it." Veda's voice was low and hesitant.

All eyes focused on Veda.

She blinked up at them. "Dez made a request that could solve all our problems."

Cyra darted her gaze to the silent male seemingly fascinated by his food. She turned back to Veda. "Explain."

"Excuse me, Captain." Dez stood. "I will let you discuss this plan privately with your partners."

"Dez, wait," Veda said. The door slid closed behind him and she briefly laid out his offer.

"Absolutely not." Cyra didn't even look up to see if anyone had a different opinion and continued to shovel down her food despite the guilt that choked her.

"Now, wait just a second," Rhysa spoke up. "It's a reasonable request, benefitting both us and him. Is there a risk, sure? But what is that compared to the reward?"

"Don't know." That sexy...*cargo* was messing with her plans. "Not willing to take the gamble."

"You're willing to chance us being stuck in the middle of space with no food or no fuel, but you're not willing to risk losing the cargo?" Blaize jumped in on Rhysa's side, earning her a surprised look from Rhysa.

"She has a point, Captain," Rhysa said.

Blaize continued as if Rhysa hadn't said a word. "If we stock up here at these inflated prices, the greater probability is that we won't have sufficient credits when we get to Cassan, and if we try to make the run to Kolben, we could run out of food and fuel. Varik won't have to steal our ship—he can just come collect it and eject our dead bodies into space."

Veda nodded.

"First, Varik is not a real threat." Cyra glared at her crew, daring them to call her out for the lie she spewed. She should tell them about the penalty for not delivering Dez on time. But if she admitted the ridiculous timeline, they would insist on traveling through ER bridges. She stifled the shudder of dread of being pulled to pieces in one of the unpredictable rends in space.

"You're dreaming if you believe Varik would give up so easily," Blaize interrupted.

"Second, how is stocking up on Din' Gale going to be better than stocking up here?" Cyra stood and dropped her empty bowl in the recycle bin to keep from licking the residual sauce.

"We can't fully provision here." Rhysa leaned forward, locking her gaze on Cyra's. "We don't have enough funds, even with your ridiculously high deposit. Apparently, we underestimated just how much more everything would cost here."

"Fuck." Cyra dragged her fingers through her hair, uncovering her gills. Her partners were right. Stubbornness could get them killed. But Dezmuhnd, while nice and a decent cook, was an unknown. She cursed Auvi for dying before she was ready to be the captain. "I'm not agreeing to this until I talk to him."

Cyra banged on the door to Dez's quarters. A low rumble reached her ears before the door slid open.

Dez stepped back, allowing her to enter.

Cyra cursed her body's response to being alone with him. She glanced around the small room. There was nowhere to sit other than his bed. She turned from the temptation, and guilt crept up her spine. "You could have chosen more well-appointed quarters."

He nodded but did not reply.

"May I discuss your request with you?"

"Yes, Captain." His voice was scratchy.

If he was getting sick—no. That wasn't an option. "You asked to go to Din' Gale, where your family lives. Why should I agree to that?"

"My home has excellent food—there are farms that grow grains and vegetables along with plentiful animal protein. You have to feed the thuringies. And the other women. And me. We have a long journey ahead. Wouldn't it be best to make it as pleasant as possible?"

Great argument, but it didn't address her concern. "If I take you to your home, what would possibly compel you to reboard?"

"I won't harm you. In any way." His yellow gaze turned hot, searing into her. "Your livelihood, your future, is secured by transporting cargo for others." He scanned her body, and her breath caught while her core heated. "I will honor my contract as I have for the past five g-years."

Cyra swallowed hard, aching for the cool waves in her pool. She studied him the way he'd done to her. Everything she knew about him confirmed his words. He'd saved her ship from the spiders. He'd helped with the dogs. He'd cooked the first decent meal she'd eaten since they left Cassan. Despite his appearance, he ate carefully, spoke respectfully, and was nothing but kind to everyone on board.

On the outside, he was designed to be an unstoppable predator. But he resonated a sense of calm and control. Peace. "I will take you home to visit," she said, rising. "Veda will return with more water."

"Thank you, Captain," he said as she retreated from his room. "I will show you good food." His gaze filled with heated promise. "You will eat like a queen."

CHAPTER 16

Cyra glared at the launch panel on the bridge of *The Treasure*. Blaize and Rhysa were with her but focused on their own displays. The minimal fuel and goods they'd purchased were loaded. Rhysa had set their course for Din' Gale in the navigation systems. The ship's internals were working the best they had been since they were new, but Cyra was worried about how she would launch. They hadn't needed to break out of atmosphere on Cassan, but to leave Morgual required a big launch boost to get up to the critical speed for the exotic matter engines could take over. Hovering over the launch pad while the ground crew squawked about how *The Treasure* was holding up traffic didn't help.

Cyra wasn't about to masturbate on the deck to try for an orgasm, nor was she going to ask one of them to bring her to the energy release the ship required. "How the fuck am I going to make this piece of shit work, Auvi?" she screamed out and slammed her hands on the deck.

"That's it." Blaize spun in her engineer's chair to face Cyra. "Do that again. There's almost enough energy for a push."

"Seriously? It works on anger too?" Cyra couldn't believe Auvi hadn't shared that with her.

"Seems so." Blaize went back to monitoring the systems.

"Why the fuck didn't I know that, Auvi?" She let all the anger that she felt at losing Captain Auvi, being sabotaged by Varik, and being kept in the dark on the ship's special "push" system funnel through her body and into the panel.

"Yes," Blaize hollered.

The ship lurched from where it had been hovering into hyper-speed, tossing Cyra back in her chair. She clung to the arms as the ship bucked out of the atmosphere, though not nearly as smoothly as she was used to. At least *The Treasure* was finally underway.

"Damn, I was hoping you'd have to break down and let me get you off, Captain," Rhysa said with a teasing wink.

"I'll keep that in mind for future emergencies." Cyra slumped in the captain's chair, drained of her anger and dreading what she'd have to face next.

"What the hell was that, Captain?" Veda's voice barked over the internal ship comm. Growls and snarls filled the background. "We nearly died back here. The thuringies are not happy."

Cyra grimaced and pressed the comm button to reply. "Sorry. Rougher than I expected."

"Next time, warn us when you're going to splat us like bugs against the wall."

Cyra made placating noises, promising the next one would be smoother, although she had no idea how she would keep that promise.

Within a few cycles, *The Treasure* neared Dez's planet of Din' Gale. The closer they got, the more Cyra second-guessed her decision to let Dez visit his home planet. Especially after she'd listened in on his call to them. It sounded like he hadn't been in communication with them at all, and his parents lavished him with love and praise, thrilled with the prospect of seeing him again. How would they be able to let him go again?

That one decision could leave her and her crew stranded on the remote planet. Cyra didn't really have a home besides *The Treasure*, but without transport jobs to sustain a crew, food, and fuel, she would have to sell it and find something else to do. She'd never lived anywhere else in her adult life.

They docked at the Din' Gale Royal Space Port, and it was clear that the native vegetation had to be pruned away regularly to keep the port open. Through the numerous windows of the circular building that garaged *The Treasure*, a landscape spread before her unlike anything she'd ever seen. Rocky plains covered in trees and vines provided a lush but rugged backdrop. Waterfalls filled the air with mist. The planet was almost as wet as her home planet, but the foliage was so different. Flocks of colorful birds punctuated the deep blue sky, swooping and diving through the naturally forming rainbows. The sheer beauty of it held her captive.

"Rhysa," Cyra called out to her navigator as she descended into the bay. "While we're here, would you try to secure another transport job if you get the opportunity? I have to stay close to our—"

"Dez won't run off. Even I believe him when he says he'll come with us after a visit." She narrowed her pink eyes. "And I rarely trust anyone."

"I'll just feel better if I can keep tabs on him."

"No hardship. I'll take any excuse to rub elbows with the locals. Especially if they look anything like Dez." Rhysa winked at Cyra and sauntered toward the exit where Blaize waited.

Cyra clenched her jaw to keep from saying something she'd regret, like warning Rhysa to quit looking at Dez.

Veda and Dez had left earlier to work with the space port team to manage the canines. At his request, the facility provided them with a large, fully enclosed pen where the animals could exercise outdoors while still providing shelter. Cyra had questioned the cost, but Dez waved her off. Apparently, his sister's royal status covered their expenses too. Worry weighed on Cyra's shoulders. After all the chaos, the visit to Din' Gale was too easy. She'd have to remain on guard for the unexpected because there was no way the detour to the cargo's home planet would work out for her.

Dez led them to a small hovercraft that would take them to his home. The pilot flew between the cliffs. The dark gray rocks jutted out from the dense forest.

"Your planet is beautiful, Dez," Veda said with a touch of awe.

"I loved it here." His voice held a note of wistfulness, putting Cyra on alert. "This is the wilder side of the planet. Farther out, away from the deep rivers and jagged mountains, is rich farmland. The forest has many delicacies I hope to share with you during our brief visit."

"Food. Good food. I can't wait." Rhysa rubbed her hands together gleefully.

How would Dez ever be able to leave his planet again, knowing he was going to a frozen planet to work in a mine? Cyra wouldn't be able to do it. Although she'd given up her beautiful water planet for a metal ship. Despite the effusive call, maybe he wasn't as close to his family as he seemed. Or perhaps this would be her final decision as the captain because she would forfeit on Auvi's last contract.

The hovercraft zoomed into a dock on the top level of a series of circular buildings stacked like mushrooms on top of each other, each one smaller than the one below it. Tubes radiated out from the bottom building, connecting other similarly configured buildings. The structures had huge windows, much like the port where they'd landed. Were these buildings homes or businesses? Did they have entrances to the outside forest, or did the inhabitants remain inside and only travel in the tubes? Everything about the planet intrigued her.

A group of people emerged from a nearby tube when the hovercraft landed, answering one of Cyra's questions. Two couples waited, an older and a younger. The older male appeared to be an aged version of Dez but lighter gray. The younger couple wore fine, brightly colored fabrics with gems that winked in the sunlight.

"My family." The reverence in Dez's voice warred with the expectation of what it would be like to return to her own family. She doubted they would greet her with smiles and open arms. He embraced the younger woman who had run to him. Most likely his sister, the princess, based on the jewels she wore at her ears, neck, and wrists to accent her fine shimmering-green garment. She was stunning with light charcoal-gray skin accented with bloodred markings. Her hair fell in a perfect black silk waterfall down her back. The man by her side, the prince, was almost as tall as Dez but not as muscular. He had dark, almost black markings like Dez and also had no hair. Dez's parents were dressed more humbly than the royal couple. He clutched them close, taking each one in his arms, tears running down his face. His mother grazed her fingertips over his cheeks, his shoulders, his chest, as if she couldn't believe he was real. She was an older version of Dez's sister—her skin was just a little looser, her red markings a little fainter, and her hair had a bit of gray. She was still strikingly beautiful.

He broke away from his mother and turned to Cyra. "Captain Meajzur, may I introduce my mother, Azhume? Mother, this is the captain of the ship that will take me to my next assignment."

Assignment? Dez was sold to the mines. Did his family not understand that he was a slave?

"It is an honor to meet you," his mother told Cyra, bowing slightly but keeping her distance. Cyra couldn't blame the woman who must hate her for taking her son so far away to a place that would more than likely mean his premature death. Cyra tilted her head in acknowledgment and tried to push down the sour ball that bubbled up in her throat.

Dez continued with introductions, moving to his sister, her husband, and finally, his father. He introduced her crew to each of them in the same order, starting with Veda, Blaize, and finally Rhysa. Cyra was sure she was missing some cultural message. She would discuss it with Veda later. All she felt from the group was kindness and acceptance—two things she didn't deserve.

"We have prepared a meal for you in honor of your visit, Brother." The princess's voice was warm and sweet. "Would you all please join us?"

Dez's gaze shifted to Cyra. She gave a quick nod of silent approval. A note of tension Cyra hadn't been aware of released in everyone but her. With Veda by her side, she followed the prince and princess through a passage in the lower level leading to the structure's center. An elevator in its core let the residents move from building to building. Dez explained that there were no businesses in the residential zone. Work centers and markets were located farther out between the green zone and the farming land. They rose to the top level in the stack and exited into what was obviously the home of the royal couple.

Finely crafted carved-wood furniture cushioned in rich fabrics filled the open space. Cyra stepped out of the elevator and onto the polished light wood floors, partially covered by a colorful woven rug. A bay of windows called for her to admire the breathtaking view. Standing in front of the perfectly clear panels, it was as if she was still outside. An unobstructed vista led to a valley with more waterfalls than she could count.

There must be a river below, but she couldn't see it through all the trees. The birds—their variety and huge numbers—once again left her in awe. Din' Gale was paradise.

Dez's mother, Azhume, approached her at the window. "I never tire of the beauty."

"Having seen it in person, I can't understand how your son left."

Azhume smiled, her eyes crinkling her light gray skin. "We didn't always live in the prince's palace. Our daughter bonded with someone beyond her reach. But since the day she was born, Dez never denied her anything." The warm approval radiated through her words. "He's always been very protective, especially of his little sister."

"She's lucky to have a brother who would sacrifice so much." And a family that recognized it instead of expecting it.

"We're all lucky. My husband would have taken on the burden if Dezmuhnd had not dissuaded him. He insisted Daymuhnd must remain by my side to care for me." Her voice trembled the slightest bit, and a whisper of regret and relief rose from the woman.

Cyra said nothing. What could she say? When she'd left her family, it had been a selfish act to avoid remaining in her crowded home. She hadn't thought of anyone other than herself. She was embarrassed when she thought back to her actions compared to what Dez had done for his family.

"Come eat. You must be starved. Dez mentioned during his call that you and your crew have no chef and don't eat well."

"It's a long story."

"You will share it while we dine." Azhume held out her arm, indicating the direction to go.

The food was amazing as promised, and the conversation flowed easily. There were four or five courses, Cyra lost count. Each dish was fresh and expertly prepared. She was so full she could hardly see straight. The wine they'd had probably wasn't helping her eyesight either. No wonder Dez complained so bitterly about the food on the ship.

The love that the family had for each other flowed over the table in their words, their thoughtful glances, even the way they shared the dishes placed on the table. She'd enjoyed the obviously oft-told stories of his childhood and the descriptions of their planet just as much as the food. The more she learned about Dez, the less she understood how he could ever leave.

She yawned but tried to be discreet.

"You seem tired," Daymuhnd, Dez's father, said. "Please, let me escort you to your rooms."

"Oh no, we were planning on staying on the ship," Cyra told them, although they really hadn't discussed any plan. Staying in their home would only add to her guilt.

Seated next to her, Dez leaned close. "You must stay with me and my family. After all, you don't want me running away, do you?"

She wanted many things from him, but none of them involved him running away. Her inappropriate ideas had to be a result of the wine. She shouldn't think of him that way. "I'm sure that after that exquisite meal, I'll sleep so deeply you could run away no matter where I am. I don't want to be a burden to your family."

"It is not a burden," Azhume said, making Cyra realize their private conversation had been overheard, and all eyes were on her and Dez. "We live in the lower levels and have plenty of guest rooms. It would be more difficult to find a hovercraft at this time than to have you stay." Azhume was so gracious, it was difficult to argue.

Cyra turned to her crew for backup. All three of them were begging her with their eyes to stay. Traitors. "If you're sure..."

"I'm sure," Azhume said warmly and rose from the table.

She kissed her daughter good night and patted her son-in-law, the prince, on the shoulder. Daymuhnd took her hand and escorted her from the room. Cyra and the rest of the crew thanked the prince and princess for the fantastic meal and wonderful company. They were invited to come back anytime their ship was in the solar system, even if Dez wasn't with them. Another stab of guilt twisted deeper into Cyra's belly.

Dez walked with her to the elevator, his hands clasped behind his back. "Would you like to see the forest before we leave?"

"I would love to see everything. It seems like so much is hidden."

"I'll take you after our morning meal. Your crew can go with us or attend to loading the ship, as you wish."

"Thank you, Dez." Cyra resisted the urge to touch him or say something more. What could she say? She'd been paid to drag him to another end of the galaxy, and she would complete her job, no matter how attractive she found him or how completely she adored his family and his beautiful planet. He was cargo, and her future, the future of her crew, and *The Treasure* required her to deliver him to Kolben.

CHAPTER 17

"Fuck." Varik snarled at the comm display. Still no word from the pharmaceutical company on Morgual. After so many cycles, odds were Cyra had delivered *his* spiders on *his* ship and taken *his* money. The tracker he'd planted on *The Treasure* showed that she had launched from Morgual. Somehow, she'd put together enough funds to get fuel and food to make the delivery. And clearly, despite the conversations he'd had with his contact, the company had paid for the spiders.

He smacked his fist on the desk. Unable to sit still, he paced the tiny quarters on the *Harlan Johnson*. Captain Twalley was still dawdling about leaving, and somehow Cyra kept moving. How the fuck was she doing it? Varik would have been hard-pressed to get the fuel, food, and pay the crew, and he had Auvi's funds. Well, *his* funds. Because Auvi promised to leave everything to him. Including the damn *Treasure*. But Auvi had lied. One false step and Varik had been cast aside without a backward glance. That wasn't love.

Auvi had moved on as if everything they'd shared was meaningless. He'd given Cyra Varik's rightful place. And she took to it like a fish to water. Finding a crew. Delivering the deadly spiders. Getting off Morgual.

If she wasn't using his rightful property to do everything, he'd almost admire her tenacity.

A knock on his door froze him mid-stride. He rolled his shoulders and shaped his lips into a welcoming upturn. On the other side, he found Jarn, assistant to Captain Twalley. Varik's heart leaped at the site of the beautiful copper-skinned male, and his smile shifted from being a mask to a genuine reflection of his mood. Jarn was young, or at least younger, with a strong jaw, molten brown eyes, and a lean body that begged to be worshipped. Varik leaned forward to catch the scent of his soft male musk. Footsteps echoed farther down the corridor.

Varik stiffened, wiping the smile from his face. "What?"

"Uh... Mr. Pectori," Jarn stuttered. "Captain Twalley requested your presence in his...um... his quarters." Jarn's face deepened to a heated bronze color.

Gods, what Varik would give to make the male stutter for real, to choke on his cock, to swallow him deep. But he had to focus on the captain and the seduction he'd started in an attempt to convince Twalley to leave the station. Until they were in space, Varik's hands were tied. If he bedded Jarn the way he dreamed of, he'd hold no sway over Twalley and would likely lose his ride completely.

Once they launched, anything and everything would be possible. Varik smoothed his hands over his shirt, tucking it tightly into his flight pants. He tugged his collar, enjoying the way Jarn's eyes traced every move. He would fuck this sweet boy and bring them both untold satisfaction, but not soon enough.

"Tell the captain I'm coming." Varik paused on the loaded word. "Just need to finish one thing." Varik closed the door in Jarn's face before he dragged the assistant across the threshold and ruined everything.

On his comm, he closed the tracking app and sent yet

another placating message to his quickly dwindling crew that he had a meeting with Twalley and to remain at the ready because they could be leaving any cycle. It was a lie, or maybe not, depending on how the meeting went, but he had to keep as many of them engaged as possible. To wrest the ship from Twalley, he'd need more than Jarn's amorous devotion.

Varik checked the time. He'd made Twalley wait long enough. Varik strolled down the pristine cream-colored corridors that reminded him more of a hospital than a spaceship. The *Harlan Johnson* was a research vessel, not a working ship. But as soon as he was in charge, this little tug would be working overtime to get *The Treasure* back under his command where she belonged.

He knocked on the captain's door before adopting a casual pose against the frame. A single breath after Twalley opened up, Varik rolled into the room, giving the captain his best-heated stare. "You need me?"

Twalley swallowed, his throat visibly constricting. "Varik."

Varik smiled a half smirk and let his eyes go soft. "What can I do for you, Captain?"

"We're almost ready to embark. I wondered if you might review the travel details with me one more time. You're so knowledgeable about the ER bridges and the best fuel rates, travel costs..." Twalley's gaze roamed Varik's body.

"Of course."

Twalley sat behind his desk. Varik dragged a soft ottoman beside the man and sat as close as possible—his head at the captain's chest, his leg pressed tight against Twalley's leg, and his eyes locked to the screen as if he wasn't teasing his target.

Jarn cleared his throat and moved from a far corner of the room. Varik resisted the urge to move away from the captain and comfort the lover he desired. He had the lover he required against his body. Jarn could wait. Hopefully would wait. If Jarn truly cared about him, he should wait.

"If you need me, Captain, I'll be in my quarters." The note of bitterness in Jarn's voice scraped against Varik's skin.

Twalley murmured assent, barely acknowledging his assistant's exit.

Varik's heart recorded Jarn's leaving with an intense ache. He lifted his gaze from the closed door to Twalley's. "Show me."

By the time Varik returned to his own quarters, his back was stiff, and his brain was glazed over from reviewing the unchanged plans and costs. He and Twalley had reviewed the details a dozen times. Much more of the anxiety-driven bullshit and he'd put his fist through the man's face, then leave and find another fucking mark.

A ping from his comm had him darting across the room. *The Treasure's* trajectory meant she was likely headed for Din' Gale. It would require almost no fuel for her to get there, but landing would be difficult. The planet restricted incoming vessels that didn't originate on Din' Gale in an attempt to reduce the risk of viral, fungal, and non-native plant invasions. The fact that her flight path eliminated almost any other destination told Varik that she had either picked up a contract in Morgual or secured one from Din' Gale. Something he and Auvi had worked on for g-years but never been able to achieve. If she got a contract like that, she might build up enough funds to keep *The Treasure* going as a business, eliminating his potential to reclaim the one-of-a-kind ship.

"Fuck," he barked out, drawing back his arm to hurl the comm at the wall but thought better of it before he released. One fucking disaster was enough.

CHAPTER 18

THE FOLLOWING MORNING, Cyra followed Dez through the building levels and several tunnels before exiting into the forest. It was cooler than she'd expected. The canopy of trees let only small amounts of light reach the forest floor. Birds called to their mates, filling the humid air with melody. Despite the birds and the other unfamiliar sounds, a stillness settled inside her as a quiet peace. Serenity that could never be found on her ship with its different systems constantly whirring and beeping. If she'd been alone, it might have been unnerving. But Dez led her with strong, self-assured movements. His natural patterns blended into the shadows. If not for his clothes, he would've been nearly invisible if he stood still.

Dez's silence let Cyra get lost in her own thoughts. She followed him, unaware of how far they traveled. Heat slowly warmed her skin. She rarely had the luxury of walking on anything other than a motorized treadmill on the ship. It was different to walk without artificial gravity, using muscles she'd forgotten she had.

The smells were different too—dirt and the plants—so different from the ship and even from her home planet. And

Dez's smell fit in here perfectly. When had she become aware of his scent? They'd been traveling between the station and the planets for such a short time, and she'd tried to avoid him as much as possible. Somehow, his uniqueness to anything she'd known before had registered deep inside her. He made perfect sense there, in the forest of his home planet, unlike when she visited him in the cargo bay where he definitely didn't belong or in his equally unsuitable quarters. An alpha predator, he moved silently, alert to every slight movement hidden by the forest growth. Following his focus, she caught small animals and insects she would have otherwise overlooked. He was breathtaking in his element.

As they continued to walk, Cyra detected a new sound—one she knew intimately—the splashing and rushing of falling water. A wave of aching anticipation flowed through her. The smell of the water became stronger. She breathed deeply, appreciating the sweet humidity that hadn't been pumped out of a mechanical system entering her lungs. Life thrived in the natural water that was never present on the ship, even in the water chamber. She followed Dez around a large outcropping of dark gray stones, and there, in all of its cascading glory, was an enormous waterfall. It flowed down a sheer cliff face, a living thing moving on its own. Actual water. The vines followed it down, reaching with their tendrils into the mist. The sky, so deep blue, appeared purple. Faint rainbows flickered into view as the spray danced in the unobscured sunlight.

Tears gathered in her eyes at the beauty of it. The loss. She'd given up such beauty when she ran away to *The Treasure* all those g-years ago.

"Come, sit here." Dez patted a smooth, somewhat flat rock.

Cyra settled beside him, close enough that a tingle of energy filled the gap between them. "This is perfect. Paradise."

"It's always been a favorite spot of mine. My childhood home was in the opposite direction and quite a bit farther. It's different to sit on this side of these falls. It's the place I dream of when I dream of home."

"I can see why. Thank you for taking me here." The words weren't enough.

Dez said nothing for a moment. "Do you have a place you dream of when you dream of home?"

"My planet's very different from yours. It's almost entirely salt water. I was born on one of two main landmasses. My family lives near a beach." A twinge of loss arced across her heart. She swallowed it down. "I swam every day I could. I love being in the water." Needed it to survive.

"If we had more time, I would take you to Lake Gal' An. It's too far to walk, but the water is crystal clear and not as cold as this waterfall."

"I would've liked that," Cyra said quietly, wishing things could be different for Dez.

They sat wordlessly for a long time before Cyra rose and asked him to take her back to the palace. It seemed like a longer walk back, and Cyra was tired when they reached his parents' home. She left Dez to rest and dream of what her life might be like if she hadn't run away so many years ago and instead had agreed to take a mate and have lots of babies. But as much as she missed nature, she couldn't honestly romanticize the life she'd left. She'd never have met Dez or Veda. She'd never have had the chance to see new worlds like Din' Gale. She'd never have been independent and the captain of her own future. And as much as she loved—even lived for—the natural beauty of a planet like Din' Gale, her life was meant for more than pretty walks in nature and family meals.

Besides, she had obligations to her partners, to the people

who'd contracted her to deliver the dogs. And even to Auvi—to honor what he'd given her and to finish the commitment he'd made with the contract to deliver Dez. Life wasn't always rainbows and waterfalls. *The Treasure*, the unforgiving metal behemoth, would give her a life much more substantial than mist in the sunlight.

Veda knocked on Cyra's door what seemed like moments after they'd returned. She hadn't been aware that she'd fallen asleep so quickly and deeply.

"They're hoping you will come down and share a meal with the family before we leave," Veda said from the doorway.

"Of course, just let me get myself together."

"Are you feeling well? You don't look good." Veda's eyebrows pinched together.

"I'm fine, just tired. Must be the air on this planet. It makes me want to sleep." With Dez. *Where had that come from?* She scrambled from the bed as if she'd found him in it.

"I'll let them know you're coming."

Nope. Not coming. Or rather— "Yes, I'll be there shortly."

The tension at the table settled heavy on Dez's shoulders. His mother was unhappy. He hated when his mother was sad, but he couldn't do anything to change it. Circumstances had changed for his family, but they had changed because of his decision. He couldn't second-guess that decision now. He'd made promises. One when he entered the indentured servitude and a second one to Cyra.

Cyra entered the room, and once again, her beauty captivated him. He noted that her eyes were tired but stunning—like the ocean was captured in her orbs. Her loose, dark green hair appeared black except when the sunlight hit it at just the right angle. The more time he spent with her, the more attractive she became.

"My son," his mother began after everyone was seated and eating. "You must consider staying."

"I cannot, and I wish to discuss something other than my remaining."

His royal brother-in-law spoke up, saving the lunch. "I have a proposition for Captain Maejzur."

"Please, call me Cyra, your highness."

"Captain Cyra, I've been seeking a reliable method to sell goods to Cassan. Din' Gale has an abundance of food and selling fresh items to the space station can be very profitable, or so my brother informs me. We're able to ship within our solar system with our own transport ships, but none are rated for such long travel."

"We have the latest technology in refrigeration and preservation systems in our cargo bay. *The Treasure* is specifically designed for transporting live and perishable cargo." The pride in her voice swelled Dez's chest even though *he* was her cargo.

"I was told the same thing by Dez."

Dez continued to eat despite the weight of Cyra's gaze on him.

His brother-in-law cleared his throat and took a sip of water. "Would you consider a trial contract for one delivery to Cassan? If all goes well, perhaps we can create a regular shipment schedule. I wouldn't want to ship too often. Scarcity keeps the revenue high. Also in farming, there are ups and downs. But selling our surplus to Cassan a few times a year has an appeal."

Cyra straightened in the chair, shifting from her role of guest back into captain. "Of course we would be interested in a contract, your highness." Authority and confidence laced her voice, making her even more attractive. "Perhaps we can discuss the details after the meal. We have to leave soon due to contractual deadlines. The fuel and other provisions are being loaded now. Right, Veda?"

Veda nodded.

Dez smiled, remembering the look on Veda's face when she saw the medical supplies his parents had included as a gift. His family had been very generous in honor of his visit. It was a small thing, but it would make the trip a little safer. He didn't expect he would be using any of the medicinals himself, but it was good to be prepared for the unexpected.

The next day dawned with a brilliant red sunrise. Dez savored the spectacular view, imprinting the image to warm him when he was cold on the mining planet.

"It's time to go." Cyra's soft voice was filled with guilt and a hint of concern.

"Yes, Captain."

"Dez, I'd understand if you refused. It would ruin—" She glanced at where Veda, Blaize, and Rhysa waited in the hovercraft.

"I only need a moment to say goodbye."

Dez's mother cried quietly. Devastated tears trickled slowly down her face. His heart broke, knowing that would be the last time he saw his family. He held each one of them.

His sister whispered in his ear, "Don't go, Dez. I never should have let you sell yourself. I was too selfish."

He held her face and forced himself to smile. "I would do it again to see you this happy with your mate. It was worth it."

The prince pulled him into an unexpected embrace and told Dez, "You are an honorable male. You will be rewarded in this lifetime."

Dez never expected to be rewarded beyond seeing his family cared for. And how would he receive any further rewards—working in a mine on an ice planet at the other end of the galaxy from everyone he loved? But it was a nice thought. Finally, there were no more goodbyes to be said. Dez walked onto the ship behind Cyra. Each step killed the last bit of hope for his future. No sunshine and waterfalls. No family. No mate.

He headed directly to his quarters to be alone. To be cargo.

CHAPTER 19

"Countdown to launch." Cyra used the familiar phrasing Auvi had always used. The memory of his voice as he used her for his launch sequence fired up her feelings.

"Engine's go." Blaize gave Cyra a thumbs-up.

Cyra guided the ship out of the hangar and braced as they lifted into the air.

"Now, Captain!" Blaize called.

Cyra slapped her hands down on the launch panel and let every bit of anger flow through her. She was still angry with Captain Auvi and Varik. She was angry with Dez for putting her through such an emotional scene with his family. She was angry with herself for feeling any guilt for a situation she didn't create. And most of all, she was angry that she chose her security and her crew over a family. It made no difference that Dez hadn't asked her to choose.

She had no choice.

She wasn't a heartless leader. But she couldn't choose to be dependent on others in a cold universe that wouldn't care for her one iota. She had a single opportunity for independence and security. She'd make it work, even if it broke her heart to be the instrument that parted Dez's family again. It was just the way of the universe, and she was only one small being within it.

The ship lurched through the planet's atmosphere on a path for Cassan. The chaotic thrusting knocked the crew around in their seats, but they had strapped in tight this time. A few minutes into their long trip through space, Cyra released her restraints. Blaize and Rhysa had everything under control. Cyra left the deck, intending to rest in her quarters for a while, but instead found herself walking down the long corridor to the back of the ship. To Dez.

She paused outside his quarters, the door open. He was stretched out on the lower bunk, torso bare. The dark black stripes that swirled around his body like tattoo art mesmerized her momentarily. She shook off the strange, lusty haze. "Dez? May I speak with you?"

He rose from his bunk all stealth and grace. "Of course, Captain. What can I do for you?"

"I wanted to talk to you. I... I'm sorry."

"You have nothing to apologize for." Except he wouldn't meet her eyes.

"Maybe not, but I'm still sorry that you won't see your family again. It is clear how much they mean to you." And she hated that leaving them hurt him.

"If not for your generosity and trust, I would not have seen them at all. You have given me a gift I could never repay."

His calm acceptance only made her more agitated. "But you did. You talked the prince into using us for a transporter."

"Well, I talked him into trying you out. I have no idea if you'll get another contract or not. That's up to you." He briefly met her gaze, and a slight smile flashed across his full, dark lips.

Unable to maintain the eye contact, she dropped her chin. "I wouldn't have had the opportunity if you had not created it. So, thank you, Dez."

"It was my honor." His deep voice pressed the words into her heart.

He was honorable, and all that was good in a male. If only they'd met in a different way, under different conditions, there might have been a chance for them to have a different relationship. But it was just wishes. Cyra reached out and touched his shoulder. He flinched slightly at the electric jolt that transferred through her. She should have recoiled, but his skin was warm and his muscles strong. Perhaps her brief touch would convey all the admiration she had for him and offer some comfort. Tears pricked at her eyes. She dropped her hand and rushed out.

There was nothing else to say.

After a long session in the water tank, Cyra went to the galley. It was her turn to attempt to cook their meal. It would be damn disappointing after dining with royalty on Din' Gale. Her crew would have to tough it out. She wasn't a chef, and they had to eat. At least they had better ingredients now.

Cyra's attempt was a complete failure. The protein was slightly burned on one side and undercooked in the center. The vegetables came out better, but not by much. She sighed as she sat down with the crew. Dez was notably absent, but he probably wasn't up to company. "Sorry. I did my best."

Rhysa laughed. "You're a damn better captain than you are a chef, that's for sure. I'm just happy I didn't have to be the first one to cook after leaving Din' Gale. They spoiled us."

"They did," Blaize agreed, looking sadly at her meal.

"I'll take some food to Dez and be right back." Veda stood, taking her untouched plate and adding to it for him.

The others were picking at their own plates and choking down a few bites when an alert sounded, followed by Veda's voice over the ship's loudspeaker. "Captain, we have a medical emergency in crew quarters. I need you now."

Cyra's heart lodged in her throat. She jumped up from the table and ran into Dez's room. What if he had tried to harm himself? She shouldn't have left him earlier. She should have insisted he join the crew for meals. If he died, she wasn't sure what she would do. Veda had sounded frantic. Veda was never frantic. She was calm in an emergency. It had to be horrible.

"Veda?" Cyra called out as soon as she hit the crew corridor.

"In here," Veda replied from inside Dez's room.

Cyra was afraid to look. His grunts and whimpers of pain hurt her ears, but at least he was still alive. She stepped inside tentatively. Dez was on the ground alternately writhing in pain and going board stiff. His eyes were rolled back in his head. There was no blood and no obvious injuries. "What's going on? What's wrong with him?"

"I don't know." Veda pressed her hands to his shoulders. He howled in pain and she retreated. "I found him like this when I brought him his plate. He didn't even take a bite."

Cyra didn't miss the insinuation that her food was so bad it could have caused him this much pain. Dez's scream ripped through her. He went completely limp.

Veda put two fingers to his neck. "He's passed out. The pain must have been too much."

Cyra warred with indecision. Should they return to Din' Gale? What if he died? What if he remained in pain and they couldn't fix it? She needed answers. "What can we do?"

"I don't know," Veda barked at her. "If we can get him to the medical bay, I can run some tests. I tried to calm him when I first entered, and he was more aware. When I touched him, he threw himself to the other side of the room to get away from me. He hasn't been able to say two words to me."

"I'll stay with him while you get the gurney."

Veda turned and ran out. Cyra prayed she would be able to help him.

As soon as Veda returned, they managed to get him onto the gurney. Cyra watched him for any signs of awareness as they guided the floating table back to medical. It was crazy, but it looked like his skin was writhing. Or at least his tattoos were—they were changing, moving, and rearranging themselves on his body. She didn't know much about Dez or his race, but his condition couldn't be normal.

Veda locked the gurney into place once they reached the lab. Bright white floors and fixtures reflected the strong overhead lights.

"Do you see what I'm seeing?" Cyra asked Veda.

"You mean the fact that his markings are changing?" Veda removed the med probe from his ear and placed a sensor on his chest.

"Exactly. What the hell is going on?"

"I'm not sure. I couldn't get much out of him, but he did say the word 'mate.'"

"Mate?" Cyra retrieved her comm. Maybe she could ask his family. *Damn.* The signal was too weak. She'd have to try from the bridge. What she wouldn't give to have a communications specialist who would know how to route the signals across vast space.

Veda kept taking measurements and staring intently at the display mounted on the wall. "His vitals indicate stress, but not in a range that could be dangerous. I need to do some research. I'll hook him up to a fluid push and stay here until we know more or he's better."

"He's not going to die, is he?" Cyra could barely choke out the question. *Please don't let him die,* she begged silently. Who she addressed, she wasn't sure. Any being with the power to save Dez.

"Based on the readings, I don't have any reason to think this is a deadly situation, but I don't know." Veda sat at her computer and pulled up a medical encyclopedia.

Cyra clutched her hands together to keep from touching Dez despite the compulsion to comfort him. "Do you want me to stay with you?"

"No, you'll only be in the way. I'll comm you if something changes."

"Take care of him."

Veda glanced up, eyebrows lifted.

Cyra glanced away, unable to deal with the feelings she shouldn't have. Dez was cargo, and any illness put her future and her partners' future in jeopardy. Any other thoughts were inappropriate and should be squashed.

"Go." Veda shooed her out. "Your nervous energy is not what he or I need right now."

Cyra left the medical bay and strode blindly back to the bridge. She'd been the last to see him before he had taken ill—had touched him, and sparks had definitely flowed. The word "mate" reverberated in her skull. But *she* wasn't his mate. Maybe someone back on Din' Gale. Maybe there was an incubation period, and his reaction had nothing to do with her. Maybe Veda misheard him.

Didn't matter. She couldn't take him home. And she sure as hell couldn't keep him. Veda would have to figure out how to fix him, preferably before they got to Cassan.

CHAPTER 20

Dez opened his eyes and quickly shut them. The light was blinding and painful. Where was he? What happened? Slowly, in flashes of images, he recalled Cyra touching his bare skin and what it meant.

Why now? Why her? He released a moan before he could stifle it. Footsteps neared and stopped.

"Dez, can you hear me?" Veda asked.

Her voice was so different from Cyra's—the voice he ached to hear again. Dez's throat was too dry to respond. He nodded.

"Are you feeling better? Can you talk?" She pressed something cold to his ear, and he shifted away. "Dez?"

"Water," he croaked out.

Veda bustled around, and moments later, a straw brushed his lips. He sucked in the cool liquid, thankful for the relief.

"Can you tell me what happened?"

If he said it out loud, it would be real. He huffed out a breath, opened his eyes, and—based on the way the appearance of his arm and hand had transformed from his ancestral stripes into something closer to rolling waves—accepted the process already happened. "The mating change."

"Mating change?"

"When Din' Gale males are born, we bear markings that indicate our family line. When we mate, when our fated partner touches us, the males—we undergo the change. The markings shift to represent our new family. We're marked for life as belonging to her."

Veda bit her lip, eyes wide. Softly, she asked, "Who's your mate, Dez?"

"Captain Cyra." He closed his eyes. The timing—the reality of his situation—couldn't be worse. That was why the unmated were not touched except by family, usually only mated family. How had he not recognized the risk? But the odds of a female from a different planet, with different physiology, being his mate was so infinitesimal that it hadn't registered in his consciousness. Until the electric jolt she'd delivered, and by then it was too late.

"When did she touch you?"

"After takeoff. She came to see me. Before she left, she touched my shoulder. The connection was immediate. It triggered the change, but she was gone before I could say anything."

"Is it always so painful?"

"Our females can do things to ease the transition, but it's always painful. It is meant to be a rebirth. Our women go through the pain of childbirth. It is only right that we understand the pain we are asking them to endure by bearing our young."

"I'm not sure Cyra is ready for all this," Veda mused, seemingly speaking to herself. She peered into his eyes. "I have no idea how she'll take this, Dez."

"There's nothing I can do to change it." She would be his mate, even if she rejected him. Even after she left him on Kolben.

"I have to let the captain know." Veda picked up her comm

and tapped the screen.

A few minutes later, Cyra appeared in the doorway. "I got your message."

His mate. Her salt-water scent washed over him. Her dark hair curled over her shoulders, uniform hugging her curves. Gods, she was perfect. Dez groaned with need.

"You're sitting up?" Cyra pivoted to her friend. "What's going on, Veda? Did you determine what happened?"

Veda clasped her hands and stared at the floor. "Dez explained it to me."

Cyra's gaze returned to him with obvious expectation.

"I have found my mate," he said simply. What else could he say? It changed everything and nothing.

Cyra looked between Veda and Dez, confusion wrinkling her features.

"Not me," Veda said softly. "You."

"No." Cyra shook her head and shifted back.

"You, Cyra Meajzur, are my mate." Dez shifted off the gurney and took a step toward her.

"Stop." She held up her hand as a barrier. "I am not your mate. I don't know what game you're playing, but this is ridiculous. I can't be your mate. We aren't the same race. I don't know you. In fact, none of us really knows you. I think it would be better if you returned to your room if you are quite recovered from... from this...charade."

"*Charade.*" Dez narrowed his eyes at the woman the universe had stuck him with in some sort of cosmic joke. "You think I could fake the primal markings changing to brand me as your mate?" Dez pulled off his vest, baring his skin to her. "Do you see these waves that now cover my chest, right over my heart? Do you think I had any control over this? I'm contracted to live the rest of my life working in a mine on a distant planet. It's not exactly the best time to discover my mate."

"How do you know it's me?"

"You touched me. My body reacted to the contact. It was instantaneous. That only happens with mates. It happened with my parents. After my sister was allowed to touch the prince, he too experienced the mate marking." And, if Dez couldn't come up with a solution to this situation before they reached Kolben, he would die.

"It can't be. I don't know if it's a lie or a mistake, but this, you and I, mates, it's not happening." She shook her head. "I already refused to be mated to the male my parents chose. I don't want a mate or babies. I left my planet to escape all that. This." Cyra flicked her finger back and forth. "You and I? Not happening." Cyra turned and left the bay.

Dez ached with the compulsion to follow her.

"That went well." Veda's words dripped with sarcasm.

It couldn't have gone worse. Dez closed his eyes and sighed.

CHAPTER 21

RAGE RODE VARIK HARD. He was impotent to force Captain Twalley into action. Something had to give. How the fuck could he get their ship off the station? He banged his head against the wall of his shitty quarters above the narrow bed.

Jarn rolled over and stretched. "Holy crap. I haven't used some of those muscles in so long, I nearly forgot how."

A smile settled on Varik's lips as his lover's words inspired the solution. The insight almost made up for the fact he shouldn't have taken Jarn to bed. If Twalley caught them, it could ruin everything.

"I have to go." Varik flipped off the coverlet and pulled on his pants. He sniffed his shirt and pulled it over his head when it didn't make his stomach curdle.

Jarn sat up, face slack, eyes pleading. "What about...?"

Varik leaned over and gave him a firm kiss. "Just need to keep this under wraps until we leave the station." He caressed Jarn's soft cheek. "Be patient, love."

Jarn nodded.

"I'll find you tonight."

"Of course." Jarn's smile didn't quite convince Varik, but he couldn't take the time to comfort the man. He had to save *The Treasure.*

Varik stuck his head in the open door of Twalley's office. "Captain?"

"Varik," Twalley's cheerful voice welcomed Varik in.

"I have a concern I should share with you." Varik rounded his shoulders and gazed wide-eyed at the man. "Get your advice."

Twalley puffed up a bit. "What can I help you with?"

Varik wrinkled his brow and filled his voice with worry. "It's about your ship, sir. It's been in the docking bay for a while now, right?"

Varik had already looked up the records. Over four g-months.

Twalley murmured agreement.

"Well, sir. There's some risk when the engines are allowed to fallow like that. I mean, they're designed to run, be lubricated, and be used. If left neglected, they could seize up on you."

Twalley's grunt carried a note of apprehension. Perfect.

"Sir, I think you should let a skeleton crew and me take it for a short trip and make sure the systems are optimal. Identify any maintenance that might be required before we take off for your extended research study. It would be horrible to finally get the approval and then have a delay we could have foreseen or prevented."

"That's a great point." Twalley picked up his comm. "I don't have any meetings scheduled for the next several cycles. Why don't you organize the necessary crew members—navigator to plot the course and so on, and we'll go out."

Shit. "There's no need for you to be involved in a technical maintenance run, sir. I know how busy you are with organizing the research plan and coordinating the grants. I'm happy to cover this routine task."

"To be honest, I've organized what I can. It's simply a matter of waiting. I'm happy about the change in routine. Give us a chance to get...more familiar." Captain Twalley stroked Varik's arm.

"Perfect, sir. I'll make the arrangements." Varik forced a seductive smile to his face and squeezed Twalley's hand with a fake promise. One he would do everything to avoid. But after fucking Auvi on the deck of *The Treasure*, a private session with one slightly balding, middle-aged mouse of a scientist was no big deal. "Shall we...share a cabin?"

Red bloomed up Twalley's cheeks. "Uh, perhaps not this time. Keep up appearances."

Varik made a pouty face. "I understand. I'll talk to the navigator and organize the rest of the crew we need."

"I'm sure we'll be able to get some alone time on the trip, even with separate quarters." Twalley winked.

"I look forward to it, *sir*."

Twalley's grin was the opposite of everything Varik was feeling. Not only was the captain going, meaning Varik couldn't commandeer the ship, but he'd have to leave Jarn behind because he couldn't risk the captain finding them together. Not this trip.

"I can't believe you don't want me to go." Jarn crossed his arms, concealing a large portion of his perfectly lean chest.

"Captain insisted on a skeleton crew. It's just for a few cycles." Varik glided fingers down Jarn's cheek. "I need you here. Keep our quarters together. Listen for any jobs that come up for ships leaving sooner." Varik had convinced Jarn that his funds were limited. They needed to find a crew that could take them both, and Captain Twalley's research trip might not pan out. If nothing else, it kept his expenses low and gave his young lover something to focus on besides Varik's seduction of Twalley.

"Fine."

"I'll make it up to you when I get back." Varik shifted his hand under the cover and grasped Jarn's cock, stroking the ridged shaft firmly, cupping the bulbous head, and bringing it back to life. His lover's hips twitched. Fuck, Varik was going to be late. But so what? Twalley would wait.

He flipped the coverlet back and straddled Jarn. Arms still crossed, Jarn glared up at him. Varik pressed his shoulders back until Jarn relaxed on the bed. "Before I go, I'll give you a reason to forgive me."

Varik shifted between Jarn's legs. Lifting him by the knees, Varik pulled him into the perfect position. The gasp that left his lover's lips when he tongued the sweet hole he'd used all night went straight to Varik's empty balls. He circled his lover's still gaping pucker, teasing up to his balls and wrapping his hand around Jarn's hardened cock. He squeezed and released. Spit into his palm and proceeded to stroke and lick his boy to a screaming orgasm.

Jarn was still shaking when Varik slapped his ass and rose from the bed. "Be good. I'll be back soon."

"Okay." The tiny hint of whine in Jarn's voice reassured Varik that his new lover would be waiting.

On the ship, Varik spent the next cycles checking systems and teasing Twalley. The captain tried to get Varik to sneak in and out of his bed so the crew wouldn't know what was going on. Varik used the late-night invitations to tease the captain. Sending filthy texts and even an image of his hard cock spewing. So what if Varik lied and said it was for Twalley. He sent the same image to Jarn with the message, "Miss you. Be home soon, baby."

Twalley hadn't questioned the path Varik had charted with the navigator that would lead straight to Din' Gale. But two cycles into the trip, his tracking software updated to show *The Treasure* moving in the opposite direction. He considered hurling the device against the nearest wall. Cyra was headed in the opposite direction. Back to Cassan.

Varik stormed off to the engine room. As the only engineer on the ship this trip, he could do what had to be done without eyes on him.

Later that cycle, red lights and system warnings blasted through the *Harlan Johnson*. Twalley leaped up from the captain's chair on the deck. "What's happening?"

Varik pressed his lips together to keep from laughing. Twalley was no captain. Varik spun in his chair. "There's been a critical breach in the engine room, sir. I'll seal it off immediately, but we need to turn for Cassan now. With any luck, we'll make it back close enough that a rescue ship can be called in. I'll do what I can to close the breach and keep us from further damage."

Varik raced from the deck to the engine room and cackled silently once the doors had sealed.

CHAPTER 22

"Veda, will you please take a tray to Dez when you're done?" Cyra asked while eating her own first meal of the cycle. It was just the two of them in the galley. Blaize and Rhysa had already eaten and left.

"No."

"What?" Veda never told her no.

"No, Captain. I will not take a tray to Dez. I'm not going to be in the middle of this."

"Veda?" She chastised her friend with the single word, still in shock at her defiance.

Veda left the galley without another word. Cyra would have to take his tray if she didn't want him to starve since he'd refused to come to the galley to eat. It wouldn't be right to ask Blaize or Rhysa to do it. It sort of fell under a medical director's purview as eating was required for health. At least that was what she told herself as she choked down the god-awful mess Blaize had made. *The Treasure* needed more crew.

"I brought you a tray." Cyra set it down on the narrow shelf that dropped from the wall of the small room. He really should have a chair.

"You need not have bothered. I'd just about rather starve than eat the mess you have made of the fine foods my family gave you."

"Look. I didn't even cook this morning. I can't help it if I don't have a chef. An engineer and a navigator seemed a little more important, and I don't even have the funds to pay them. They're really my partners, not my employees."

"You should let me cook—"

"I have, but we all agreed to take turns."

"All the meals."

"I can't take advantage of you. You're not an employee. You're—" She bit back the word *cargo*.

"It would be my pleasure to have a way to care for my mate, even if she doesn't want me."

The last part he said so low as to be a whisper, but it still stung. "It's not that I do or don't want you. I just think you're wrong."

"I'm not wrong." He closed his eyes briefly and took a slow breath. "Will you let me cook for you?"

"Just eat this. I'm sure it's not as bad as it looks."

"I'm sure it's worse. Have you tried feeding it to the thuringies? Did they reject it as well?"

Cyra sputtered, at a loss for words.

He stood from his bunk and crossed his arms, facing off with her. "I will not be eating another substandard meal. There is no rational reason for you not to let me cook."

Dez's arms bulged. His smooth, bald head was covered in sexy black stripes since they'd rearranged. His gray skin was no longer odd to her. In fact, he was gorgeous. Damn, she needed to get her mind out of the gutter. She was the captain. He was her cargo. Her cargo that had acquired food, fuel, and another contract. Her cargo who was insisting he was her mate. All he wanted was to cook. "Fine."

"Fine, I can cook?"

"Yes."

"Thank you, my queen."

She rolled her eyes. "I'm your captain, not your queen."

"To me, you are both."

Cyra huffed and left. There was no arguing with him, especially since he made her want to melt with a look, with his primal scent and the sound of his voice. She was gone for him. Not good.

"I'll have the mid-cycle meal ready for you and your crew, my queen," he called out after her.

Cyra busied herself with correspondence from the bank, reviewing possible flight plans to Kolben with Rhysa, and commiserating with Blaize on the antiquated state of the systems. Discouraged by the discussions, she headed to the water chamber to take a break. In the corridor, she froze. The scent of something delicious hit her, and her stomach rumbled. She checked her comm. Mid-meal. Cyra turned for the galley, where she found Dez and her partners cozied up around the table, moaning.

"This is better than the food at the palace," Rhysa declared.

"I'm going to gain back the weight I lost." Blaize sighed.

"It's better for all of us," Veda said. "Good nutrition is critical to good health."

Dammit. Cyra would have to let him keep cooking because it was the best meal she'd had that she could remember. He'd made the noodles taste decent, but since he had ingredients to work with, there was no denying his skills.

"How is yours, my...captain?" Dez asked her quietly after he sat back down with a refilled plate, nudging aside Veda to sit next to Cyra.

"It's fine, thank you."

"Fine," Dez repeated the word in the same tone she'd used.

He clenched his jaw briefly. "Fine is a very good word for many things and beings. I will accept fine," he concluded, lifting a full fork to his lips.

Cyra's attempt to emotionally keep him at arm's length wasn't working. She couldn't even slight him successfully. The beast would not take offense. She would have to find another way to keep her distance because the urge to wrap herself around his warm muscles and express her thanks for the amazing food with kisses, lots of kisses, all over his body, a particular part of his body, was nearly irresistible. Refusing to so much as glance at him, she finished her food as quickly as possible and left the galley to soak in her water chamber—away from him.

Despite her best efforts over the next few cycles, she learned it was next to impossible to avoid him.

Cyra peeped out into the corridor and found it empty. She made a mad dash for the bridge only to slide to a halting stop.

"There you are, my...captain." Dez held a small tablet Veda had loaned him to track inventory and plan meals. She dreaded the sight of that device. He grinned at her.

She scowled and slipped past him to collapse in the captain's chair. All that running for nothing.

"What are you making us for mid-meal, Dez?" Rhysa asked from her position at the navigator's deck. Did she have to sound so seductive? And who cared? Whatever he made would taste good, but he insisted on reviewing every meal plan and demanding Cyra's approval.

"I was just about to discuss that with our captain."

"You two need some alone time? I could make myself scarce." Rhysa stood.

"That's not necessary." Cyra closed her eyes and rubbed her temple. "What do you need, Dez?" Better to get it over with so she could clear her head and focus on work.

Dez approached her, coming so close she could smell a hint of his musk, the tiny bits of moisture that carried his wild scent. His nearness warmed her. She itched to run back to the salt tank to keep from trailing her fingers along the planes of his muscles, followed by her tongue. He spoke, rattling off details about the food, the recipes, the menu, but all she registered was his low tones deep in her belly.

"Is that acceptable, my queen?"

She shook off the mesmerizing stupor he created. "It's fine."

His smile was too wide. Did he know what he was doing to her? She scowled at him.

"Fine. I'll take fine." His fine backside as he left held her captive. Damn that male for being so sultry, so smug, so satisfying. In the galley.

Not anywhere else.

She shook her head. She couldn't entertain even a hint of what her body desired from him, even if her thighs did ache. And she still had one more meal-planning session with him to endure this cycle. And three more the next. "When do we reach Cassan?"

Rhysa laughed.

Finally, after several more cycles of cat and mouse, which Dez, the apex predator, won every time, Cassan loomed ahead in the digital display. It was so huge it appeared closer than it actually was. Despite the additional cycles it would take to reach it, Cyra was grateful to nearly be there. It meant more space away from Dez than the ship allowed. His meal-planning antics had progressed to include *accidental* touches.

She ached to grab him with both hands and do very non-captain-like things to him, like stroke his entire body and find out what he liked. But she couldn't. He was cargo. She had a contract to deliver him. He was cargo. He would be living in Kolben while she would be traveling all over the galaxies. He was cargo. And she was so over the moon for him. She couldn't get off the ship soon enough.

"Rhysa, what's our ETA?"

"The same as the previous time you asked me, minus the few seconds since then."

"Can't we get there faster?" The whine in her voice hurt her own ears.

"Not if we don't want to blast right through the dock. They might be unhappy with us if we rip off part of the station because we came in too hot."

Dammit. Her skin itched with unmet need. "Call me when we're going to land. I'm going to the water chamber."

"You're in there so much you're going to prune."

"It relieves stress."

"I know of some other things that relieve stress..."

"Not interested." Cyra paused in the doorway to the bridge. "Oh, and when we get to the station, we need to send out inquiries on a communications officer. We did okay on this trip, but we need to fill that slot. I think we should add to the staff now that we have a regular contract, or soon will."

"What are we doing about galley duties?"

"Nothing." Cyra left the deck without further explanation.

Returning from a long soak, Cyra found Veda waiting for her in her quarters. Something was up, but Cyra would delay asking as long as possible. She walked by Veda and opened her wardrobe. There was nothing in there she wanted to put on. If Veda hadn't been here, she would have had some personal alone time, which wouldn't have necessitated clothes.

"What?" she gave in and asked Veda.

"I was wondering when you were going to acknowledge me."

Cyra didn't say anything. She just looked at her.

"I think you and Dez should go to dinner while we're on Cassan."

"What? Why?"

"Because he's been cooking for us. Because he's your mate. Because you can't keep running from this situation. You need to resolve it."

"How is having dinner together going to resolve the fact that he's contracted for delivery to Kolben, even if I am his mate?"

"You're being stubborn. There's always another solution, another plan."

"This is plan B. I was never supposed to be captain this soon. I'm making that work. How many alternate plans do you think I can support? Eventually, I just have to go forward. Perhaps it isn't the best decision. Maybe I'll regret it later. But this is what I have. This is what Auvi left me. He knew me better than anyone."

"Better than me? Really?"

"No. Not better than you. You've been my best friend. You are my best friend. I just..."

"I get it. He was your savior. He left you this ship, and you think it's your only lifeline. Maybe that's true. But maybe Dez can be a part of that. Maybe he's your next great thing."

"He can't be."

"You don't know that. You at least owe him a thank you for the transport contract, for feeding us, and for being honorable. He kept his word to you."

"If I promise to take him to dinner, will you let me be?"

"For now."

Veda left, and Cyra was no longer in the mood to prove that she knew what Rhysa suggested for stress relief. Rhysa probably didn't mean for her to relieve her stress alone. But alone was how she would be for a very long time. Dez was beautiful. He could cook and probably do a lot of other things. But the bottom line was the ship was her only safety net. The only way she would keep the ship was to be the most reliable transporter. It was tough enough being a female in a male-dominated industry. She couldn't afford to fail.

CHAPTER 23

THE SHIP DOCKED in a sector of Cassan different from the one they'd left from. Without the spiders, they didn't have to pay for the secure dock with additional security—an expense Cyra was happy to be relieved of. Rhysa and Blaize had taken off in separate directions. Cyra was sad that they weren't closer, but they were so different. At least they didn't fight. After g-weeks together on the ship, getting time apart was good.

"Veda, I'm going to take care of the Din' Gale delivery, then contact some of the bartenders here and see what the gossip is. I need to put out the word we're looking for a communications officer. Do you want to go with me?"

"I'll stay and keep watch over the thuringies. Why don't you see if Dez can go with you?"

"Subtle."

"I can be less so if needed."

"You aren't going to let this go, are you?" Cyra huffed.

"You'll thank me for this someday."

"No, I won't."

Cyra paused in the open entry to Dez's quarters. He was sprawled out on the too small bunk, reading something on the comm display. "Dez?"

Dez held up a finger to her before using it to tap the screen. "I have been reading the most excellent stories about how other beings find and seduce their mates."

"Romance?" He was reading romance novels?

He held up the screen and showed her the cover of two half-naked beings wrapped in an embrace. "Veda loaned them to me." He rose from the bed. "You require my services?"

"I'm contacting the receiver for the Din' Gale goods, and then I'll take care of some errands and grab a meal. Would you like to go with me?"

"It would be my pleasure, my queen."

"Captain."

"That, too."

Cyra stomped off the ship. Between Veda and Dez, she was getting frustrated with them not accepting her decision. She didn't have time to argue with him. Her errands were critical, and if at all possible, she'd try to secure another contract and get back on track for delivering Dez. Kolben wasn't coming to her. And the cycles before the penalty kicked in were ticking away with alarming speed.

They traced their way through the crowded marketplace filled with vendors and shoppers, laced with the scents of exotic foods and the echoes of too many languages. She found the office of the buyer that the prince had contracted with.

"Captain Cyra. Right on time." The thick male grasped her hand with stubby fingers. Did Dez growl? She glared at him over her shoulder. "And you are?" the man asked Dez.

"Dezmuhnd Cuocua, brother-in-law to the crown prince of Din' Gale." Dez gave the slightest bow.

"Royalty." The man smacked his hands together. "I can't tell you how happy I was to make this deal. I've been working on it for ages. How soon can we receive the order?"

"Now, if you have a place to receive it. The goods require some reasonable refrigeration as they're fresh."

"Yes, yes. I have room in our storage."

"Do you wish to inspect first?" Cyra asked, not entirely certain of the expectations of the buyer. She hadn't accompanied Auvi on many deliveries.

"Not necessary. If the prince sent his brother-in-law to oversee the deal...well, then." He held his arms wide in an accepting gesture. "I'll send my men to your ship to retrieve the goods."

Cyra considered pointing out that his delivery wasn't the reason Dez was present, but why bother? She texted Veda to expect local warehousers to arrive shortly. "There's just the matter of payment."

The buyer settled in his chair, which had retained his shape while standing. He tapped a few keys. Cyra's comm pinged, and she checked her account. The credits had arrived. Her half of the deal. She already felt lighter, having a small cushion of funds not allocated to getting to Kolben.

"When can I expect another delivery?" the man asked Dez.

"It'll be a while before we get back to Din' Gale," Cyra answered. "We have to go to Kolben next."

The man shivered. "Why would you go there?"

"Other contracts." It was none of his business.

"Good, good. But don't forget to contact me when you can run another shipment." He rubbed his jowly chin and peered at his display. "Actually, this will keep the goods rare and in demand." Cyra could almost see the credits stack in his eyes.

"Great. Well, I'll be in touch." Cyra and Dez left the man to his schemes. When they were outside the office, back in the streaming mass of public, Cyra turned to Dez. "That went well." There was no time to celebrate, but maybe some time to eat? "We need to put the word out for a communications officer. Let's grab a mono-tram and head to some popular hangouts."

Dez nodded, his gaze swiveling around the space.

"You okay?"

"There is no air here. It's worse than the ship. Nothing grows."

"Not true. They have greenhouses with grow lights on a different level. Hydroponics and waste reclamation growing a variety of crops."

"It smells dead." His face wrinkled.

"It's not that bad." It was. She recalled having the same reaction to Cassan the first time she'd been there with Auvi. She'd acclimated. Their trip to the retail district, where the cheaper bars were found, was brief and wordless. Dez seemed deep in his thoughts, and Cyra wasn't sure what to say to him. It didn't matter if he got used to the station because he'd never be back.

They visited several of her favorite watering holes. The bartenders were happy to see her and more than willing to chat with her. They didn't care about her reputation, only that she tipped well as Auvi had taught her. None of them knew of a communications specialist looking for a contract but would keep the word out. They had the same story for contracts to Kolben. Not many transporters would go there, so they didn't see a lot of demand from the suppliers. Many expressed shock that she would be willing to travel so far. She shrugged off their doubts. Time was going to pass either way. Better to pass it with paying contracts.

"Are you hungry?" Cyra asked Dez. He had been her quiet shadow during her visits. Not far from her body, but not intrusive in any way. She had to admit that it was nice to have his company, and she felt more secure than if she'd been by herself.

"I'm always hungry," Dez answered. It sounded to Cyra as

if he was talking about more than food. She chose to ignore the subtext of his statement.

"Great, we're near my favorite Chalcanth-themed restaurant. You shared your home with me. Now, I will give you a taste of my home."

"Is there a reason none of your other crew mates are willing to dine there with you?"

"I didn't invite anyone else to go with us. But I'll admit, it's not Veda's favorite."

"Take me, and I will decide for myself."

Dez followed Cyra to a small eatery tucked away in a remote corner a few meters from a residential section of the station. The restaurant walls were painted a deep cobalt blue, and bright green strips of translucent fabric hung from the ceiling. Dez's head swam a bit at the contrast of the artificial gravity and the sense of being underwater. The server had similar features to Cyra—blue skin and gills, and dark green hair tied up on her head. She didn't spark any attraction.

Only his queen existed in his heart. If only he could find a way into hers.

Cyra ordered for them both. Dez was nervous about her selections, like sea snake and raw bittlefish. He was willing to try it. It was the food of his mate's childhood. The meal would bring him a new understanding and provide new details for him to contemplate as he pined for her alone in his room.

Once the meal was served, Dez started with a small bite of the sea snake. At least it appeared to be cooked, unlike the other morsels on the flat wooden serving platter. He placed the cooked piece of snake gingerly in his mouth. Cyra studied him the entire time, and tense anticipation built between them.

Flavor burst over his tongue. Salty, a bit sweet, and some other indescribable flavor that only food that once breathed actual life contained. The texture was flaky and delicate. "It's delicious."

"They make it in the traditional way at this place. Slow smoking it over salt-saturated driftwood. You can taste the ocean and the land in every bite. Nothing reminds me more of my planet than this dish." Cyra's approval was evident in her tone. Dez warmed at her words. He would have faked enjoying the meal if he had to. Luckily, it hadn't come to that.

"Do you ever visit your home?" The last visit to his own home planet was too close to the forefront of his mind.

She glanced away. "No, I didn't leave under the best of circumstances. I don't know if I would be welcome."

Impossible. "Your family is still there?"

"As far as I know. I've never heard otherwise."

Maybe she really did need a communications officer desperately if she hadn't been able to figure out how to contact the planet. It explained all the running around they'd done earlier.

"Why did you leave?" Something horrible must have happened.

"I wanted to be more than a baby factory. I wanted to have adventures. I thought I knew more than I did and could take care of myself."

She left to avoid her family obligations? Not what he had expected. There was probably more to the story, something she wasn't telling him. "You seem to have taken care of yourself quite well."

Cyra smiled at him, but it was a little wistful. "I don't know if I should take credit for where I am right now. I'm struggling to make the best of a situation I wasn't prepared for."

Dez could relate. His vision of what his life would be after he sold himself into servitude hadn't been close to the reality. It had been a huge adjustment when he learned he would be treated as if he held very little value and warehoused with others until the owner had taken a liking to him. The few years he'd spent as a personal companion had been closer to what he'd anticipated. Too bad it hadn't lasted longer. "It's difficult to be completely prepared for any circumstance. It's more important to be adaptable and creative. A plan is only worthwhile as long as all the variables remain unchanged. That is rarely—if ever—the case, in my experience."

"I had a lot of help to get to this point. Captain Auvi gifted me the ship after he saved me as a runaway. Veda has been incredibly supportive and taken care of details I would never have been able to handle, like feeding those damn spiders."

"Her tiny frame belies her brave strength." Dez chuckled.

Cyra's face lit. "I think she might be the smartest, bravest person I've ever known. I love her more than a sister."

"I would like to be this kind of friend to you too. Someone who helps you. Someone you rely on."

She tilted her head, and the light left her face. "You're going to be gone soon."

"We have several g-months of travel ahead of us. Would you be willing to let me do more than cook meals?"

"Like what?"

She didn't say no. "I'd like to continue to help look for a communications officer for you while we are on Cassan. Perhaps I could secure another contract as well?"

She shook her head slightly. "I don't want you to feel obligated to help me. I've been paid to transport you. It seems like I'd be taking advantage."

Did she not understand she couldn't take advantage of her mate who wished to give her everything and care for her in every way? "We may not know each other well, and we may not have long together, but you are my mate. It would bring me pleasure to help you."

"If you want to do it, I won't stop you. But you don't *have* to do anything. You don't even have to cook." She served herself more colorful pieces from the platter.

"I disagree. I absolutely have to cook." Dez grinned, relieved that she was able to give in, even if it was a tiny amount. He selected two more pieces, more colorful and much less cooked than the sea snake, tasting her planet and enjoying every moment of the shared private meal. He rarely saw his mate alone for more than a few moments.

"Did you get enough to eat?" Cyra asked, shifting the empty platter on the table by millimeters.

"I did. It was wonderful." She lifted her gaze, and a hesitant smile teased her plump lips. "Thank you for sharing your food with me." If only he could kiss her.

"Do you want to go with me to one last stop? There's one more bartender I need to connect with."

He stood and held out his hand. "I would be pleased to accompany you."

When she placed her hand in his, he tried to memorize the feel of it so he would never forget her willing touch, the shape of her fingers, the warmth of her delicate grip. They walked down the row of businesses. Her skin pressed against his was a small balm to his aching heart, his demanding soul. His mate hadn't touched him since she'd changed his markings. He was starving for her. The simple connection eased his never-ending pain. If only she would give him more. The kiss of her sensuous navy blue lips. His hands through her dark green locks. His naked body against her soft blue skin. But he could settle for holding her hand.

The bar she led him to was crowded. They stood near the seats that surrounded the bar itself. Every seat was filled with a variety of beings. Short and dark like Veda. Pale and lean like Blaize. Thick and muscled like himself. All chattering in the common language, tossing back drinks and searching for some measure of happiness at the end of a long day or longer journey.

The two bartenders moved so fast as to be running, making and serving drinks to the demanding crowd. A band tuned their digital instruments at the back of the room, adding to the overall noise. He and Cyra would have to wait to speak with her contact.

Dez stepped closer to Cyra. He made himself as big as possible to appear as imposing as he could. He wouldn't allow anyone else to touch her. If only he could wrap her in his arms, but there was no way she would permit that. Finally, one of the bartenders acknowledged them. They ordered a couple of drinks, but this male was not her contact. They continued to wait. A bar this busy had to be a good source for networking.

A drunk male stumbled toward them. He stared at Cyra. There were four others with him. A pack moving toward his mate. "Cyra, we should go?"

"What? No." Cyra remained focused on the man mixing their order at the end of the bar. "We have drinks coming, and I still need to make contact."

"Please, my queen." Before he could continue to present his reasons for leaving, the group was on them.

"It's her," the male slurred loudly. "This is the tentacle slut. Varik told me about you. We may not have tentacles, but there are five of us. It will feel like tentacles when we fuck you like the slut you are."

"Apologize." Dez stepped forward out of the shadows and moved Cyra behind him.

"You don't have tentacles either. How are you going to pleasure that fucking slut all by yourself?" He grinned his stained toothy smile and winked a red-rimmed eye before shooting his arm out toward Cyra.

Dez roared and hit the male in the face so hard that the breaking of bones was audible over the sounds of the bar. The unconscious male flew back into his buddies, knocking them down in a writhing pile. Dez roared at them again. They scrabbled and pulled their leader with them, leaving the bar as they made fear-filled noises of apology. They never turned their back on Dez. Their eyes were as wide as saucers.

Dez turned to check on Cyra. Her arms were wrapped around her middle.

"Your—your eyes," she stuttered.

They must have gone red-orange. He consciously lowered his lips from the fearsome grimace and pinched his flared nostrils. He'd meant to be menacing, but she was nervous—scared of him. He reached for her.

She gasped and cringed away from him.

"I would not hurt you, my queen." Although he'd exposed his brutal predator side, it was only to protect her.

"They were just talking."

"He tried to grab you. They would have attempted to harm you. There were five of them." He crossed his arms to keep from reaching for her again. How could she not perceive the threat? "They were not in their right minds with drink. And I would never allow you to come to harm."

She tilted her head, her gaze raking him. Finally, she stepped closer and placed her hand on his forearm. "Thank you, Dez."

Dez wrapped his arm around her torso and tugged her close, noting the bar had gone quiet. The band and all the patrons stared at them. There was no way she'd be able to communicate with her contact. He'd had no choice but to protect her, but maybe he'd gone too far. "We should go."

She glanced around. "Right."

They returned to *The Treasure.* Dez guided her through the halls of Cassan by the hand based on memory and his innate sense of direction. He kept her closer to him than he had when they left the restaurant. He couldn't make himself let her go, even after they were safely on the ship.

"Are you alright?" Dez asked her once they were in his room and he could finally release her. He shifted his gaze over every inch of her, confirming she was truly unharmed.

"Yes, thanks to you." She shivered. "They really did want to hurt me, didn't they?"

"They did, my queen."

She leaned forward and wrapped her arms around his shoulders. Her touch sent an arc of desire shooting across his skin. Her breath teased his lips, and, before he could move, she kissed him. A moment of her delicate lips pressed to his so chastely, but she kissed him. His heart and brain exploded. His mate had voluntarily touched him and kissed him. He embraced her around her waist, holding her close, prolonging their kiss, tasting the salt of her soft skin. She allowed it for such a short time before she pulled back and put her forehead to his. His breath came in pants as if he'd chased her through the station. He loved that she was almost as tall as him. He could look her in the eyes. Or he could have if her eyes were open. Her shuddering breath heated his skin.

She lifted her head and opened her gorgeous ocean-blue eyes. "I have to go."

She freed herself from his hold and left.

He flopped back on his bunk. It wasn't perfect, but it was progress. He could still feel her on his lips. Slowly, he licked them and savored her taste. With a groan, he rolled over, pressing his erection into the thin mattress. She would kill him before they got to Kolben.

CHAPTER 24

Cyra escaped to her water chamber. She could have visited the salt pools at one of the station's spas, but she preferred to be alone. Alone, she could let her skin release the feel of him. Release the energy she'd absorbed from him.

Their impossible connection clawed at her.

She couldn't do it. She couldn't sacrifice everything she was to be someone's mate. If she was going to end up tied down to a male for life, she could've stayed with her family. Never had an adventure. Never been a captain. Never had a chance of having a successful career. She ached for this male. He fuddled her brain and captured her heart. But what she wanted most in this lifetime was her freedom. Her independence.

Her body was a traitorous bitch, demanding she return to his arms to let him give her an orgasm that didn't involve tentacles or an audience. But that wasn't what she'd studied so hard for, what she'd sacrificed for. He could be a temporary distraction, but no more than that. Except that she liked having him with her when she went off-ship. The way he protected her from a danger she hadn't recognized.

She wasn't much of a people person to begin with, and once Varik had trash-talked her to anyone who would listen, she had a bigger target on her back. She already stood out from most of the other transporters—tall, blue, and female. Not like she could blend into the crowd with those characteristics.

In the past, she'd kept to herself and avoided any possible threats. As captain, that was no longer an option. She had to interact with the key players in the industry—the bartenders, the dock workers, the vendors. She wouldn't leave it to her crew to handle everything the way Captain Auvi had done.

The gelatinous water held her aloft as her thoughts tried to drag her down. Why couldn't the answers ever be easy? Her entire life was a struggle between what she wanted and what she could have. She closed her eyes, allowing the solution to come to her, letting go of all the tension. Hours might have passed before she found her less-than-perfect resolution.

For as long as she could, she would let Dez help her. It would hurt to let him go when the time came, but it would hurt them both if she shunned him in the meantime.

An imperfect compromise, but it was all she had. She continued to float around, letting her thoughts wander until she was completely relaxed. She returned to her quarters and fell asleep as soon as she settled into bed. Dez filled her dreams.

During the next cycle, Cyra stumbled into the galley. With Dez on her brain, her sleep had been anything but restful. But she had a business to manage. Blaize and Rhysa were at opposite ends of the table. Dez was at the food prep station, filling the room with amazing scents. His thick legs and taut backside clenched and rippled with every shift of his body. Cyra's mouth watered.

Veda came in and sat next to Cyra.

She purposely looked away from the temptation of Dez. "Do we have any leads on a communications expert?"

"Nothing," Rhysa answered.

"I talked to everyone who would listen, putting the word

out, visiting at least thirteen places. I even talked to the shop-keepers, and no one knows of anyone who's looking. It's incredible. You would think there would be *someone*. It seems like it should be a solvable problem. I mean, aren't new officers graduating regularly and don't they need a contract if for nothing else than to pay their living expenses? I can't believe that nobody knows anybody who is looking..."

Dez cut off Blaize's ramblings by placing a plate of hot food under her nose. Cyra was grateful. It was too damn early for all that jabbering.

"We'll need to restock and get going then." The time had come for *The Treasure* to make the trip she dreaded. "Rhysa?"

Rhysa paused her fork mid-bite. "Captain?"

"Can I ask you to help us with getting the fuel?" It was awful to ask, but every credit counted since there were far too few in the business account.

Rhysa chewed and swallowed. "Absolutely." She grinned and wiggled her white eyebrows. "I was planning on a quick visit to my guy. Having a valid reason works to my favor."

Cyra glanced up as a dark arm holding her tray of food entered her vision. His smoldering look was warmer than the meal he'd given her. "Dez? Would you be willing to go with me to select provisions?"

"I would be pleased to assist you." Why did his answer sound sexual?

"Veda, do you need anything?"

"Dez's family was incredibly generous. And since no one was sick or injured, even the thuringies are well, so, no. I don't need anything," Veda replied.

Dreading what might be a long-winded answer, Cyra ate a few more bites of the delicious protein and vegetable mixture Dez had made. "What about you, Blaize? Need anything?"

Fortunately, Blaize was still eating and just shook her head.

As soon as she finished eating, Blaize would be all over the system checks. Cyra's crew was experienced and talented. She didn't need to instruct them what to do every minute of every cycle. It made being the captain simpler.

Cyra and Dez spent the day shopping and revisiting their contacts. There was no contract to be had to deliver anything to Kolben, and they struck out on any leads for the communications position. Cyra was discouraged, but her time wasn't a total loss. Dez held her hand for most of the day. He touched her shoulder or her back if she was busy with her hands. He was in contact with her all the time and she liked it. The warm energy that came from him wrapped her up and soothed her almost as well as being in her water chamber. She couldn't get used to it, but she would enjoy it while it lasted.

"Hello?" Cyra called out as she and Dez walked down the main corridor of *The Treasure*. They'd already found the bridge empty. "Veda?"

The med lab was empty. So were the engineering areas of the ship. "They must have had errands to run after all."

She hadn't been uneasy all day, but being alone with Dez on the ship had an air of intimacy she hadn't experienced being with him in public.

"Hungry?" she asked, heading back to the galley.

Dez tugged her hand that he hadn't let go of. She stopped and gave him a questioning glance. He embraced her and his lips hovered so close to hers. She couldn't resist and pressed forward, accepting his silent offer. His lips were warm and gentle but determined. His hands went to her hip, pressing her body to his, while he teased her lips with his tongue until she opened for him.

The corridor disappeared. There was only Dez. His kiss deepened as he feasted on her, savoring her. He teased her tongue until she responded, just as hungry for him. She would never end their kiss if she had the option of forever. His erection pressed against her mound. Their clothes were the only barrier preventing them from having sex there in the hallway.

The realization of where she was interrupted her desire. She dreaded getting caught making out by her crew, and with a great draw on her internal will, she put her hands to his muscular chest and pushed him back, instantly missing the sweet connection of their lips.

Dez sighed, dropping his hand from her hip. "I'll begin preparing our last-meal."

"Dez..."

"There is nothing to say." He held up a hand, his eyes briefly closed. When he opened them, they weren't focused on her but on some distant point on the ship. "I understand. Do you think everyone will return to eat?"

"I'm sure they will." His food was delicious, and credits were dear. "Can I help you?"

He shook his head, and her gut clenched as if he'd punched her.

"I think I would prefer a few minutes alone to regain control of myself. If you are with me in the galley, I may not feel like cooking." Dez finally met her gaze and gave her a panty-melting grin.

She took her first conscious breath since she'd pushed him away. His smile warmed her almost as much as his touch. He wasn't mad at her like she would be if the situation were reversed. She couldn't have him, and she didn't deserve him. She left to go to her quarters and find her own control or, more likely, release. The water tank wasn't going to cut it. She stripped down once she'd locked herself into her room, lay on the bed, and used her fingers as she imagined what they could have done if she'd let the kiss go on. Her orgasm was like her cooking—barely adequate to sustain her and only left her craving what he could give.

Later in the galley, after everyone had returned, Cyra slunk in and took a seat, still worried about how Dez really felt. His grin had been convincing at the time, but could he really be okay with her ever-moving boundaries? If she could get control and keep her hands and her lips to herself, there'd be no room for misunderstandings. But she didn't have the willpower. Even her eyes betrayed her as they roamed over his thick muscles, cataloging every bump and shadow.

"So, Rhysa, did you blow the fuel guy again? Or did we have to pay full price?" Blaize asked, interrupting Cyra's fantasy life.

"Funny, bitch," Rhysa replied lightheartedly. "He gives me a good price because he wants to, same reason I blow him. Besides, I wasn't in such a hurry on this trip. Everyone got theirs." She winked a pink eye at the redheaded engineer who was blushing deep red.

Cyra assumed their banter meant they were forming an odd sort of friendship. She was relieved that Rhysa didn't take offense to Blaize's snarky comment. She'd expected Rhysa would blow up about giving a blowjob. Not so much. Of course, she hated that Rhysa was trading sexual favors for their fuel even though she appeared happy to do so.

"By everyone, I hope you mean you got yours," Cyra blurted out. "There's selfless, and then there's stupid. I personally need a lot more upfront before I go down on my knees for someone."

"Good to know." Dez turned and put a plate in front of Blaize.

Despite being blue, her cheeks heated with her blush, and she was likely purple. She bit her tongue. The same appendage that had explored his sexy mouth. She stuffed her mouth with seared meat. Talk of blowjobs and people getting theirs made her uncomfortable. Not because she didn't like sex talk, but because she was aching for a sexual release. A real one, not a mini-gasm on the tips of her fingers.

Dez caught her quick glance in his smoldering gaze. He took her hand in his and kissed her fingertips. His tongue teased out so briefly and then he broke into a huge grin. She'd washed her hands, but somehow he knew what she'd done. Maybe he had some super predator sense and could smell her arousal, or maybe he was empathic and could sense her feelings. He released her hand. "You could have asked for my assistance."

Cyra's breath caught. She'd have to be careful around him if she would hide anything. Especially anything having to do with imagining fucking him. Veda cleared her throat, bringing Cyra back to the galley. Dez freed her, and she released the breath she'd been holding. She might have to give in and have a brief affair with him. Not too brief—it was a long way to Kolben. But no strings attached. The more she toyed with the idea, the better it seemed.

"Where did you go this afternoon, Veda?" Dez asked as he sat with his own meal.

"Oh, I went to run a few errands. I sent a message to Doc just to check in. I needed some personal items. Oh—" She startled and shifted in her seat. "I was thinking about starting a hydroponic garden. It would be nice to have some fresh vegetables on these long journeys. I know this guy who knows all about the lights and the soil and the plants that do best. I didn't buy anything. I wanted to talk to you about it first, Cyra."

"That's a brilliant idea." A hydroponics project could be the perfect distraction. "What do you think it will take in credits to get started?"

"Don't worry about the credits. Everyone else bought into a

partnership, and I want to do the same. I just wanted to make sure that you would be okay with me setting up the system."

"Blaize?" Cyra asked. "What do you think? Can our systems absorb the hit for the power and water?"

"Depends where on the ship you're doing this." Blaize took a breath to continue, but Veda jumped in.

"I was thinking I might take over one of the cells. The other option is one of the empty crew apartments, but that would be harder since the furnishings are built in. A cell is the perfect space. I'm spending so much time back there anyway with the dogs."

"Actually, that works. The systems are designed to climate control those areas within pretty tight parameters. As long as it's not too big an area."

"Of course you can have a couple of cells. Maybe the set of four that can connect to form one larger space," Cyra replied.

"I would be happy to assist you with this project, Doctor," Dez added, making Cyra fall for him just a bit more.

CHAPTER 25

VARIK SLUNK DOWN to the docking bay once the *Harlan Johnson* had made it back to Cassan. Twalley deemed him a hero for limping the ship all the way back, avoiding a rescue hauler. Varik leveraged every bit of the captain's reaction, confirming how smart it had been to take the ship for a test run, even putting in a new part on order to complete the deception. It was the captain's fault that the situation had come to this. If he'd only let Varik take the ship when he'd asked instead of insisting on tagging along. As it was, Cyra had returned to Cassan an entire cycle ahead of them.

There she was, his *Treasure*. The huge ship filled the large docking bay, one of the largest available on Cassan that wasn't for a pleasure cruise or other passenger vessels. He ached to run his hands over her, make sure she was being taken care of, but he had to stay hidden. The ramp was lowered as if in invitation. Varik took a single step and froze. The blue bitch who'd stolen his ship strode out followed by a giant male, her literal shadow. The Din' Gale native Auvi had contracted to deliver to Kolben. What was Cyra up to?

The male should be in the cargo hold unless she'd canceled

the contract. But how could she pay back the deposit? Not to mention the forfeiture fee?

Following them around for the entire cycle netted him no information. They'd gone to various vendors and bars. Nothing unusual. Probably seeking more crew. To go to Kolben? She'd obviously delivered the spider cargo based on the fact *The Treasure* was no longer in the quarantine bays. If only he could have seen them struggling to round up the creepy-crawlies. If she didn't have another contract, she was prodding the wrong wormholes. The bars she visited were for crew, not distributers. She made it to Morgual and back. So what was she up to?

His comm beeped. Jarn. Another love Cyra was keeping Varik from. He should be sharing meals with Jarn, especially after leaving him on his own during the fake test run. Cyra and her shadow appeared to be returning to the docks. His surveillance would have to be on hold until the next cycle. He sent a message to his lover that he would be home soon. First, he had to check in with Twalley.

"The part should be available in a cycle or two at most." Varik lounged in the chair in Twalley's cluttered office as if he wasn't aching to get back to Jarn.

"No rush. There's been another delay in the research funding." Varik masked his frustration. It was clear Twalley was nervous with his hair on end and his avoidance of Varik's gaze.

Fake sympathy was called for. "Oh no. What's happened? Can I help?"

Twalley puffed out a breath and blinked up at Varik. "Nothing technical. A form that was missed with the university's accounting office." He waved his hand. "A minor setback. I'm sure it will be fixed in a cycle or two."

Varik had heard that before. "Excellent." He stood. "Then I better check on that part. I don't want any delay to be my fault."

"Thank you so much, Varik. You're a lifesaver." Twalley beamed at him.

Varik barely contained his rage when he exited the office. A cycle or two meant ten based on the previous delays. If Cyra left Cassan before he could follow—

Killing Twalley and taking his ship was an option. Except that was a high-risk solution when they were on Cassan. Station security would get involved. There would be questions and complications with the title transfer he wasn't prepared to address. Better to subdue Twalley once they were underway, distanced from security, and staffed with a crew loyal to Varik.

The bigger issue was figuring out where Cyra was taking his ship next. She should be going to Kolben. Din' Gale had been a surprise, but still within his tracker's perimeter. How could he make sure *The Treasure* and the *Harlan Johnson* wouldn't pass each other coming and going?

He couldn't.

Yet.

Jarn waited at the door of their room like an excited puppy. If only he could take him out in public and treat him to a restaurant meal at a nice place. But he had to maintain the image of a mostly unemployed engineer, hungry for work. If Twalley should spot them...well that would be a disaster.

"Hello, love." Varik tugged Jarn to him, petting him and kissing him. The boy was so loyal and once Varik had his treasure back, he would treat Jarn like the prince he was. "Hungry, baby?"

"For you." Jarn gave him a soft smile.

Varik stroked his cheek. "I have to feed you or you'll waste away to nothing." Varik released his lover with a slight nudge. He checked the food replicator. Basic nutrient paste only. The basic foodstuff would keep most beings alive and was unlimited in all modern replicators, but damn was it nasty. Not even to keep up appearances could he face another serving of that slop. "What are you in the mood for? Anything? I'll order delivery."

"Can we afford that?"

Jarn had no idea Varik could afford that and much more. "Twalley gave me a bonus for getting the ship back to Cassan without having to call for rescue." Or he should have, the cheap bastard. "Let me spoil you for once."

"Could we go out?" The wheedling tone grated. Give the boy an inch, and he took a mile.

"Unfortunately, I have an early morning appointment. I need my rest. If you don't want me to order—"

"I do. I do. What about this place?" He held up his comm opened to a menu that featured historic Earth comfort food.

The synthetic animal fat would give Varik the shits, but whatever. "Sure, baby. Order me some of whatever you get. I'm going to wash up." He dropped a promising kiss on his lover's lips. They'd eat, fuck, and sleep before Varik left to track Cyra. Eventually, he'd get his opportunity and a plan would come to him. But he had to stay focused.

Varik returned to the dock in time to see Cyra and her shadow depart. Shortly afterward, a Blaque Poll native, based on her disturbingly pink eyes, trotted down the ramp. Her movements were seductive. Varik wouldn't mind getting a piece of that ass. How had Cyra secured one of the best navigators around? Because that's what anyone from Blaque Poll did. Captains paid a fortune for their services, and Cyra had no credits. Unless she'd gotten a huge contract with his ship. Varik clenched his jaw and waited. Veda was still on the ship. Following Cyra had netted him nothing. If he could get into the systems, he could find out everything.

About the time his patience had run out, and he'd been ready to abandon his hidey-hole, Veda appeared, along with his ex-lover—Blaize. He recognized the redhead in full light. The ramp closed behind them. Varik's blood heated.

The ship was empty, and he'd didn't need a ramp to access his treasure. After ferreting his way through the external access panel into the main systems, he whistled. Blaize had been spending some significant time down there. She was such a tight-ass about everything, but that didn't make her the better engineer. The surfaces were spotless. Connections tight and labeled. The cables neatly bundled and suspended in anti-gravity sleeves. All the stuff he'd planned to do when he got around to it once *he* possessed *The Treasure*.

Good. It would be that much nicer when he took her back. First, he had to put some insurance in place that he didn't lose track of her again. Then he'd see what direction they headed.

Barking drew Varik's attention. What the hell? Was the cargo full of dogs? Sweat broke out on his forehead. He hated canines after a particularly vile incident with a married lover's spouse g-years ago.

He finished up quickly and disappeared the same way he'd come in, fortunate no one had returned before he'd had a chance to put everything in place. Because finding *The Treasure* when she crossed into the godforsaken galaxy that contained Kolben would have been like searching for an atom in a black hole.

Varik wasn't sure if he felt like celebrating or drowning his sorrows. It didn't much matter since he was in a bar and had lost track of the number of drinks he'd had. Every attempt he'd made to secure a contract on another ship had been a failure. Either the captain and crew were not the type that he would be able to manipulate, and Varik backed out. Or they would balk once they found out which ship he used to work on. The stories of what the slut Cyra had done somehow tarnished his reputation, and he couldn't get an offer. It was as if fate was working against him.

How the fuck was he going to get to Kolben? Even with the insurance in place, no way would Captain Twalley not see a deviation of that magnitude from their planned trajectory. It was questionable if his tiny ship could make such a voyage.

Varik had heard Cyra had been asking around for more goods to deliver, so she couldn't have a full load even with the beasts he'd heard. He should have sucked up his fear and checked the cargo bays before he left. No matter what they were transporting, it would require a fuck ton of fuel. Especially with the slight *modification* he'd made. But he'd have to get to *The Treasure* before salvagers found her floating in deep space. *After* everyone and everything had perished.

How had Cyra gained the upper hand when he had all the finances and the experience? The situation was so unfair. He scowled, cursed Auvi, then threw back his drink.

CHAPTER 26

Cyra searched the ship for Dez.

"There you are." His half-naked body mesmerized her as he worked out on the gym equipment in the cargo bay. He was sweaty and bulging, and she wanted to make him more sweaty and bulging in a completely different way, in a different room, and in several different positions.

He sat up, and his gaze bored into her, heating her between her legs. "I needed to work off my...excess energy."

"Have you thought about moving into a bigger room?" She shouldn't care. "The one you're in is too small for the long journey to Kolben. It doesn't even have a chair."

"I was not invited to stay in the room I'd like to occupy during the trip."

The breath in her lungs left on a word. "Dez."

"You do not need to provide me with a reason, my queen. I'm capable of waiting patiently for what is inevitable."

There was his alpha arrogance. "I think you're a little optimistic. Nothing is inevitable."

"We are."

His confidence in their relationship and the tone of his deep, warm voice tempted Cyra beyond reason. She would love nothing more than to abandon her responsibilities and her future and the future of her crew and take this male to her bed forever, or at least the next hundred g-years. But she wasn't impulsive, generally. And anytime she had been in the past, it hadn't been the best decision. She couldn't afford to give in to her desires completely. But maybe partially. "The room next to the captain's quarters is available."

"That works. For now." Dez lay back down on the bench and resumed pressing the virtual grav bar above his chest.

"Veda said you've been working with the dogs."

"Keeping them fit and engaged. A bored animal is dangerous."

Cyra glanced at the kennels. All five thuringies were lying down, head on paws, staring intently at Dez. She couldn't blame them because she struggled with taking her eyes off him herself. "Thank you."

"It's my pleasure, my queen."

"Captain."

"That too." Dez continued lifting the bar up and down, muscles straining, trails of sweat tracing paths between each one. It would be awkward if Cyra remained staring at him. Besides, the water chamber called her name.

Unfortunately, the relaxation she'd sought there had been short-lived, and after a long, restless night, Cyra finally gave up on sleep and got up. She wasn't certain Dez had moved, but she had a sense of him through the wall. She pressed her hand to the panel as if she could feel him. The decision to invite him to move closer might've been a mistake.

In the galley, she found nothing but the scent of the earlier meal and her wrapped divided tray. Of course Dez saved something for her. After quickly eating and tidying up her mess, she went to the deck. Blaize was doing system checks, and Rhysa was plotting navigation based on updated dust cloud data.

"Hey, Captain. Are you sure you don't want to jump there with some bridges? We could entirely avoid this class five cloud." She pointed at the screen displaying the latest NOAH data. The official organization for all things space travel related.

"Rhysa, you know I hate those things."

"It would be infinitely faster."

"Yet we could get there later. Only we might benefit from the time shift. We wouldn't age, but we could be well into the future or possibly the past. Although it's less likely, I don't like either option. Not to mention the possible damage to the ship. Those things aren't entirely reliable. I would much rather take the longer, surer route since we have the means." Her argument was weak. Ships used them all the time with rare complications. Even Auvi had used them whenever he could. But she dreaded the experience every time. And she had a living, breathing reason not to get to Kolben faster.

"Whatever you say, Captain."

"Blaize?"

"Yes, Captain, we're ready to launch when you are."

"Let me just do my own final checks and talk to Veda. I'll return soon, ready to leave. Get authorization from the docks for liftoff."

The med lab was vacant. Cyra hadn't seen Dez either. She headed for the cargo bays.

"Veda? Are you in here?"

"Back here."

Cyra found her nestled among boxes of various sizes and states of unpacking.

"They delivered my hydroponic setup earlier. I'm just checking out all the lights and grow pots. I need a plan before I start setting it up." She plucked a light bulb from a pack and inspected it before returning it to the protective casing.

Cyra bit her lip. "I need your help."

"What's wrong?" Veda came out from behind the pile of stuff.

"Am I being unreasonable about not using ER bridges?"

"Did Rhysa push you to approve a route with them?"

Cyra rubbed her forehead. "Not pushed exactly."

"Logically, the risks are minimal but not zero. And to be fair, your physical reaction to them seems to be unusually strong."

Cyra shivered at the physical memory of being pulled and stretched to her limits when Auvi would use them.

"But are you sure this isn't about something else?"

"Like what?"

"Like that handsome male who calls you queen, saved your meal for you, and is now living in the quarters next to yours?"

Cyra crossed her arms. "What does Dez have to do with worm holes?"

Veda waggled her thick eyebrows. "I'm sure he'd be willing to help you with *all* your holes."

"Funny. Did I say I liked you? Get ready for launch, Miss Comedy." Cyra turned and left as the sound of Veda's laughter followed her.

Speaking of Dez, she should verify that he was actually on board. She'd spoken to everyone other than him. He needed to be prepared for takeoff.

Cyra knocked on the door to Dez's quarters. During her final visual inspection, she hadn't seen him anywhere else on the ship to make sure everything was stowed away and safety doors were closed, so he had to be in there unless he was gone. She heard his deep voice before her mind could run down that dark corridor.

"Coming."

The word held more promise than it should have. The door opened and all ability to speak left her. Dez wore a tiny pair of form-fitting briefs, leaving nothing to her imagination. And as good as her imagination had been when she'd thought of him, it was woefully inadequate. He was huge—everywhere. She'd already seen his sculpted arms and suspected he had a washboard stomach. But he was so much more than her imagination had teased. She trailed her eyes over his bulging biceps, up to his broad shoulders, down his muscular pecs with the dark, almost black, flat nipples that made her mouth water. She continued down the center of his abdomen that was like a valley chiseled in stone between a series of boulders that made up his core. The dark markings trailed down to his shorts. Everything pointed at his enormous cock that seemed to be growing larger the longer she stared. She couldn't draw her eyes away.

Dez stepped closer, forcing her to meet his dark yellow eyes. He was breathing just as heavily as she was. "Did you want something, my queen?"

Well, fuck. Could he have made an innocent question sound any dirtier? She paused and took a deep breath. She shook her head slightly, trying to get the blood flow back to her brain. "To make sure you were prepared...for launch."

"Do you require my assistance with launching the ship?" His tone was teasing. She was sure he knew exactly how *The Treasure* functioned after all the stories and the personal attacks. He had to have overheard the whispers while they'd visited all the bars looking for a navigator.

"We don't have to clear atmosphere when leaving the station. Just wanted to make sure you were ready."

"I'm ready. And willing. And able. For whatever I can do for you, my queen." His deep voice held so much dirty promise.

So many images raced through Cyra's mind. A tawdry to-do list that heated her cheeks. "Your captain."

"That too."

Cyra spun and left him standing in the door of his quarters. If she hadn't, she wouldn't be authorizing their departure anytime soon. She'd be wrapped around him like seaweed on a pier. All the reasons that was a terrible idea floated away on the tides of her desire. Except for one. She had a ship and a business to save and people counting on her. No pressure.

A couple of cycles after leaving Cassan, well on the way to Kolben, Cyra's crew had settled back into their routines. Veda focused on establishing her indoor greenhouse, and Dez helped with the construction and took point on working with the dogs. Cyra strode down the wide, empty corridor to the deck to review some administrative communications. She trailed her fingers against the locks on the built-in storage embedded in the walls, still in awe that *The Treasure* was hers. On deck, Blaize and Rhysa were at their stations. It would be a smooth trip, even if it was a long one. As soon as they delivered, they would continue to work to find more crew and more contracts. It was the life she'd dreamed of.

If only—

"Captain? I think we have a problem?" The concern in Blaize's voice made Cyra stiffen. "We're burning fuel at twice the expected rate."

"Are you sure?" Not good. Her gills flapped as she gulped air.

"I ran the calculations several times and verified the requirement with Rhysa. We loaded sufficient fuel with a buffer. I would never have let us leave without a sufficient reserve. But we've burned through the buffer and are still consuming at an unexpected rate. I originally discounted it as launch overhead, and I expected the usage rate to stabilize. It hasn't stabilized at all. In fact, if we continue to see the same trend, we will continue to double our usage every few cycles—"

Cyra interrupted Blaize to get to the critical issue. "Is the ship in danger?"

The worst possible scenario was the ship imploded—a quick death. Or slightly less worse, they had to shut down the engines and die a slow death unless a rescue ship reached them in time. Neither option comforted Cyra.

"The ship is in no danger according to the other readings and system alarm states. There can be only two reasons for the excess burn. Either we purchased substandard fuel or we have damage to the fuel inlet or the turbopump that is undetectable with the current system monitors. I've disproven every other theory."

"Which is more likely?"

"If the fuel was just substandard, the rate of use would have stabilized by now, I believe."

Blaize was so careful with the ship. Cyra had inspected the engine rooms, internal and external, and they had sparkled. But maybe the cleaning was to mask incompetence? She struggled to believe that about Blaize based on the previous legs of their journey. She was meticulous. "How could the damage have occurred? During liftoff?"

"No. Everything about the launch was normal." Blaize crossed her arms. "There's no sign of a hull breach. We didn't cross any debris fields or dust clouds." She bit her lip briefly. "It's my opinion we were sabotaged."

Cyra let that gem settle.

Sabotage.

It wasn't completely unlikely. She hadn't seen Varik on the station but heard he was still there. He would have known they were at the station. And it was possible someone other than Varik had a reason to resent the situation with *The Treasure* or one of her crew. *Why* wasn't important to their safety. "What are the possible solutions?"

"The problem is that there is no guarantee I'll be able to make a repair on the fly, even if we identify the issue. Ideally, we find a place to land that's within the range of the remaining fuel based on my conservative estimate."

"Rhysa, are you aware of this situation?"

"I am, Captain. I've identified two possible destinations. We can return to Cassan, and we should be able to make it all the way there. Or we can change our trajectory slightly and stop at a planet called Arbotriz."

"Recommendations?"

"I think we would be better off going back to Cassan. There are known suppliers there to get the parts we need to fix the ship and get more fuel," Blaize said.

"I disagree, Captain." Because of course Rhysa disagreed with Blaize. Cyra blanked her reaction and let Rhysa continue. "We should be able to repair the ship and refuel at Arbotiz, and that would require less fuel than turning around. It's a shorter distance, not by much, but shorter nonetheless. And we don't have the loss incurred by reversing direction, making Cassan a higher risk."

Cyra considered the dilemma. It was a risk to stop on Arbotriz, not knowing how they would get the repair done. Returning to Cassan was a bigger gamble, not only because the fuel usage would be greater, but their saboteur was there. At least, she had to assume that was true. "Go to Arbotriz."

CHAPTER 27

CYRA BREATHED a sigh of relief when they were granted landing authorization on Arbotriz. She hadn't been to this planet previously, but her hasty research told her that it was primarily females living on the planet. There was supposedly a strong agricultural industry, and the majority of the population lived in tightly packed communities. She'd asked Dez what he knew about the planet, and he'd just chuckled and said it was safe, but she should see it for herself, and he wanted to witness her first reaction. She couldn't understand what would be so odd about the planets or the inhabitants that he would expect a reaction. She'd been plenty of places and seen all matter of beings. She wasn't going to be surprised by some odd-looking humanoids. Obviously, they spoke Galaxian, the universal language, so they couldn't be that odd. Could they?

After disembarking, she admitted Dez was right—she was a little shocked. She hadn't seen a population with wings before. At least, not wings that didn't seem to function for anything. They were small and translucent and looked delicate enough that they could rip if they were breathed on too heavily. Apparently, one of the original NOAH exploratory shuttles that landed there found the most advanced species to be an insect—

a bee population. Whichever NOAH team had come to Arbotriz galactic centuries ago must have been amazingly talented. The humanoids looked similar to walking bees. Would their social structure be similar too? Cyra wanted to meet the locals, but she needed her ship fixed and refueled before anything else happened.

"Blaize, will you be able to get eyes on this failure and figure out what it will take to get it fixed as soon as possible? I need to know the cost of any required repair."

"Rhysa, please investigate what ER bridges are available to take us closer to Kolben with less fuel."

"You hate worm holes, Captain," she argued.

"We may not have another option."

Rhysa spun in her chair. "I'll see what I can do."

"Dez?" Dez had come to the deck after they landed. What did he want?

"My queen, I would like to see if I can secure a contract for your ship to help with expenses. My knowledge of this planet indicates that males are highly valued, and I may have more success talking to potential customers than the rest of the crew."

"You know about this planet?"

"I studied many of the inhabited NOAH planets in neighboring galaxies as part of my basic education. Didn't you?"

They must have covered those topics on the days her mother kept her home from school to help with the babies. "Not that I recall."

"I will provide you with any information you require, my queen."

"If you think you can have more success without us, then fine, go. But I'd rather you go with Blaize or Rhysa."

"I will do better as an unattached male. They have no way of knowing I'm already mated."

"You aren't already mated."

"I would hate to say you are wrong, Captain." He lowered his eyelids along with his voice. "But my status is mated. Although my mate denies me."

"I'm not denying you. I'm just not your mate." Because if she was—

"As you say, my queen."

"Ugh! Go see if you can find a contract." She shooed him away.

Dez leaned forward and kissed her lips quickly but pulled back before she could react. Kissing her in front of her crew left her embarrassed and speechless.

"Wow. I don't know why you're arguing with him over the mate thing, Captain. I would have already given him the full inspection and launch test." Rhysa wiggled her eyebrows over her bright pink eyes. "Twice."

"I'm not concerned with what you would do in my place in regard to Dez. I'm concerned about how we're getting to Kolben."

"On it."

Cyra needed time in the water chamber. Her ship had been sabotaged. Her cargo was insisting he was her mate. Her navigator couldn't open her mouth without a disagreement falling from her lips, and she was stuck on some backwoods bee planet that barely had a landing pad large enough to accommodate *The Treasure.* She needed to drown her sorrows in salt water.

Dez took a small shuttle from the space port to the business center. He passed through rich farmland that seemed to be growing a variety of crops. The crops weren't huge but were well on their way to producing. It must be late spring, at least on this side of the planet. As they approached the center of activity, the similarities and distinct differences from his own home planet became obvious. There were tall buildings, but they were packed closely together instead of spread out with tunnels. Instead of just green vegetation growing naturally around the structures, it seemed to be a riot of color. The closer they got, the more colors he could distinguish. There were flowers everywhere in every shade.

The shuttle stopped, and he stepped off, trying not to walk around with his mouth open as he looked at the wild complexes. Flowering vines and bushes planted at every level camouflaged the edges of every structure. Businesses occupied the lowest levels. Above that were hexagon-shaped rooms—apartments, houses—he wasn't sure what to call them. Every space appeared to have an outdoor balcony. The balconies were filled to overflowing with the pots that supported all the plants. The balconies themselves were of every color, either paint or something organic he couldn't tell. No two buildings or balconies were alike. The lack of symmetry and open space unsettled him. He took a moment to look his fill and then focused on the surrounding businesses, determined to help his mate.

A crowded beverage bar offered squeezed local produce. Dez wandered past a clothing boutique displaying beautiful clothes for females in the window. He would love to buy Cyra one of the gauzy dresses in a rainbow of watercolored dyes. She would rather he support her ship with his credits. But she wouldn't allow him to do that either. She would be unhappy if he bought her something so impractical. She was under too much pressure to appreciate a luxury. He would find a way to ease her stress soon.

He came upon a market that sold various produce, most of which he'd never seen nor heard of before—exactly what he'd been seeking. Inside, he asked to speak to the owner. Fortune smiled on him. The female who emerged from the back room undressed him with her eyes and licked her lips upon first glance. He lifted his chest, tightened his abs, tilted his head ever so slightly as he eyed her up and down and gave a slight smile. Her wings fluttered.

Perfect.

Dez left a long while later with a very profitable contract to deliver goods to Kolben and a deposit on the first shipment. The owner had been trying to break into new markets, and one message exchange with a contact she had in the Kolben Mining Company—the same that had purchased his own contract—secured the deal. Cyra would be pleased. Perhaps he could ask for a reward. He deserved one for flirting so shamelessly when he had no desire for anyone but his queen.

Dez finally found Cyra floating in the water chamber. She was completely submerged, completely relaxed, and completely naked. Her green hair fanned out behind her, light as downy feathers and glistening like silk. His fingers twitched with the desire to run through the beautiful strands. Her delicate gills at the side of her long, slender neck flitted in and out on an invisible tide. Her toned legs languidly kicked up and down. He could almost imagine them coming around his hips, tugging him to her as she pressed her sweet body to his, owning him. Slowly, she rose, rolled, and lifted her head from the watery gel. He focused on her eyes, expecting her to be angry that he was there while she was unclothed.

"You're back." She inspected him as he'd just done to her with no hint of concern about her state of undress.

He widened his stance. "I secured a contract."

"What?" She bounded out of the tank, grabbing a towel to dry her hair. "How did you do that? For what? Tell me."

Dez smiled. "I'll give you all the details at last-meal, my queen."

"Captain."

"That, too."

Cyra's comm clanged. An emergency hail. Dez tensed as she darted over the device, pulling on a dressing gown. "Veda?"

The doctor's voice came through the speaker. "There's a problem with one of the dogs. I could use some extra hands and my scanner."

"I'll be there in a moment," Dez answered before darting out of the water chamber and racing to the med lab. He prayed that the dog would be okay for her sake and Cyra's.

"It's in this cabinet." Cyra, dressed in a loose robe, reached past him to open the small door.

Dez retrieved the unit, grateful he hadn't had to search. They ran together to the kennels. Veda knelt by Queen's side. She reached for the scanner. "Get some blankets, Cyr."

Cyra didn't balk at being ordered around by her friend. Dez petted Queen's head as Veda ran the scanner over the dog. Cyra returned with a stack of blankets and towels, breathing so hard her gills fluttered. She was so beautiful, she took Dez's breath.

"I'm pretty sure Queen is in labor."

"What?" Dez's attention went to the doctor. "How is it possible?"

Veda lifted an eyebrow. "Are you really asking me where babies come from?"

Dez's cheeks heated. "No, but the dogs were in separate kennels. They haven't been left alone. She didn't show signs of being in heat."

"It's possible she was pregnant when we did the intake. I didn't get a blood sample, and I wasn't looking for pregnancy. If she's like most canines, she likely had just been bred when we got her. It's been about sixty cycles."

"What do we do?" Cyra asked, the panic thick in her voice.

"Wait." Veda took some of the stack from Cyra's arms. "Make her comfortable and let nature to take its course. Her body knows what to do."

Dez freed the rest of the load from Cyra's arms. He arranged a soft nest for the panting dog while ignoring the warning growls. Queen immediately dragged the various items, pawing them, circling before lying down. Dez petted her. "You'll be fine, girl."

"It's going to be several hours before things get interesting. We might as well give her some space." Veda stood with the scanner in her hand.

"I should prep last-meal," Dez said.

"Call me when it's ready. I'll stay here." Cyra shifted one of the folded blankets and sat down. "Keep an eye on things and do some research." She held up her comm.

"I'm going to take a power nap, then." Veda moved toward the exit.

"Use the ship system to page me if you need me, my queen."

Cyra nodded, already refocused on her screen.

Later, the crew gathered for the meal in the galley. There had been no change in Queen's condition, but Veda planned to eat quickly and take the next shift.

"What about this contract you got, Dez?" Cyra asked.

All eyes turned to him. He explained what he'd been able to negotiate, but as good as his news was, the cost of repairs to sabotaged fuel regulator and replacement rods tempered it.

"And we'll need to upgrade the refrigeration cells in the cargo bay, I think." Veda winced and shot a quick glance at

Cyra. "They were fine for the relatively short trip between Din' Gale and Cassan. But Kolben…"

"It'll be worth it if we can make a little profit and the delivery goes well. We could get additional contracts. Dez said this vendor has a ton of overage. She even opened juice bars, but still, they have to toss so much. And Kolben will pay a fortune. Maybe we could even expand the refrigerated cells." Blaize took a breath.

Dez swallowed his laugh when Cyra jumped in before Blaize could continue. "I agree. We should take the contract for this shipment. We'll run the numbers before deciding any future business."

His mate. So smart, so practical. So resistant to being his. Time wasn't on his side, but she would be. No matter what he had to do to convince her. She would recognize him as hers before she left him forever.

Dez cleared the remaining items from the table as the crew left.

"Let me help." Cyra wiped down the table. Everyone had already cleared their places. There wasn't that much to do. "I want to check on Queen with you."

"Veda would have called us if anything was happening."

At that moment, Cyra's comm chimed. A note from Veda. *It's time.*

Cyra clung to Dez's hand as they rushed down the hallway. "If anything goes wrong—"

"It won't. Queens know what to do. They always come out okay." Dez smile when Cyra glanced at him.

Veda had a towel in her hand, but Queen seemed to be in charge, licking the newly born puppy clean. "It's a girl."

Dez and Cyra stopped a respectful distance away from the new mother. Cyra asked, "Is there another one coming?"

"We'll know in a few minutes, but this species typically

only has one, maybe two, according to the journals I found," Veda answered, her eyes never leaving the animal. Twenty minutes later, the afterbirth expelled, and Veda confirmed there would only be one and that both dogs were healthy. The puppy was already nursing.

Cyra slid down the wall and sat. "What am I going to do with a thuringy puppy?"

"What do you mean?" Veda asked.

"It's not part of the contract, and a puppy is of no use to the mining company. They purchased guard dogs. Fully trained guard dogs."

"For now, the only thing to worry about is giving her a name." Dez sat by his queen. "Anything come to mind?"

She turned her wide-eyed gaze to him. "Princess?"

Dez laughed. "Perfect, my queen. I will see to her care and training. There is no rush to decide what should be done with the little one."

"Captain," she responded in a shell-shocked tone.

Dez let it go unanswered. She was that too. But first and foremost, Cyra was his queen.

CHAPTER 28

Cyra yawned as she made her way to the galley. Rhysa and Blaize were there, along with someone she'd never met before. The woman's small, translucent wings flitted lazily as she chatted with Cyra's crew as if she'd known them forever. Cyra peeked over Dez's shoulder to see what he was cooking. It looked unusually fresh, and the smell made her mouth water.

"I picked up some produce at the market while finalizing the contract." Dez kept stirring the contents pan.

She hadn't slept well and kept tossing and turning, seeking another few minutes of rest. "How long have you been awake?"

"I awoke quite early. We have much to do today to prepare to leave."

A sliver of resistance trailed down her gut along with the hot drink. "Are we going to be able to get the refrigeration upgrade installed today?"

"They're scheduled to arrive shortly, as will the parts for the fuel system repair."

"Thank you, Dez," she said quietly. He was making it very hard for her to remember he was not part of her crew, and she couldn't invite him to stay. Parts of being a captain had never found their way into her girlhood leadership dreams.

Somewhat more awake, she approached the unknown woman. "I'm Captain Cyra Maejzur, nice to meet you?"

The woman stood. Wide-set eyes accented with dark eye stains popped against her deep golden skin. Her long black hair framed the stunning effect. "Bodicea Szerensci, or just Bodi."

Cyra glanced at the rest of her crew, expecting an explanation.

"While we were out last night..." Blaize sucked in a breath, and Cyra prepared for a long explanation. "Rhysa and I decided to check out the nightlife here. I mean, it's going to be a while, and you were already in your tank, and Veda said she'd watch the ship—"

"Where is Veda?" Cyra interrupted.

"Greenhouse. She already reported on Queen and Princess. Everyone's good," Rhysa replied.

"Anyhow, we were at this bar, and it was just buzzing with life." Blaize giggled at her lame joke. "And while we were there, we met Bodi, and it turns out she's a communications specialist. She worked on all kinds of ships for years. And she's been the communications liaison for the royal family on Arbotriz. She's beyond qualified, and she's interested in joining us."

"More than interested." Bodi's voice was low with a hint of aggression. "It's been too long since I've been off planet, and I miss it."

Cyra was torn between being thrilled and concerned about their finances. With the unexpected repair and the upgrade to the refrigeration, not to mention feeding another crew member, she wasn't sure she could afford this stroke of luck. But she couldn't afford to pass it by either.

"In fact, Rhysa and Blaize mentioned there might be a partnership opportunity?"

That option carried its own risks. She already had three partners. And what if Bodi didn't fit in? "Possibly. I'm willing to give you a temporary contract for the trip to Kolben. If that works out, we can renegotiate. If not, we can drop you here when we pick up the next load of produce."

Bodi's wings quickly flittered and stilled. "That works."

After they finished eating the omelet and fruit salad Dez had prepared, Cyra met with Bodi to go over the contract. Bodi didn't ask about any of the details, signed quickly, and returned to staring at Dez. It made Cyra uncomfortable, but she didn't address it. He could manage his own love life. It was none of her concern. At least, that was what she told herself before leaving the galley for the flight deck.

After several hours of discussing the repairs with Blaize and the fuel needs with both Blaize and Rhysa and all the options for getting to Kolben, Cyra was exhausted. Rhysa, who had argued to use ER bridges, was completely against using one to get to Kolben. But Cyra worried avoiding wormholes could set them back because they were so far behind schedule. Rhysa was adamantly opposed and insisted they would be fine traveling at the fully accelerated capacity of the ship. Blaize confirmed that, with the repair, there was no reason they couldn't avoid using an ER bridge. Cyra had finally given in. Her crew had a change of heart? Why? She was missing something. The lack of logic made her brain hurt. Rather than continue to struggle for answers, she retreated to her water tank.

The next cycle, after all the final checks were made on the fuel system and the new refrigeration unit, they launched. Cyra had no problem getting the ship out of the atmosphere by simply imagining having sex. So what if it was Dez she pictured? At least he could power her emotions without actually fucking her, thank goodness. For whatever reason, sexual energy led to a much smoother burst from the atmosphere. Sometime in the future, when she had a ton of time on her hands, she'd ask Blaize to explain the system to her in detail.

After the launch, Rhysa verified the navigation and declared nothing more to do. "I'll keep an eye on the trajectory for a few more hours until last-meal is ready."

Cyra nodded her agreement. Blaize and Bodi left. Time to find Veda and have some girl time. Her best friend would listen to all her concerns about the changes in the crew, the ongoing threat that could be Varik or someone else, and, of course, Dez. Because as much as she tried to ignore the situation, he was constantly on her mind.

The med lab was empty, which meant she was either in her quarters or working on her garden. Cyra checked Veda's quarters first since it was closer. As she entered the corridor, she heard voices—an argument between Dez and she wasn't sure who. She hurried to his quarters. His door was open. Bodi had her arms wrapped around him.

My mate.

"You know you want me to order you around. You're a natural submissive. I can see it in you. I can give you what you need, a little dominance. Just get on your knees, Dez. Or I could even spank—"

Cyra exploded. "Bodicea! Let go of him right now."

Bodi jerked her head around, and her dark eyes went wide. She released Dez and took several steps back, hands in the air. "Captain, we were just..."

It wouldn't take a minute to jettison Bodi. But if Cyra did that, the crew might mutiny or worse, send her out behind Bodi. Cyra sucked in a slow deep breath and willed her gills to settle. "I don't care what you think you were doing. I'm going to say this once, and if you understand what's good for you, you will remember it always. He's mine. Don't touch. Ever."

"Yes, Captain." Bodi's wings buzzed from flapping so quickly as she left Dez's apartment.

Cyra stepped into the room and hit the panel to close the door.

Dez didn't say a word, but his gaze was locked on her. He wore nothing but a pair of pants, his chiseled dark chest lined with markings he claimed were hers. He'd probably been changing his clothes after cooking or getting ready to work out. She didn't care. "What the fuck was that?"

"She followed me. I didn't realize—you have nothing to be concerned about."

"Really? You've been calling me your queen, insisting that you're mated to me. And the first cute bubble-butted, big-boobed badass who wants you can be in your rooms, touching you?"

"I didn't—"

"You didn't say no."

"My queen." He tilted his head and gave her a soft, pleading look. Held his arms open.

Cyra considered falling into them, but maybe he liked what Bodi was offering. "Take off your pants."

"My queen?"

"It wasn't a question, Dez. You understood the words." Would he push back? Speaking to him that way was a crazy risk.

Dez's mouth turned up in a small smile as he undid the fastener on his pants and dropped them to the floor. His gaze smoldered through her.

Holy typhoons. Cyra clamped her mouth shut and swallowed. Her gills fluttered.

His cock had been soft but hardened, lengthening for her. Apparently, whatever Bodi had done or said hadn't worked. He truly hadn't wanted her.

Cyra closed the distance to Dez, almost pressing her body to his, maintaining the smallest amount of space. She reached down and grasped him firmly.

"I'm not sharing." She stroked him. His thick, hard length filled her fingers. She teased the spongy head, squeezing it and causing a tiny release. She rubbed her hand across the top and freed him so that she could slowly and purposely lick his essence from her palm. Her gaze never strayed from his.

His breathing accelerated. She licked her hand again. His cock vibrated, shivering with his need for her. More pre-cum beaded from the head. She rubbed her wet hand over his tip and down his shaft, jacking him off—slowly. Firmly. Taking possession.

"You're mine." She sped up. Did he realize he was thrusting into her hand? The power and control over him sizzled through her, heating her core. She moved away as he tried to close the tiny gap between them, maintaining one single hand touching him, working him, drawing his orgasm from him. She moved faster and gripped him tighter.

"Please, my queen," Dez begged.

Cyra pressed her clothed body against his naked one and nudged him toward the bed without breaking contact with his cock. He sat when the back of his knees hit the edge, jerking him out of her hand. Cyra dropped to her knees and took his cock in her mouth. She held her gaze to his yellow eyes as he roared and erupted, hips thrusting in tiny bursts despite his clenched muscles. He came completely undone. She swallowed every bit of his hot cum. It was hers. He was hers.

She stood and removed her one-piece uniform. Naked as he was, she crawled on top of him, shoving his torso down to the mattress. She shifted up his body until her core was over his face. She met his fire-filled gaze and willed him to respond to her demand without being told. Dez stared back, stroked his hands gently up the outside of her thighs, over the globes of her ass, and opened his mouth.

She lowered onto his face, close enough that he could work magic with his tongue. His gentle grip on her hips wasn't controlling but connecting. He kissed her wet lips, licking deeply, suckling her like she was the only water on a desert planet. She caressed his beautiful bald head, locked into his yellow-eyed gaze.

Cyra rolled her hips, unable to hold still any longer. It had been so long since anyone had touched her intimately, privately. Auvi had never done this for her—no one had. Dez showed her everything she'd been missing. The urgency of her release beckoned her, demanding she ride his tongue like an untamed beast.

Dez's grip on her hips tightened, hanging on, encouraging her to take what he offered. He sucked on every part of her— her lips, her clit, her delicate folds. It was as if he was mapping her pussy with his mouth, taking inventory of everything she liked and finding ways to make her like it more. Time had lost all meaning when she gave in to him and exploded.

She thrust her head back, closed her eyes, and screamed out all the air in her lungs. The stars outside their ship appeared behind her eyelids. She shook and stretched and lost all connection to anything other than Dez. It was almost as disorienting as going through a wormhole the first time. But with no fear, no discomfort. Only wave upon wave of pleasure.

Holy fuck, what is he doing to me?

Dez clutched her tighter, working her through the entire experience. Until she finally found the air to tell him to stop. He immediately released the tension in his hold, resting his hands on her hips. The warm strength of his touch steadied her, bringing her back to the ground. She tilted her head down to check on him. Had she been too much? Too out of control?

"Good girl."

Cyra's core clenched.

His smiling face glistened with her release.

She shifted her leg to free herself. Dez lifted her as if she weighed nothing, and somehow they ended up aligned on his narrow bed, her body pressed to his. His arms wrapped around her, and her head rested on his chest.

"My mate," he sighed.

The room contracted to an airless cell, and her heart raced. Cyra bit back her instant rebuttal. What had she done?

CHAPTER 29

"Status, Varik?" Twalley gripped the arms of the captain's chair on the deck of the *Harlan Johnson*. Sweat covered his forehead, and his eyes were red-rimmed.

"All systems normal, Captain," Varik replied, exactly as he'd done every time Twalley asked over the past few cycles. It was true. The ship was in perfect running order. Their launch had been uneventful except for the fact they'd actually launched. Varik had to acknowledge that once the man had received his final grant approvals, he'd wasted no time getting his crew on board—well, Varik's crew—and making way.

Varik glanced over at Jarn at the navigator's station. His lover was a little green in that department, but the navigation was simple since they were following *The Treasure* instead of adhering to any plan Twalley had. Varik had helped Jarn connect to the tracker on *The Treasure,* and the navigation effort was complete.

"How much longer until we make Galiese?" Twalley asked. Their first planned stop yet not one they'd be making.

"A few cycles yet," Varik replied. "Captain, you appear not to be feeling well. Should I contact the medic?" Varik's buddy didn't know how to do much more than hand out pills. A skill he'd picked up in his youth, according to the stories he told at the bar.

"No, no. Something I ate didn't agree with me." Twalley stood on wobbly legs. "Being as everything is under control here, I'll take my leave. I'll be in my quarters if you need me."

"Of course, Captain." Varik gave a curt nod of respect he didn't feel. "Call if you need anything. In fact, I'll have the med tech check on you shortly. There was a virus going around the station before we left. I hope you didn't get exposed."

"I'm sure it's nothing. But thank you, Varik." Twalley ambled away, leaning heavily on the walls. Hopefully, he made it to his quarters so there wouldn't be a mess in the corridors. So much cleaner that way.

Jarn blocked his view of the departing, soon-to-be-dead captain. "What did you do?"

Varik stiffened. "What are you talking about?"

"Did you do something to the captain?"

Varik punched up from his chair. "Not here."

Jarn took a step back. "We can't leave our stations."

"Are you accusing me of something?" Varik hissed. "Because if so, two things. Be damn sure. And don't you dare accuse me in public unless you want me to charge you with defamation. I don't care who you are."

Jarn's shoulders slumped. "I'm sorry. The captain being sick scared me. And then you mentioned a virus, and I don't know anyone who was sick on the station."

Varik smiled gently and kept his voice low. "My darling boy, that's because I didn't want to worry you. You lost your parents to a pandemic on your home planet. I know how that word terrifies you." Varik brushed his fingers over Jarn's. "That's why I didn't want to have the conversation on deck. You can't control your emotions around illness."

"Do you think the captain is really sick?" Jarn glanced over his shoulder in the direction the captain had gone.

No. But it was perfect that his lover thought so. "It's possible. But you heard him say it was just something he ate. Don't worry. No matter what, I'll take care of you."

Varik made a big show of contacting the medical lab and having his guy check on the captain. That evening, he announced that while the captain was indisposed, he would be acting captain at Twalley's request. No one questioned him, as expected, since the majority of the crew was loyal to Varik.

"Jarn, come to my cabin after you eat," Varik whispered seductively in his lover's ear. In his quarters, Varik shed his uniform and waited for Jarn covered by a thin sheet, his hand underneath slowly stroking his cock.

Jarn smiled when he finally appeared.

"Strip. I have something for you." Varik actually focused on how good it would be to command a ship again and take back *The Treasure*. The *Harlan Johnson* was nice but small. Even the quarters were too tight. And the shared facilities for everyone but the captain were a bit too communal for Varik's tastes.

Jarn shivered, the movement bringing Varik back. He flipped back the sheet. "Come here, my cock misses your sweet mouth."

Jarn folded his body over Varik's knees on the edge of the mattress, putting his mouth exactly where it belonged—stretched over Varik's head. Jarn bobbed and slurped. Varik lifted one knee, and Jarn dragged his nails along Varik's balls exactly as he'd been taught. Perfect. Varik toyed with Jarn's sweet ass, teasing the hole and making his boy groan. The vibration tremored down Varik's cock. His balls drew up, filling with his seed. He thrust into Jarn's mouth, grabbing his hair and holding him in place to take every hot jet of satisfaction. "Fuck. That's my boy. That's my sweet love. So good."

He petted his lover and rolled him into position along his side against the wall. They kissed, and Varik savored the taste of himself on his sweet lover's lips. "Get some sleep. I'll get you off when we wake."

"What about the captain? I thought you didn't want him to know about us." Jarn blinked up at Varik with watery eyes.

"That was only until I could be sure you had the job. I couldn't leave you behind, and I didn't want to give the captain any reason not to hire you. I don't care who knows how special you are to me now."

Jarn brightened and peppered kisses all over Varik's face. Sweet little puppy. "Enough. Save that for the morning."

But in the morning, a pounding on the door awakened them. Varik pulled on pants, not bothering to tie them closed. "What?"

His med tech buddy was there, frantically glancing from Varik to the captain's door. "We have a problem, sir."

Nice touch with the *sir*. A few crew members milled around the corridor with worried expressions. Varik projected his voice so they wouldn't have to strain to eavesdrop. "What is it? What's happened?"

"It's the captain, sir." Eyes still twitchy. Good thing his back was to the audience. "I think he's succumbed to his illness."

"I'll be right there." He slapped the door panel to close it. "Hurry, get dressed."

Jarn jolted. Varik slipped into his crisply washed and waiting uniform. He didn't wait for his lover.

"Show me," he told the med tech. After officially confirming Twalley was well and truly no longer living, Varik gave instructions for the body to be treated as hazardous material and the body jettisoned. As was protocol, a report was sent to Cassan with a quarantine notice. They wouldn't be stopping anywhere.

Varik stifled a laugh. He'd had no plans to stop on Galiese. He was waiting for *The Treasure* to turn back to Cassan. Then he would redirect the research ship and beat them back since they were the smaller, lighter ship and could make better time. Unless Blaize was so incompetent she let them run out of fuel. Then he'd let some of the crew take the *Harlan Johnson* back to the station while he reclaimed *The Treasure*.

Of course, none of the crew succumbed to the same illness as Twalley. Varik thoughtfully declared their quarantine at an end a couple of cycles later. If the crew had questions about why they weren't returning to Cassan, they wisely kept their curiosity to themselves.

Except Jarn. "Shouldn't we go back? Isn't this ship part of the research grant?"

At least his lover had waited until they were in private to question him. "I believe Twalley owned the ship. I have a lawyer looking into it, contacting the heirs."

"But what are we doing?"

"The ship I have us tracking has something of mine. Something very precious. We're just going to keep an eye on it or possibly meet up while we wait to hear from Twalley's family." He pulled Jarn into an embrace and kissed him until he was breathless, then rode his ass until he screamed out his pleasure, leaving no room in his pretty little head to worry about ships and final destinations.

Varik was on a new mission to deliver—not goods. He would be delivering retribution. Cyra had stolen *The Treasure*. She wasn't qualified to be the captain. She and her ragtag crew of criminals needed to be wiped from the galaxy. Blaize and Cyra, most especially.

CHAPTER 30

Sanity rushed back to Cyra like a punch to the face. She was still the captain. Dez was still cargo.

She'd reacted on impulse to Bodi touching him. Cyra should have kept walking. She'd tried to deny her desire for him, but it kept sneaking out. And after what they'd done, their situation was completely confused. She'd claimed Dez and told him he was hers. He wasn't going to let her take that back.

Fuck.

She had to get out of there. She swung her leg up and around as she pivoted on the bed. Once free of him and off the bed, she grabbed her discarded clothes. "I have to go."

Dez didn't say anything. His face remained impassive, but his gaze held disappointment and determination. Tension squeezed Cyra's shoulders. He was still a man on a mission—one that wasn't going according to plan. What was she going to do with him? No idea. She fastened the final clasp on her top and walked out the door without another word.

Since she couldn't talk to him, she went in search of Veda for a reality check. Maybe the situation wasn't as dire as she imagined. Perhaps it was worse.

"I should have known to look for you here first," Cyra told

Veda when she found her in the makeshift greenhouse in the cargo bay.

Veda shifted her focus from her plants and smiled. "I seem to spend more time here than in the med lab. After Dez helped me set it up, the work really began. I had no idea that growing things from seed would be so challenging."

At the sound of Dez's name, a series of images of them together flashed through Cyra's mind. She mentally kicked herself for leaving when they were just getting started and again for ever starting at all.

"What's wrong?" Veda pulled off her gloves and moved to Cyra. Veda took Cyra's hands in hers and led her to the bench at the back of the room. "What happened?"

Cyra tried to tell her friend what she'd done, but the words wouldn't form.

"Just start from the beginning."

"Bodi was in Dez's quarters." Leftover rage sizzled up briefly.

"Were they together?" The shock in Veda's voice made Cyra feel a little better about her own reaction—a tiny amount.

"No. Bodi was propositioning Dez. She wanted him to submit to her. Sexually."

"What was Dez doing?" Veda asked. How could she be so calm?

"I don't know. Nothing? I didn't wait long enough to find out. I lost my shit and kicked her out of the room. Then I closed us in there and took advantage of him." Cyra dropped her head in her hands and stared at the metal panels of the floor.

"You had sex with Dez?" Veda obviously didn't believe her. And maybe she was kind of right.

"Not exactly, no penetration."

"Were you naked?" Her doctor voice had kicked in.

Cyra gulped and met Veda's gaze. "Yes."

"Was he naked?"

Another image flashed through Cyra's mind. All those beautiful markings. His thick, veined cock glistening with desire. "Yes," she answered breathlessly.

"Okay, so aside from wishing I owned that memory, I need you to explain. What exactly happened that has you so upset?"

Cyra dropped her head again, unable to face her disastrous actions. "I took advantage of him. I told him he was mine and no one else could have him."

Veda rested a hand on Cyra's shoulder. "Does Dez think you took advantage of him?"

"I don't know." Cyra put aside her pride and shame and faced her dearest friend. The only person she trusted to help her. "After he, after we— Afterward, I told him we couldn't do this, and I left. He looked sad."

"Of course he's sad." She tilted her head, and her gaze softened. "His body knows you're his mate. He's convinced of the validity of this. You finally gave in and had a sexual encounter and then immediately rejected him again. He's going to be sad."

Veda's words stabbed Cyra in the gut. "It sounds so bad when you say it that way."

"I'm just explaining it from his perspective." Veda barely lifted a single shoulder, a hint of a shrug, as if all of what she said was obvious.

"I can't do this, Veda." Cyra stood. She paced the short distance to the tables where palettes of growing medium held a smattering of tiny green shoots. "If I give into my lust or mating or whatever this is, I lose everything. Am I supposed to just toss my life away with no concern about your future or my future or the rest of the crew? Am I supposed to just park *The Treasure* at Cassan and let Varik have it? What would I do then? Live on a jungle planet, dependent on my in-laws while making black and blue babies that look like bruises?"

"Just because you're blue and he is charcoal doesn't mean your babies would look like a bruise. You're just being dramatic." Veda laughed.

Cyra couldn't pull back from full meltdown mode. "It wouldn't matter what they look like. You know I would love them dearly. But don't you see, that isn't *my* future? I gave up my whole family and my life on Chalcanth not to stay home and make babies. I wouldn't be happy. *The Treasure* is my home. Being on this ship makes me happy."

"How do you know that being with Dez means the end of your transport business?"

"Because I'll have defaulted on his contract. The contract that I'm now responsible for, not Auvi. If I don't deliver Dez to the mining company on Kolben, on time, I'll owe them the entire amount that was already paid, plus a stiff penalty. It will kill us financially. No recovery."

"Dez has negotiated two contracts for us since then. Recurring contracts that will bring in revenue for far longer, and they don't require you to give him up."

"I know that. And I appreciate him doing that." Cyra scraped her hair away from her gills. "But it won't be enough." The amount was astronomical. "I don't see a time when I will *ever* have that many credits."

"Cyra, there is always a way." That was Veda's faith talking. Faith Cyra didn't share, having grown up differently.

"Not in this case, there isn't. There is only one way this can go. And it doesn't end with me and Dez and purple babies."

Veda sighed and clasped her hands. "Your stubbornness is your greatest asset and your worst weakness."

"I'm sure you're right."

"I am." Veda paused and pressed her lips tightly together before she continued. "And you have to talk to him."

Cyra's stomach soured. "I don't like you right now."

"Don't have to, but you do have to talk to Dez. The sooner, the better." Veda guided her to the door. "I have to check on Queen and Princess."

Cyra would love to stomp her foot and refuse to face Dez. Not very captain-like. The better option would be to go back in time and not interfere with Bodi. Or have left instead of closing herself in with Dez. Where was a wormhole when she needed one? "How are the dogs doing? Maybe I should check on them with you."

"They're fine. But Queen isn't ready for visitors. She barely tolerates me and Dez," Veda said. "Quit trying to distract me and go talk to him, Cyr."

Cyra rolled her eyes. "I'm going."

Dez strode to the galley as if his heart was still in his chest and every muscle didn't ache for his mate. They should still be in bed together, making love. But Cyra had run. No matter, he still had a crew to feed. He would find a way to connect with her again, to bring her back to his bed. He froze. As if his thoughts had called her, there she was, head down and mumbling to herself. She stopped and turned but still hadn't made eye contact. "Cyra?"

She startled and spun back. "Uh. You. I mean, I was coming to talk to you."

How could she be on her way to him when she had turned around? Dez let his confusion twist his expression.

"I mean, I was as soon as I figured out what to say."

If he said the wrong thing, he could push her away. He held still, patiently waiting for her words.

"I'm sorry I rushed out."

He nodded in agreement. That had sucked. He'd planned

to show her how perfectly their bodies would fit together, how whatever pleasure she may have experienced before was nothing compared to mate-bonding sex. Tasting her had set his world on fire. He'd traveled the stars when she sucked him into her warm mouth. Couldn't she tell how different sex was with her mate? Dez had nothing to compare it to, but he'd heard the stories. He'd never touched another unmated female, saving himself for his true mate, but then he'd given up on finding her, only to discover Cyra.

Could she not feel the joy?

"I don't know what to say, Dez." She crossed her arms in a protective move. "Nothing's changed about our situation."

Dez closed the distance, and she backed against the wall, eyes wide. "I disagree. Everything has changed, at least between us." He stroked his fingers through her deep green locks. "I know what you taste like. I know how you shake when you're riding my tongue." He caressed her shoulder. "I know how your breath changes right before you let go."

Her breath hitched, and her pupils expanded.

"I know what it is to erupt in your throat and have your sweet mouth all over my cock." He kissed her neck, just below her shivering gills, teasing her skin with his tongue.

"But Dez." She clasped his shoulders, clinging to him. Her knees trembled. "I can't— It's wrong when I know this can't last."

So it was guilt, not fear. She didn't understand that as fated mates, they would be together for as long as possible. "I." He kissed the dip at the base of her neck. "Don't." He kissed up her skin to the edge of her chin. "Care." He clutched her hips and tugged her to him, pressing his hard cock to her soft lower belly as he took her mouth. There would be no changing her mind with words. Besides, he couldn't explain why he had faith that they would be together for as long as they were both alive. If she let him, he could show her what he felt.

She turned her head and pushed against his shoulders. He stepped back, releasing her.

"But I care. I care, Dez, and I don't want to hurt you or imply promises I can't keep."

He smiled. "Of course my queen. But while we are here, on this ship together, I will show you what it means to have a mate who loves you."

Cyra's mouth dropped open, and her eyes went wide. She shook her head the tiniest bit.

Dez refused to remain an audience to her arguments. He turned his back and gathered ingredients, already late to prepare the mid-cycle meal. Her footsteps rang in his ears as she walked away.

The urge to follow her was hard to resist, but he remained focused on his tasks. There would be plenty of time between wherever they were in space and the godforsaken planet of Kolben to create a lifetime of memories for his mate. Because it was nearly impossible that she would succumb to the mating illness the way he would once they parted.

CHAPTER 31

LOVE? Had Dez really told her he loved her before walking away? Technically he'd said he'd show her what it was like to have a mate who loved her. Was that the same thing? She wasn't sure. Did she love him? She couldn't. Could she? If she did, and she left him on Kolben, what did that say about her?

Her job shouldn't be this difficult.

Veda told her to talk to him. She'd planned to but hadn't been ready for their conversation. Then he'd dropped a love bomb on her. She paced back and forth in the corridor, torn between retreating to her salt tank, going back to Veda, or taking her position in the captain's chair. Maybe there was a way to fix her mess.

She took her place on the bridge and logged into *The Treasure's* financial tracking software. As Auvi trained her to do, every detail of every transaction was recorded. The amount of Dez's contract, the sky-high price that had included extras for food and medicine. The fuel costs. The contract from Din' Gale. Her payment for goods to the prince. There would be more contracts like that, but the net income, while it was profitable, wasn't near enough not to only pay back Dez's travel costs, but the indentured servant contract to the mining company, the broker's fee, and the penalty for breach of contract. Even with the new contract with Arbotriz, she didn't have enough credits to cover transporting goods to Kolben, which was costly. The upgrades to the perishable goods systems had wiped out the income from the first Arbotriz delivery. It only made future transactions more profitable. Clearly a good investment, but they still wouldn't realize the kind of credits she needed to buy back Dez's freedom. And even if she did, her partners would have to give up their shares.

She took a breath. It was as if Blaize had taken over her thoughts. *Slow down. Look again.* But the more she poked at the numbers, the worse the picture became. She groaned in defeat.

"You okay, Captain?" Rhysa asked from her station.

"Fine." If only she could come up with something. Maybe she had an error. "Bodi, can you get a link back to Cassan so I can check our bank balances at the Milky Way Credit office?"

The Treasure was fairly far from the station. It was a crazy request, but it was the last possible piece of data Cyra hadn't triple-checked. Maybe by some miracle, the credits Auvi had left her had been returned. Right. As if Varik would ever do the right thing.

Hours later, across the slow but solid link Bodi had formed, Cyra confirmed that Dez was screwed. There was no possible way for her to change his circumstances. "I'm going to soak."

"Aye, Captain," Rhysa responded.

The title stabbed Cyra in her back as she left. She might be in charge of *The Treasure*, but she had no power to do the one thing she most wished she could, which was to save Dez.

In the galley, Dez arranged Cyra's meal in her preferred divided tray, making sure all her favorites didn't touch. His mate was particular about certain things. He adored accommodating her preferences, and he liked any small thing that brought her a bit of joy. More and more frequently, she retreated to her water tank. The stress of being captain, keeping the crew focused, and financial issues weighed on her. He'd done what he could by bringing her contracts and kept trying to do more for as long as possible.

The others had already gathered around the table filled with his prepared dishes. His mate remained absent. Should he cover her food and put it in the warmer?

"Veda, how's the greenhouse?" Rhysa asked as she filled her plate.

"Slow but good. I have some sturdy sprouts now. But I'm holding out for the second set of leaves before I get too excited."

Blaize moaned. "I can almost taste the fresh tomatoes now."

"Slow down. A lot can go wrong, and it's my first time trying something like this. In fact, I didn't find any recent documentation on growing crops on a ship. All the data I could find was from ancient Earth data repositories. Most of the data is before quantum gravity became standard. There were some studies from a few colony ships. I'm trying to replicate their methods."

"If you need help, just ask. I have a fairly green thumb." Bodi held up her golden thumb as if it would suddenly appear green.

At least the crew was getting along and focused on a project together. The more they came together as a team, the easier it would be for his mate.

Cyra came through the door, hair wet and twisted up on her head. Her eyes met his, and he cringed at the fatigue he saw in the moment before she glanced away. Despite the space he'd held for her, he slid her tray to the spot she'd taken between Veda and Blaize.

"Thanks." Her voice was heavy and low. What had happened since he'd told her he loved her? He gritted his teeth. Should have known better than to drop that on her in the middle of the galley after they were already unstable. Saying "I love you" never strengthened a weak relationship. It only cemented a strong one. His declaration must have added to her stress. To be fair, he hadn't planned it. And there was no way he'd take it back because it was true to his bones. He loved her. Even if he couldn't have a lifetime with her. But like the crew coming together around the fledgling crops, he would do everything he could to support Cyra with her fledgling business.

"I checked on the produce stores," Dez said as he leaned across the table to focus on Cyra.

"Everything okay?" Cyra's forehead wrinkled.

"Great," he quickly assured her. "In fact, the refrigeration unit is working perfectly. I even had Blaize run diagnostics to make sure the power use was within spec."

"You didn't have to do that. Blaize would have told me if there was a problem, right?" Cyra nudged Blaize.

"Of course. But it was a great idea to isolate and test. I didn't mind at all. And the numbers look amazing, really. I didn't realize upgrading our systems would actually lower our fuel use. I mean, it makes sense." Blaize's attention pivoted between Dez and Cyra as she spoke.

"We'll make so much moving goods to and from Kolben. Especially if we can figure out the best bridges to use," Bodi added, fork in the air. "Damn, this is delicious, Dez."

Dez nodded his acknowledgment, unsure what to say to the woman who'd accosted him in his quarters.

"Don't get used to it. None of the rest of us can cook." Cyra stabbed into her noodles before twirling her fork.

She might as well have stabbed Dez in the heart. Did she have to take every single opportunity to remind him of their challenges? She lifted her fist to her chest and rubbed a slow circle as if she could feel his heart hurting. Maybe hers hurt too. That made the situation worse. He could leave, knowing he'd still be connected to her, but not if it hurt her. True mates would always find their way back to each other, even in different lifetimes. At least that was what he'd always been taught to believe. But if he left her in pain, lacking for anything once he was no longer on *The Treasure*, that thought would kill him faster than the severed mate bond.

There had to be something more he could do before they reached Kolben. "I'd like to start working with Princess in a few more g-weeks. Thuringies mature incredibly quickly, and she should be ready for basic commands."

Veda nodded in agreement. "It would be good to keep her occupied. Also, we'll need to provide her plenty of chew toys as her chompers come in."

"I probably have some tubing and things that might work. If not, I can print some," Blaize offered.

Cyra shook her head. "You shouldn't have to do that, Dez. It's not your job."

"But it would be my pleasure, my—"

"Fine." Cyra cut him off pointedly.

He grinned at her even though no part of him was happy. He wouldn't show how much he ached for her in front of her crew. In private, she would be reminded of exactly how he felt about her, her resistance, the short time he would have with her. If she let him.

CHAPTER 32

Varik clenched his jaw and glared at his screen on the deck of the *Harlan Johnson*. *The Treasure* wasn't moving, and it wasn't back on Cassan. They weren't moving at all. If they were incapacitated in space, they would still be drifting.

"Jarn," Varik barked at his lover, who occupied the navigator's chair. "What is at these coordinates?" He called out the numbers and repeated them. A few of the crew glanced over, but as long as Varik sat in the captain's chair, they could all keep their opinions to themselves. Especially if they wanted to make it back to the station and get paid.

Credits, or really the threat of losing them, did a lot for maintaining order on the commandeered ship.

"There's a tiny planet, Arbotriz, there, Captain."

Varik enjoyed his lover calling him by his title. Even better than sir. But the pleasure was quickly dissipated with the information he found on the planet. Female ruled. Agrarian. Monarchy. With a full-service space port.

How the fuck had they managed to get *The Treasure* there? Or even known the planet was there? Varik had no idea. According to his calculations, they should have taken the only alternative and turned back to Cassan. The effort to turn the ship would have caused them to run out of fuel nearby, and he could have retrieved *The Treasure* easily.

"Program a course to take us there," Varik told Jarn.

"What?" The communications officer tossed off his headset and stood. "This is too much. First, you take over as captain. Then you don't return immediately to Cassan. Now we're heading to some unknown planet. I didn't sign up for this."

Varik narrowed his eyes. "You're welcome to go. Take anyone with you. I'm happy to open the airlock."

The communications officer strode across the deck to get in Varik's face. "Don't you dare threaten me. I've already sent a message to the authorities about Twalley's passing and notified the grant committee. If you know what's good for you, you'll turn this ship around to Cassan."

Varik stood. "Get off my deck. You're relieved of duty." He shot out his arm, pointing at the exit. "And you're confined to quarters."

"And how do you think you're going to enforce that?"

At that moment, the two junior engineers, Varik's people, appeared at the entrance to the bridge. "Problem, Captain?"

Varik smiled. "Your escorts are here. They'll be happy to enforce my orders." He glanced over at the other crew on deck. "Anyone else?"

All heads turned to their screens.

"Good. Jarn? Is the course for Arbotriz laid in?"

"Aye, Captain."

At least someone on the ship had the right attitude.

"I'm just worried, that's all." Jarn paced the length of Varik's quarters. He really should take over the captain's lodgings.

They weren't much bigger, but it was the principle of the thing. Later. After he got rid of the mutinous busybodies.

"Did you hear me?" Jarn paused and glared down at Varik.

Varik stroked his cock to keep from letting the situation soften him. "Do we have to keep rehashing this? I'd much rather listen to you gagging on my cock than lecturing me about what I should do with my ship."

"But that's the point." Jarn put his hands on his hips. "It's not your ship. Technically." Nice save, but Varik caught the chastisement. "The grant committee was notified."

"The comms officer sent a message. This far into space, that's not the same as the grant committee receiving the message. It could take cycles for that message to be received by some low-level clerk. By that time, if you do what I tell you, we'll have *The Treasure*." In fact, they would land on Arbotriz in the next two cycles, depending on approvals and space at the landing port. "Don't worry." Varik tugged his lover into his bed and freed him of his clothes and his ability to speak. Much better. Varik thrust his cock deep into Jarn's throat until he found his release.

The next cycle, they received word that they would be allowed to land at the auxiliary space port on the far side of the planet from where *The Treasure* was docked. Varik fumed.

"How did you not know they had two space ports?"

Jarn's cheeks turned shades of red. "It's not documented in our databases on this planet, so it's probably a recent build. I don't know. This is my first time being the lead navigator, and I've never worked in this galaxy. Why is it always my fault when *your* plans don't work out?"

Varik saw red. "Just get us docked."

It wasn't like he had any choice. The rebellion had seethed through all the crew Varik hadn't personally contracted. He had to get them off the *Harlan Johnson*. He could not rely on them to do what needed to be done to overtake *The Treasure*. Landing held its own risks. They had to report the captain's death and the brief quarantine. Medical officers swarmed the ship dressed in biohazard suits, swabbing everything and everyone.

While they waited for results, Varik went to his former comms officer's quarters. He was the lead rebel. If Varik swayed him, the rest would follow. As soon as he opened the door to his quarters, Varik said, "I'll pay you the full price of your contract if you get off this ship as soon as we're cleared and take your buddies with you. No accusations, no filing of reports, no bullshit."

"Why would I do that?"

Varik stepped into the man, forcing him inside and closing the door. "Because if you don't, you're going to become very ill, and it could be life-threatening."

A glance at the syringe in Varik's hand made the man back up, hands raised. "I don't want any trouble."

"Good. Then we agree. Your contract's paid out, and you go away quietly."

The man's head bobbed in agreement.

"I'll deposit half of what you're owed now. In ten cycles, if I have no...trouble...you'll get the rest."

That would give Varik plenty of time to catch up to *The Treasure* according to the routes he'd calculated with Jarn using ER bridges. Hell, he might get to Kolben before *The Treasure*, be ready and waiting to take her back. He had to assume she was fixing the fuel problem he'd given her and that she would resume her path to Kolben. The deadline was looming. If she'd bothered to read the contract, she'd be in a hurry to get there, but would she get over her aversion to using a wormhole?

There were too many fucking variables. And once she delivered the mining slave, she'd have the funds to keep his *Treasure* from him and there would be nothing he could do about it.

CHAPTER 33

Cyra pulled out the bottle of grain alcohol she'd found in Auvi's quarters. Last-meal was over, and everyone was sitting around the table in the galley. Everyone but Dez, who'd left as soon as he'd finished eating. He was avoiding her, using the dogs as an excuse. She didn't care. She *didn't*. She just wanted to have a drink with her crew and relax. It had nothing to do with him. She set up five small glasses and poured a healthy shot into each one.

"To the crew of *The Treasure*." She lifted her glass and threw back the drink in one swallow. It burned her throat, and based on the four sets of watering eyes staring at her, she wasn't alone.

"The second shot is always better." She poured them another round.

"Goddess bless, this stuff is horrid. What the hell is it? Cleaning fluid?" Bodi asked after the second shot was gone. Her golden skin flushed copper.

Cyra was wrong. The second was just as bad. But it was starting to have the desired effect. The ache in her heart eased a little, growing numb, which was fine with her. "Have you ever liked someone you couldn't have?"

They were her crew, and she probably shouldn't be discussing personal feelings with them. Too late. After the two drinks, she didn't really care. She probably just needed another drink. She filled their glasses, drinking quickly to maintain a buzz. Even with the strong liquor, her metabolism would process it rapidly, and she would be sober before the next shot. She didn't want to be sober.

"I've never wanted anyone like that," Veda admitted.

"You've never been with anyone?" Rhysa asked.

"Nope."

"Aren't we a pair?" Rhysa nudged Veda with her shoulder. "I've been with everyone, and you've been with no one. But neither of us have wanted anyone the way they want each other."

"What are you talking about?" Cyra demanded.

"It's obvious that you and Dez are gagging for each other. If the sexual energy was any hotter when you two are in the same room, we'd need to be issued sun shields to work on this ship."

Cyra wrinkled her forehead. "You think our sexual energy is hot?"

"Yes!" A chorus erupted from the entire crew.

"Well shit. How am I supposed to get good advice about how to avoid a sexual entanglement with him when all of you seem to be in favor of it?"

"We're in favor of it," Veda told her.

"I only hit on him to test if he was really into you after they told me the story," Bodi admitted. "Curiosity always gets the better of me."

"You weren't going to fuck him?" Cyra didn't quite believe that. She couldn't have misunderstood so completely.

"Oh, don't get me wrong, Captain. I absolutely would have fucked him if he was willing. I just wanted to find out if he was willing. He wasn't, by the way. He was on the verge of pushing me out of the doorway and running if you hadn't shown up."

Cyra gaped at Bodi. "I can't believe you did that."

"Sorry." Bodi's wings flittered.

"Why are you so hung up on this? You want him; he wants you. Why don't you just fuck until we get to Kolben? I mean, you shouldn't waste the opportunity," Rhysa said.

Cyra shifted her attention to Blaize. She had been quiet through all of this. "What do you think?"

"I don't know. I trusted someone once, and that has caused me more heartache than I thought I could survive. But Dez isn't Varik. Not in any way. Except that they are both fucking gorgeous. You have to do what you think is right. I can tell you that sex with Varik was awesome, and as long as I imagine him being someone else, those memories still supply context for my personal sessions. If you know what I mean."

Cyra disagreed with Blaize about Varik's bedroom skills, but she didn't interrupt.

"It's difficult to form relationships in space. You're traveling, and they're either on a station, planet, or another ship. It doesn't lead to long-term things. You need to find a way to take pleasure when it's offered. At least I think that's what you should do. I'm kind of too drunk to even know if I'm making sense." Blaize hiccupped.

Everyone at the table laughed. Blaize was cute when she was drunk, and she clearly was, based on her slurring words. Yet even drunk, she spoke the truth. Varik was decent in bed, but it was all performance with him. No emotion. With Dez, it would be the complete opposite. He was all genuine emotion and would give her anything she wanted. What was Cyra doing, squandering a chance at happiness just because it was temporary?

She rose from the table. "You're right. I'm going to find my happiness."

Bodi poured another round of shots. They lifted their glasses, and she hollered out after the captain, "Go get 'em."

"To happiness," Blaize said, and they slammed their drinks.

"However fleeting," Rhysa called.

"To love." Veda's words echoed in the hallway.

Cyra made her way slowly down the corridor to Dez's door. She moved slowly to give the alcohol a chance to clear her system and to see if she would change her mind. It cleared, and she didn't. She knocked on his closed door.

CHAPTER 34

Dez stood in the doorway after pressing the panel to open it. He was still breathing a little heavy from running down the corridor ahead of Cyra. He had been listening to the women outside the galley, hoping to get some insight as to what was going on in Cyra's mind. He hadn't heard what he'd wanted to, but at least she was there. It was up to him to capitalize on the opportunity she gave him. She may not know it, but her temporary affair was going to last a lifetime. At least for him. "Would you like to come in?"

"I'd like to come."

"I'm sure that can be arranged, my queen." The door slid closed behind her. He opened his arms, and she launched herself into them. He kissed her upturned face gently and then deeper. He pulled away. "This isn't a good idea."

"Are you kidding me? I finally get the nerve to come back here, and you're going to stop me?"

"You've been drinking." The strong alcohol remained on her lips.

"I have, but I'm completely sober."

"You don't taste sober."

"Alcohol burns off in my system super-fast. Right now, I'm

experiencing a bit of a sugar high, but even that will pass in a few more minutes. I promise, Dez, I know what I'm doing."

She was destroying him in the best possible way. "And you want this? You want to be with me?"

"Desperately. It's all I've been thinking about since—"

He couldn't make her beg. "I need you so much, my queen."

Cyra leaned into him and kissed him again. Hunger clawed at him. He let her claim his lips and his tongue. They were hers. His hands moved over her body, caressing and mapping the lines and curves that made her uniquely Cyra. He ran his fingers gently through her dark locks, which were like water flowing through his hands. Her shifting caresses covered his body.

"Too many clothes." He had to touch her skin. It had been too many cycles. He released her while still giving her his mouth. He pulled the bottom of his shirt up to his chest. Cyra followed his actions and tore the shirt out of his hands and over his head.

Finally, his mate's hands were on his skin. He came alive under her restless touch with electric awareness of every millimeter of her path. She stroked his chest, following the lines of his natural tattoos that were a testament to his belonging to her. She didn't understand exactly how critical to his health she was. He would explain it to her when the time was right. Later.

She stroked the sides of his abdomen, squeezing his sides and embracing his body so tightly as if she were trying to find a way inside him. He'd gladly take her in. She moved her hands lower to his hips. Her fingers found the indents of the muscles and traced the V-shape down toward the waistband of his pants. She released him and grabbed his pants, ripping them apart. He didn't care; he could fix them tomorrow. He struggled to toe his shoes off his feet as he pulled his pants down his legs.

The conflicting action sent him careening to the floor in a heap. She freed her tangled limbs a moment before she followed.

She was barely upright, and her hands went to her gaping mouth. "Oh my god! Dez, are you okay?"

Dez met her worried gaze and laughed. He was sure he was a sight. His naked ass pointed in the air, his pants around his knees and one of his shoes half on. Cyra's tentative giggles blossomed into full-blown laughter. She lowered herself to the floor and clung to him.

"In a hurry, my queen?"

She sucked in a steadying breath. "I'm so sorry."

"Let me finish undressing, and I will join you on the bed."

"Good idea." She stood, letting the rest of her clothes fall to the floor with his.

Dez pulled off the remaining shoe. He attempted to rise as gracefully as possible after sliding his pants off.

Cyra sighed. "You're so gorgeous."

"I'm pleased that you find me so, my queen." Dez clasped her hand and brought it to his lips.

"Why do you call me that?"

"Because you are the ruler of my world. You are my queen. I am your humble servant."

"You aren't my servant, Dez. You wouldn't be anyone's servant if it were up to me." The anger in her tone touched his heart.

"It is our way. We revere our mates. They provide life, and we must, as their males, provide for them." He sat next to her on his narrow bed. "There's nothing I would not do for you, Cyra."

"Would you make love to me, Dez?"

"I thought you'd never ask."

Beginning with her beautiful blue feet, he kissed his way up her leg to her hip. He stopped, knowing what she wanted but increasing her anticipation by making her wait. He returned to the beginning with her other foot. He savored the taste of her, the feel of her skin. She was cool to his touch and slightly salty. He craved more. He would never get enough.

Cyra spread her legs farther apart. Her core opened to him, so dark and inviting. Not yet. First, he would build her arousal until she was as hungry for him as he was for her. He ached to be inside her. But he could wait to give his mate something he suspected she'd never had before. He would give her undivided attention and unselfish pleasure.

If what he understood about her relationship with Captain Auvi was true, her needs had never been first. It had only been about what Auvi required to launch his ship. And whatever Varik had done, the selfish bastard set a low bar, one that Dez was about to raise to astronomical heights. No one would ever please his mate like him. She wouldn't want anyone else to try.

He took her hand and sucked the tip of each digit. He licked between her fingers and cherished her muscular arm all the way to her neck. He nibbled her there for a moment when she giggled. He noted the ticklish spot.

"Please, Dez," she begged.

"Yes, my queen. I will give you everything you need. Everything I have is yours. Let me love you." He repeated his attention to her other hand and arm while caressing her breast. The peak stiffened under his fingers. He nibbled at her neck. She was delicious. He could spend a lifetime just tasting her skin. She smelled like water, like the rain that fell on his home planet. He wanted her scent all over his body, and he shifted until every possible bit of his skin was against hers. She moaned, and her moisture poured from her core coating his cock, making him wet before he'd even entered her.

He shifted back and down, kissing down her chest between her firm breasts. Her nipples were a deep blue, almost purple.

He licked each of her berries and then suckled one firm tip deep into his mouth, teasing the other with gentle pinches and tugs. "You taste like heaven."

He moved to her other breast. He imagined their future children that would suckle here. She would be a magnificent mother. He moaned with the thought.

"Oh fuck, Dez. You're making me gush." He noted that she liked the vibration of his moan against her tit. Unable to resist, he reached down and dragged his fingers through the lips of her saturated pussy. Noting every twitch, shift, gasp on his heart as he built a record of his mate—her likes, her loves—he would study her until he mastered her pleasure.

Unable to resist, he released her sweet beaded nipple long enough to suck her cream from his fingers. His cock released its own lubrication at the taste. Not enough. He kissed down her belly, moving faster as he got closer to his treasure.

He nudged her legs farther apart with his shoulders and buried his face deep.

"Dez," she cried.

He thrust his tongue deep inside her and tasted from the source. Her rain became ocean, salty and tangy. More. There could never be enough to satisfy his craving for her. He added his fingers, beckoning her to come. Lips wrapped around her clit, he teased it with the tip of his tongue.

Cyra screamed and arched up off the bed as her core clamped down on his fingers. She exploded. He'd done that. His chest swelled, and he lapped up as much as he could, not wanting to waste a drop of her precious liquid. Finally, she went lax.

"I want you inside me, Dez. I love your tongue, your touch, but I want you. All of you." Her blue eyes burned with need, setting his body on fire.

He slid his wet hand up and down his cock a few times,

picking up his own pre-cum to add to the slickness. He tilted his hips forward and put his head at the opening of her—the place he'd dreamed of every time he slept. Tenderly, he rubbed her up and down a couple of times and pressed into her clit. Tentatively, he slid the tip into her folds. The wet heat invited him in and left him panting to dive inside. But not before she was ready. Slowly, he went in and out, a tiny bit deeper with each pass. The control it required not to plunge into her made his legs shake and his brain fog.

She begged incoherently. No words formed, but her tone told him she wanted him as desperately as he did her. He had to give his mate what she required. On the next pass, he didn't pause but slowly pushed forward. She expanded to take him in, centimeter by centimeter by centimeter.

She wrapped her legs high around his hips, dragging him deeper. He resisted her pull, continuing his slow, controlled entrance. He would always give her what she needed above what she wanted. Their first time would be slow, an exploration of how they worked together and where the pleasure hid. No way would he risk hurting her with an uncontrolled release of passion. Not this time. He would give her wild abandon if she demanded it, but not yet. There was no hurry. His life existed to please her. Finally, seated fully inside her, he held still until she opened her eyes and met his.

His heart clenched, and tears pricked his eyes. Her beauty overwhelmed him.

Never breaking eye contact, he rolled his hips, coming out of her a small amount, then back in. Slowly, the momentum built. His thrusts came faster with each pass, her legs still locked around him. Their gazes never faltered.

The pleasure was too much. He shuddered as her eyes fluttered closed. He pressed his fingers to her clit, and she clenched around him like a vise, milking his hot release from his throbbing cock. Would his seed prove fertile? She would probably shoot him out of an airlock if she knew what he was hoping. He kissed her, prepared to overcome that resistance too, should the fates grant him such an opportunity.

"Dez." She blinked up at him. "I don't think I can feel my lips."

He laughed. "Which ones."

"Neither. My body went to space again. How do you do that? You send me into the stars."

"You are always among the stars, my queen. You are the sun, and I am the planet held in your thrall."

She kissed him. A sweet smile plastered on her face when she closed her eyes. Dez left her body regretfully. If he could find a way to live between her legs, he would do it. He settled for wrapping his warm body around her cooler one and held her tight to him as she slept.

Dez woke to empty arms.

She'd left.

That didn't bode well. Their night of spectacular love-making should have changed things. Should have made her finally admit that she was his mate. Her absence had him suspecting he'd been unsuccessful at changing her mind.

There was no time to wallow in his misery. He had a crew to feed, dogs to train, and a mate to seduce. He would continue the path that had led her to his bed. She might have been able to leave, but he would do his damnedest to make sure she ended up spending every night they had together with him. He couldn't give up. He wouldn't. He believed in true fated mates.

CHAPTER 35

Cyra sat at the table, eating the breakfast Dez had prepared. She refused to give her crew any insight as to what had happened in Dez's quarters. She asked them questions like a captain should. Unfortunately, she couldn't seem to focus on their answers. The things Dez had done to her body kept playing through her mind like a video. He was the best thing that had ever happened to her and her worst mistake. She had to find a way to keep him at arm's length if she would keep her sanity and stay focused on her goals. She couldn't let one night of fucking ruin her entire life.

It hadn't been *fucking,* though. It had been the most intense lovemaking she'd ever experienced. She didn't know sex could be like that. Maybe it wasn't like that with anyone else but Dez.

That would be horrible.

To have tasted and never taste again. To have seen color and now be blind. To have sailed weightless among the stars only to be forever grounded. She refused to believe it. Dez was just a young, virile male. Yes, they seemed to have a connection, one he insisted was once in a lifetime, but she traveled the galaxies. She would find it again, or something like it. It would be good enough.

"Cyra? Hello, Cyra? Anybody there?" Rhysa waved a hand in front of her face.

Damn, she'd been caught, lost in her own thoughts. "What?"

"I just asked you three times if you wanted to review the revised flight plan with me. We were able to pick up some new data on dust cloud coordinates, and I made some modifications."

"Of course. Right after I finish here."

"Fine, I'll meet you on deck." Rhysa rose to leave.

Apparently, the rest of the crew had already finished eating and left.

"I'll come with you." Cyra hastily stood and followed Rhysa rather than be alone with Dez in the galley. What could she say to him? *Thanks for the orgasms, but you're still cargo.* She couldn't be that much of an asshole, even if it was true.

Cyra managed to keep herself occupied the entire cycle. She spent more time than required discussing the flight changes with Rhysa. She reviewed the systems with Blaize until her eyes glazed over. That female could make the dead rise just to escape her never-ending verbal spew. She met with Bodi. They discussed her duties and set up some communications to be transmitted as soon as they were within range of a communication satellite. She visited with Veda and learned more about hydroponic gardening in space than she'd ever wanted to know. She even updated logs that no one would ever see until her eyes ached. Her thoughts were filled with Dez during every moment. She had avoided checking on the dogs to evade him. But she couldn't resist any longer.

She pressed her hand to the access panel on his door, requesting entrance. The door slid open almost instantly. Dez stood in the middle of the room. He appeared to have been waiting for her.

"Come with me."

"Yes, my queen."

"Your captain," she said firmly, moving toward her own quarters.

"That too," he said quietly in her ear.

She shivered. He was right behind her. So close he was almost touching her as she placed her hand on her room's sensor. Once the access panel acknowledged her, the door slid open to reveal her own more spacious quarters. She stepped inside and grabbed him by the shirt, dragging him in behind her. The door closed, and she pressed him up against it, kissing him deeply. More, she craved more of his taste. Craved the feel of his bare skin against hers. Craved the feeling of him stretching her as he thrust inside her.

She stepped back.

"I missed you this morning, my queen." His gaze seared through her.

"I had things to attend to." She tugged off her clothes. "I don't want to talk, Dez."

Dez yanked his shirt off and dropped it on the bench at the end of her bed.

The sleeping platform was wider than the one in his quarters and not mounted to the walls on three sides. The padded headboard ended below a large portal with a view of the stars.

She planned to use every square inch of this big bed. He sat down and carefully removed his shoes. Her laughter bubbled up as she recalled the header he had taken when they were trying to strip in his room during the previous cycle. He glanced up, heat smoldering. His arm muscles rippled, and the breath left her body. The awkwardness between them had burned away, leaving heat and hunger.

He freed his stiff cock from the confines of his pants. Her mouth watered, and her pussy gushed. "Get on the bed."

Dez followed her instructions and sprawled across the mattress, his gaze never leaving hers. She crawled over him, and as her pussy met his mouth, her mouth met his cock. She wrapped her hand around the base and directed him deep into her throat. He gripped her hips, tugging her lower until his tongue parted her wet lips, lapping at her opening. She gasped around his length, finally fulfilling the fantasy she'd played with the entire cycle.

She licked at the open slit of his head, savoring his strong flavor. More. She sucked him hard and milked him with her hand. She would make him release his cum in her mouth and pull his essence into her body. Anything to get closer to him. The longing for him was inexplicable.

She ran her gaze from the tips of his long toes and up his meaty calves. His thighs supported her arms, and her blue skin looked even bluer against his charcoal shade. She dragged her hand slowly up the inside of his leg, committing the smooth warmth to memory. She discovered his sac and caressed his balls. With her nails, she scratched lightly over the skin, the texture so different from the rest of his body. There were no markings on his sac, just solid black. She rubbed her knuckles down the skin behind his balls toward his firm ass.

He rumbled in appreciation, the vibrations going straight to her core and causing her pussy to flutter toward orgasm. Not yet. She stroked the sensitive area again, sucking him deep at the same time. A third time, she pressed against that smooth strip of skin right before his ass. His rumble shifted to a roar. Her pussy spasmed. He erupted, and his salty stream shot deep in her throat.

A scream of ecstasy tore through her. Her whole body throbbed and vibrated. Her core clenched around his fingers as his tongue continued to work her clit until she had to shift away. She was spent. She rolled off him. Dez spun around and took her in his arms and held her, his front to her back.

"Thank you, my queen."

"You don't have to thank me, Dez. If anything, I should be thanking you for the best orgasms of my life."

"I am glad that we both found equal amounts of pleasure with each other, once again."

She caressed the muscles of his arms, tracing the dark lines that traversed his warm, gray skin. "Where were you today? I was all over the ship, but I never saw you."

"I worked out. Did some light training with Princess. Exercised the other thuringies. I tried out your water chamber. It isn't as relaxing without gills. I took inventory of our food stuffs and planned out the meals for the next several cycles. I helped Veda with her plants. They are growing quite nicely. We should have our first harvest soon."

"You were busy. I'm amazed we didn't run into each other at all."

"I didn't wish to interrupt your work. When you were in the same room as I was, I retreated into the shadows to allow you to work without the demands of your mate."

A tinge of regret that she couldn't be his mate stuck in her throat. She swallowed it down. "You were in the same room with me today?"

"Yes, my queen. My markings allow me to use the shadows better than others. As your gills allow you to enjoy the water more than others."

"I wish you would have interrupted me." And at that moment, she did. But that sentiment would become a problem once they arrived on Kolben. She'd spoken from her heart, but she shouldn't.

"I will remember that in the future." Dez kissed her neck where it met her shoulder. He continued to nuzzle her, kissing her hair, her earlobes, sucking gently. He took the tip of his tongue and traced the edge of one of the flaps of skin that separated to reveal her gills. She moaned involuntarily and thrust her hips back into him, finding his growing erection. He was so much warmer than her. He grabbed her hip and kept her ass pressed tightly to him. His cock was almost in her cleft. It was so good, so naughty. He should be inside her already.

Cyra raised her leg, opening herself up, and tilted her hips back farther, taking the tip of his head between her wet, needy lips. Dez released a potent growl. He moved his hips and shifted his tip inside her.

"More," she demanded.

He responded by pressing inside by the tiniest amount, still licking and kissing her skin. He released her hip, shifted his leg to open her completely, and squeezed her breast. His other hand was in her hair. She couldn't move, and he wouldn't move. He was making her insane with unfulfilled need. "Now, Dez. I need you to fuck me. Now."

"How, my queen? How do you want it?"

"Hard. Now."

He rolled her forward so that she was face down on her bed. He released her breast and her hair and pulled her hips up and back, and he thrust hard, fully seating himself inside her.

"Yes," she screamed and braced her arms so that she could push back to meet him. He wasn't making love any longer; he was ass-pounding fucking her exactly as she demanded. Exactly what she needed to get out of her head. He was all the way inside her, filling her and making her forget that they didn't have forever.

He thrust faster and harder. The tension in her body built and built, straining her skin to hold her together. He leaned forward and bit her neck below her gills, overpowering every other sensation. The pinch hurtled her atoms through a billion quantum bridges, scattering her through space.

Wetness pulsed over them where they were connected. Jets of hot cum filled her spasming cunt. She screamed again as another wave ripped through her, leaving her boneless. He held her together, anchored to the bed until she quit shaking. They lay there without moving, his soft cock still sheathed inside her.

Cyra wasn't sure when she fell asleep or for how long, but she had the best rest she could remember. She freed herself from his embrace and went to her private bathroom for a quick clean-up before she retreated to the deck. She didn't wake Dez. She had no words for him. How could she acknowledge what they had and what they would ultimately lose?

She tiptoed past the bed to retrieve a fresh uniform.

"Are you avoiding me?" His deep voice startled her.

"Hardly, I'm right here," she lied.

"You haven't said two words to me. I would have liked a kiss on waking up."

"I've never had someone stay with me overnight." She sat on the bench and put one foot into her pants. "I wasn't sure what the protocol was."

"It's not about protocol. It's about affection." He crawled along the bed behind her, swiped her hair aside, and kissed the back of her neck. The touch of his lips shot through her body.

She turned in place and kissed him on the lips. "I just don't know what to do with you, Dez."

"How about we decide not to decide? For now. Just enjoy the time we have."

"I didn't know I would like sleeping with someone."

"Not someone, Cyra. Your mate."

She closed her eyes and turned away. "So you say."

"I'm not going to argue with you." His hands skimmed her shoulders. "I'm going to spend as much time with you as possible. I want to sleep with you every night you will allow me to do so."

"Okay."

"Truly?"

"Yes."

He kissed her neck again. "I'll go cook for your crew, my queen."

"Your captain."

"That too."

<hr>

"Cyr?" Veda had found Cyra.

Did her best friend realize she'd been avoiding her?

"You can't hide from me any longer," Veda said as she stepped into the galley.

So much for eating at an odd time. "I haven't been hiding."

"Have you come to your senses yet?"

"About what?"

"Really, Cyra? You're going to play it that way. Dez. Have you made the correct decision about Dez?"

There was no decision to make. "I'm delivering him to Kolben, along with the dogs and the food from Arbotriz."

"Are you insane? You've been spending every night with him. He's your mate, and you're in love with him." Veda crossed her arms and raised a judgmental eyebrow. "Unless you're just using him as a sex slave."

The words slapped her. She gaped at her friend's harshness. "I would never use a sex slave. I've never treated Dez as a slave or used him in that way. We're enjoying each other, for now. We both agreed to this."

"So you love him."

Love was such a huge word. Dez hadn't dropped it for

cycles, but it seemed Veda was ready to take over. "I never said I was in love with him. We agreed to spend the time we had together. That time is ending."

"You are so ridiculously stubborn, I can't even begin to understand how you think. You have a male who worships you. He adores you and has done nothing but help you as you took over as captain of this ship. Yet you plan to drop him on a godforsaken planet and leave him to die." Veda shook her head.

"I'm not leaving him to die. Don't be so dramatic." Cyra picked up her empty dishes and cleaned up the galley, hoping Veda would let the conversation drop.

"He hasn't told you." Veda's voice was low as if she was talking to herself.

Cyra glared at Veda. "Told me what?"

"I did some research. His people...they can't be without their mate for very long or they'll die."

"Oh, please. Just because you read that on some site doesn't make it so. He would have told me." Wouldn't he? "Besides, I'm not his mate."

"Don't be dumb on purpose." Veda huffed and left.

Cyra stared at the empty doorway. She dreaded their arrival on Kolben, but she couldn't change anything. It was unfortunate that Dez believed she was his mate, not a dire medical emergency. They weren't the same species. She couldn't be his mate. It was impossible.

CHAPTER 36

Varik darted back to the engineer's station on the deck of the *Harlan Johnson*. Thankfully, the small ship allowed him to skip from station to station. More of the crew remained on Arbortriz than he'd calculated, including some who had previously claimed loyalty to him. Let them rot on that flowery little fuckfest of a planet. Wait until those idiots realized it was a female-dominated society, and they'd be expected to act subservient. They'd be begging him to come back and pick them up. As if he would return for traitors.

At least Jarn was still with him, along with a couple of maintenance tech types and the junior comm tech. Maybe a few others. It didn't matter.

"We're at the entrance to the bridge, Var— I mean, Captain." Jarn shifted in his chair, his face reddening. Varik would spank him for the slip later.

"Make the announcement, Karnek."

The comm tech instructed the crew to prepare. Everything should already be locked down. They'd had plenty of warning.

"Proceed," Varik told Jarn. He clicked his safety harness into place. He'd never bothered on *The Treasure*. The rugged ship was designed for bridge crossings, but as the first ER trip on the *Harlan*, Varik wasn't sure what to expect. Didn't matter what happened. As long as the ship stayed in one piece, it should put them at Kolben just in time to meet *The Treasure*. Or possibly a few cycles ahead.

The stretching sensation struck, pulling Varik into his safety straps and crushing his balls. He gripped the arms of his chair in an attempt to shift away from the pain but was unable to move. The entire ship vibrated violently. A panel from the ceiling crashed down centimeters from where he sat. For the first time, he second-guessed his plan.

With a shudder, they lurched out of the bridge. Varik shifted up in his chair and released the painful harness. "Crew check, Karnek," Varik barked out as he massaged his aching balls.

"That was intense." Jarn rubbed his shoulder, his face ghostly pale.

"Check your nav systems. See how far we are from Kolben." Varik didn't have time to coddle his lover. "Karnek, get a galactic time stamp." If they'd lost time going through the bridge, Varik would end someone. He ran system checks as he waited for confirmation that the ship was in one piece and when they would arrive. A blown temperature sensor near the engines. Could be a loss of structural shielding. He glanced at the ceiling panel lying on the floor. Not an unreasonable assumption.

"Karnek?"

The comm tech replied with the timestamp that confirmed they'd lost no time. Perfect. "Contact Kolben. Ask for emergency port access. We have damaged shielding."

The reports would support his assumption. The emergency authorization would get him on the planet in time to retake *The*

Treasure. Although with the limited crew, it would be a challenge to fly her. He could get the engines going with Jarn's help. But Jarn wasn't an experienced navigator. And Karnek couldn't be at two stations at once, assuming he had any engineering experience. *Fuck.*

Varik would figure out the logistics once he had his ship back.

The tracker on *The Treasure* wasn't pinging, but there was nowhere else they could go this far out. As it was, they'd need more fuel. In fact, so did he. It would be much easier to fuel the *Harlan* than *The Treasure.* Much easier to fly with his existing crew.

"We have permission for a three-cycle repair stop, Captain." Karnek interrupted Varik's spiraling plans.

Three cycles should be plenty. *The Treasure* should arrive shortly. Then it was just a matter of taking Cyra out of the equation. Except did he want to staff *The Treasure*? Spend all his time grasping at transport contracts, shaving his fees down to the bare minimum? Technically, he had a ship. The *Harlan* was in need of some repairs, and the grant organization might come looking for it. Or not. Twalley had the ship before he received the influx of credits. Who owned the *Harlan Johnson*?

Varik laughed.

He did, for the time being. And perhaps he could make that permanent. A black market GID chip, some paint on the freshly replaced panels, and the ship would no longer be the *Harlan Johnson.* Or he could rig a transfer of ownership predated to Twalley's death. He had options. And none of them required repossessing *The Treasure.*

But just because he'd changed his mind about what he wanted didn't mean he was giving his ship to Cyra. She didn't deserve it. Didn't earn it.

"Prepare for entry," Jarn announced over the ship's speakers.

Varik settled into the captain's chair. First, he'd fix the *Harlan*, then he'd figure out how to freeze Cyra out of her theft of *The Treasure*.

CHAPTER 37

KOLBEN CAME into view on the screens mounted like windows on the deck. A frozen round ball floating in a dark cocktail but much more deadly. Cyra shivered as if she could already sense the horrible cold air crossing through space and filling her heart. It was nothing like Din' Gale. The complete opposite. Dez would hate Kolben.

The contract that had seemed like such a lifesaver was actually killing her. Leaving him there would break her and, if what Veda said was true, kill him.

She still hadn't asked him about that. They'd spent their rest time making love as if they had all the time in the universe.

"Captain?" Bodi's voice roused Cyra from the sweet memories of Dez. "You missed first-meal?"

Cyra checked the time. She'd been on deck a lot longer than she realized. "Did you need something?"

"Dez doesn't look good either. You should talk to him." Bodi took her position at the comms station. "I'll contact Kolben and get authorization to land. I'll verify with Rhysa, but I think we're about twenty clicks out."

A twist of dread knotted in her stomach. A single cycle before they landed. She stood from the captain's chair, stiff from not moving and from everything Dez had done to her body. Had he known how close they were to parting?

"I know it's not my place, but if I were you, I'd keep him."

"If I did..."

She didn't finish her explanation but turned for the exit and walked slowly through the halls of the ship. Her feet dragged along the textured floor, and she inspected the pattern for the first time, noting the detailed valleys and mountains that created the anti-slip surface. The shine had long worn off the metal panels riveted together, creating the hive of storage behind the extents of the corridor. The lighting, set for daylight circadian rhythm, would dim later in the cycle, a nod to their planetary origins that circled various suns. *The Treasure* was huge and had flown for g-years before Cyra had ever joined Auvi's crew. Ships like her weren't made anymore. Owning her had been more than a dream come true.

But as she lingered in the galley door, her gaze locked on Dez. Mesmerized by the way his muscles shifted and bunched as he cleared the remains from the earlier meal, she may have stopped breathing.

"Hungry, my queen?"

How did he know it was her? He didn't even turn around. And yes, she was ravenous, but not for food. For him. "Yes."

"Sit, I'll make you something."

His movements were sparse, directed, economical. He must have rearranged the contents of the cabinets at some point. Another item on the list of things big and small he'd done to make her life better. The thump of her heart filled her ears, every part of her body weighed down by the reality that he would be gone too soon. Forever.

He placed her tray of steaming food in front of her. She lifted her chin and met his heated yellow gaze. Guilt twisted her stomach in a knot. "Eat."

He sat down across the table from her, waiting for her to lift the fork to her mouth. She couldn't deny his gift, his nourishing of her body. But the food, which was probably delicious, tasted like dust. She ate it anyway, if only to keep her mouth from expressing her regrets. Her apologies. Her excuses.

"We're nearly at Kolben."

She froze with her fork midway to her mouth. After a pause, she found the courage to look at him. His eyes were sad. She set the fork on the half-empty tray. "Yes."

He nodded and crossed his arms, leaning on the table. "I'd like to see if we can secure a contract to deliver goods leaving Kolben. It doesn't make sense for *The Treasure* to travel such a distance empty. Would you let me see what I can arrange?"

"Dez?"

He closed his eyes. "Let me do this for you, Cyra. Let me take care of you until I can't."

He made it sound like he was dying. "You've already done so much for me. For the crew. For *The Treasure*."

"The least I could do." He raised his eyelids, exposing his beautiful golden gaze, and lifted the corners of his lush mouth in the imitation of a smile. Cyra clenched her jaw and willed the tears back.

"There you are." Veda burst into the galley, saving Cyra from falling apart.

"Me?" she asked, hoping for a reasonable excuse to leave the conversation with Dez.

"No, Dez." Veda turned her back to Cyra. "Could you help me check the misters? The upper levels don't seem to be flowing as well as they should, and I'm worried about the flowers not getting enough moisture to make the transition to fruit."

"Of course." Dez rose from the table. "It would be my pleasure."

"Perfect, I'll meet you back there. I just need a quick word with the captain."

Cyra winced. The conversation with Veda might be worse than the one she was getting out of with Dez based on Veda calling her the captain. Veda sidled over to the door and peeked into the corridor. She rushed across the room and hissed at Cyra, "Why haven't you stopped this?"

"What?"

"You know perfectly well what. Dez. There is no way you can leave him on Kolben. You have to fix this, Cyra."

"I can't." A ball formed in Cyra's throat, watery and spiky, threatening once again to bloom into tears. "I literally looked through every bit of our finances, and the credits to buy out his contract and pay the penalty for nonperformance aren't there. Won't be there for g-years. Even if we kept every contract we have. And even if we did have the ability to pay, there's no guarantee the mining company would agree to it. They have no incentive to release him from his contract." Cyra swiped at the stray tears that had slipped out.

Veda dropped into the chair next to Cyra and tugged her into a side hug. "This is awful."

"I know." Cyra sat up tall and pulled away from Veda before she fell apart. "But there's nothing to be done. If Dez can keep a positive attitude about it, so can I. He wants to help us secure another contract with the mining company so we aren't returning to Cassan empty."

"Even now, he helps you."

Another tear slid down Cyra's cheek. She brushed it away and stood. "I need to check with Blaize on our fuel."

"I should get back to the greenhouse." They parted when the corridor forked, Veda going to the cargo hold where her tomato plants were thriving. At least one good thing was happening on the ship. Maybe Blaize would have positive news. Cyra could use some. She continued to the engine room.

"Blaize?" Cyra called over a mechanical roar. If she had ear protection in, Blaize would never hear her. Cyra searched the room and finally found Blaize back at her station. They must have been circling each other.

"Captain?" Blaize freed one of the devices from her ear canal. "What are you doing here?"

"Checking in. We'll land at Kolben within the coming cycle. Everything good for docking? Do we have enough fuel to get back to Cassan?"

"Yeah, of course. All good." Blaize's head bobbed. She bit her lip.

She was holding back. "What else?"

"It's about Dez. Are you sure you want to leave him on Kolben? I mean, he's such a great guy, and his cooking is amazing, and everywhere we go, he gets another contract. And it just seems like such a shame to leave him in such a nasty place. He shouldn't have to spend his days underground mining in dangerous conditions. He's worth so much more than that. I mean, not that he has to have a worth, but he's a really good guy, and I feel awful leaving him. Especially when it's clear how much you two love each other, and then Veda mentioned that if you leave him, he could die—"

Cyra held up her hand to stop the flow. "It's not my decision."

"But you're the captain."

"Exactly. I'm the captain contracted to deliver Dez to Kolben." The one whose stomach was in knots over the situation. "But I'm not Dez who indentured himself. I'm not the mining company executive who authorized the purchase of his contract. And I don't know what Veda told you, but Dez hasn't said anything about dying to me. And yes, I crossed a line. One

I never should have. That's on me. But there is nothing else I can do. So if our systems are prepared for a solid landing and we have the fuel to leave, I think I'm done here. I'll be in the wet room if anyone needs me."

Cyra spun on her heel and left before Blaize could start again. If she ran into Rhysa on the way to her water tank, she might just punch her to avoid another conversation about how she was failing Dez and how she should change the outcome of a situation she didn't create and had no power to fix. Not unless she was willing to sacrifice everything and everyone else.

CHAPTER 38

Dez halted at the end of the ramp when the full force of Kolben's icy winds whipped through his many layers of clothes and froze him to his bones. Each exhalation formed a cloud in the frosty air. Gods, he'd never been so cold in his life. When he'd packed the warmest clothes, made from the best fabrics available on his planet, he'd envisioned being too warm as if he was overpacking. Not even close.

He took a few more steps down the ramp. Cyra caught up to him, and he glanced over at her. Arms wrapped tight around her body, tendrils of emerald hair waving in the icy gusts, she was slightly bluer than normal. If he could, he would wrap her up and take her back to her bed. She hadn't let him in when he'd gone to her last night. He was almost certain she'd been crying when she told him to go back to his own quarters.

Despite working the issue from every angle all through the rest cycle, he'd come to no solution. So there they were on the ramp, walking to his doom. But he still had time to help his mate. "We should meet with the canteen people and get the produce delivery and the dogs handled first. We can tell them who I am after that."

"Let's ask this guy." Cyra pointed at a shape that came toward them, wrapped in a huge coat with a lined hood.

Dez decided he'd have to acquire the same outer gear. Although he wouldn't need the protection for long.

Cyra and Dez met the man midway between the landing pad and the building from which he'd come. Dez held out his hand, but the man waved him off. "Inside."

They sped up to a jog to keep up. As they arrived at the building, Cyra stopped abruptly and craned her neck toward another launch pad. Dez grabbed her arm and dragged her inside. There was a cavernous space with doors around the perimeter. Maybe offices. Didn't matter. He had to find out what caused Cyra to balk. "What did you see?"

"I thought... but that's impossible."

"What?"

"Not what—who. Varik. But it must be someone who looks like him."

Varik. Cyra had told him stories. So had Veda and Blaize. The man was Chalcanthian like Cyra. Blue. Not many of their people left their home world—the water planet. It was too hard on their systems.

Inside, the man introduced himself as Derrain and focused on Cyra once she announced she was the captain. Dez liked the man for that. Most of the people they'd dealt with over the past g-months had kept their attention on him despite his queen having all the authority. Maybe it was that her inner confidence had grown, and it was easier for everyone to see her as the leader she was. Dez shifted toward one of the thick windows next to the door they'd entered.

"There is one development regarding the thuringies." Cyra clasped her hands together.

"What's up?" The man didn't seem to be too concerned.

"You may not have been aware, but there was a female in the pack, and she gave birth. To another female."

"Huh? I don't have a budget to cover any additional medical expenses. Not sure what I'd do with a puppy." He rubbed the back of his neck.

"We are prepared to keep it, but felt you should have the first right of refusal."

"The bitch is still in good health?" The man's hands went to his hips, and he widened his stance, readying for a confrontation.

"Perfect. I'm sure you can confirm that with your intake scans."

Dez beamed as she repeated the words they'd planned.

"That works." He relaxed. "Let's sign the paperwork and get an insulated transport out to your ship to move the goods."

"Sure." Cyra nodded. "Dez, you'll be alright here?"

"Aye, Captain. I'll assist with the transport." Dez said it more for the man's instruction than Cyra's. The transfer would be his last chance to spend time with Credit, and Queen and the others. Princess was almost fully weaned, but there might be some resistance from her dam and sire to leave her.

Cyra gave a quick nod before striding away. "I'd like to talk to you about what *The Treasure* could transport for you back to Arbotriz or Cassan. Since we'll be coming out here on a periodic basis..."

Her voice became too distant to hear, but she didn't need him. She owned her role as captain. His heart expanded with pride and admiration. She was beyond amazing.

Movement out the window caught Dez's eye. Someone was running past the high tower that held the landing assistance personnel, carrying a large case. Their outerwear was even less appropriate than his own. So probably not Kolben personnel.

But the guy wasn't blue, so not Varik either. A truck pulled up, blocking Dez's view of where the man went.

Dez exited the warmth of the building. He opened the passenger side door. "You collecting the goods from *The Treasure*?"

"Sure am."

Dez climbed in and shut the door. "I'm Dez. I'll help you with the thuringies."

"Cool, man. Those things scare the tits off me." The driver was a big, hairy guy. Rhysa's type if the stories he'd heard were true. The man should be more concerned about her than some well-trained dogs.

Sure enough, Rhysa followed the male back to the cargo bays and "helped" him with the fresh produce. Dez would have waved her off, but it gave him time to muzzle each dog and pet Credit, who pressed his big head into Dez's waist. "Don't worry, boy. We'll still see each other."

Credit barked.

Dez laughed.

Until the dog barked again. Then the entire pack alerted. They pulled on their leashes, dragging him from the cargo bay. Princess followed on his heels. He released the leashes and tucked Princess in a kennel. She was too little to get exposed to the cold temps of Kolben.

The dogs raced for the exit. Had they smelled the fresh air? They'd never acted like that in all the cycles he'd worked with them. Dez ran as hard as he could. They were already on the ramp, but instead of running into the open space as he'd expected, they ran under the ship and came to a screeching halt. Single staccato barks punctuated the frigid air.

Footsteps in the snow led up to where the dogs had trampled the trail. Dez traced his gaze over the metal panels of *The Treasure*. There, on the side of Cyra's ship, a gray metal box clung to one of the access ports. Blaize's engine room lay beyond if Dez had the dimensions correct. Had the dogs heard it being placed? Or something worse? The dogs could smell things no humanoid ever could.

He placed a hand on the box—warm. And big, like one of the screens on deck, but thicker, much thicker. A red light blinked at the base.

A horrible foreboding filled his chest.

He grasped the box with both hands and tugged. After a brief resistance, long enough for doubt to shoot through him, the magnetic connection released. Dez clutched the box close.

"Vas." Dez held up his palm to the muzzled dogs. He dashed away from *The Treasure*. Away from the tower. Away from the office building, thanking the gods when the thuringies obeyed his command to stay. He reached the end of the landing pad.

The box began to beep. Dez stopped.

The red light was solid.

Dez lifted the box to throw it as hard as he could toward the open icy field.

CHAPTER 39

THE ORANGE-RED GLOW lit up the screens of the *Harlan Johnson*. The beauty of the explosive fire against the frozen landscape took Varik's breath. A moment later, the boom reverberated through his chair on the deck. He craned his neck to peer down the darkened hallway. Jarn should be bursting in at any second. Should already be here. Varik's chest tightened. "Karnek, where's Jarn?"

"Unknown, Captain."

Fuck. The smoke and kicked-up ice settled, and *The Treasure* appeared on-screen.

No.

It should be a mess of rubble. Where was the gaping hole? Where were the fire suppression units coming to douse the fuel rods in foam before they blew too? Where was Jarn?

Movement drew Varik's attention from his perfectly intact ship. Kolben personnel. "Karnek, launch."

"Uh, Captain?"

Varik darted to Jarn's seat. The navigation had already been programmed in. "Tell everyone to brace for launch."

Karnek made the announcement. Varik clicked the harness in place, the one that should have wrapped his lover in safety.

But if his lover had failed, it was likely he was dead. Jarn would want him to escape. Varik keyed in the launch sequence and braced. The *Harlan Johnson* shot into the air.

As soon as they cleared the atmosphere, he checked their fuel readings. No way they could make it to Cassan. Arbotriz would be a stretch. Would the Kolben authorities come after them? Varik hadn't seen a bunch of ships on the pad ready to launch. There had been a few small response ships in the storage units he'd sniffed around. Nothing that would allow them to chase the *Johnson*. But their comms could cross distances. Varik racked his brain for a solution.

"Captain?" Karnek's inquiry gave Varik the kick he needed.

"Find an off-books fuel depot. Darknet."

"Aye?"

"Now. Closest one." There was no point in not accepting the reality of his position. Even if he wasn't being held responsible for the bomb yet, he would be. And he had a stolen ship and was flying without an authorized flight plan or authorization to leave the planet. All of which were punishable offenses. He was officially a criminal. Accepting that fact opened doors—closed some too—but since Cyra still had his ship and *The Treasure* was still operational, Varik still had work to do.

And she had another debt to pay. Jarn. An aching hole opened in Varik's chest. He'd lost Jarn. And it was all Cyra's fault. There was no way the bomb should have failed. How had it exploded and killed his lover? Varik might never figure that out, but he knew to his bones it was Cyra's fault. She might as well have slashed a knife across Jarn's throat. Varik would get revenge for him. No matter how long it took. And instead of settling for destroying *The Treasure* as he'd been willing to do, the loss of Jarn meant war. Not only would he take back *The Treasure*, he would destroy Cyra and everyone else who dared to help her take what was his.

"I found something, Captain." Karnek pointed at his screen.

Varik rose from Jarn's chair.

"A Darknet posting for a three F."

"A what?"

"A fuel, fix, and fuck station."

Varik peered at the posting on Karnek's screen. He quickly calculated the fuel they had and the distance to the anti-authority space station. "Perfect. Send the coordinates to the nav station."

He plugged in the data to the navigation and authorized the route twice. The computer didn't recognize the location in space as a valid destination. But Varik was no longer playing by the rules. Technically, he never had. He had no illusion that the crew would keep their stop at the dirty station a secret. With this move, he would never be able to pass as legitimate again, and he didn't fucking care.

CHAPTER 40

Cyra slammed open the door to the office. Something had exploded. In her mind, *The Treasure* was in pieces, permanently destroyed. Men in parkas erupted from other doors. A vehicle with a red strobe and alarm raced across the landing pad, its spiked tires churning up the ice and snow. Her contact, Derrain, caught up to her, grabbing her shoulder.

"What?" She wrenched out of his grasp.

"Return to your ship. Run a safety scan. Now."

She turned from where the vehicle was headed to find *The Treasure* standing solid, exactly where she'd left it. A ship streaked overhead.

"Unauthorized departure." A mechanical voice echoed the announcement three times. More uniformed men appeared on the launchpad in vehicles and on foot. A dozen of them surrounded her ship, their weapons held upright, close to their chests.

She stopped, facing the one who had taken position at the base of her reopening ramp. "Cyra Maejzur, Captain of *The Treasure*. I was told to return to my ship."

The ramp touched the ground, and the guard turned sideways. Cyra marched up the ramp. Her crew stood shoulder to shoulder with the five dogs at their feet, concern wafting from them like smoke.

"Security scan is running. Nothing so far," Rhysa said.

Veda clasped Cyra's forearm. "Where's Dez?"

"Clear," Blaize said as she pressed the button to close the ramp.

"Wait." Cyra spun to the quickly closing ramp. Bodi's arms wrapped around her before Cyra could throw herself back into the chaos. "I have to get Dez. He was in the offices. I left him there to talk to the contracting agent. He should be here." Cyra begged Veda with a look. "Please tell me he made it back here."

Veda shook her head. Bodi tugged Cyra out of the bay and back to the galley.

"I'll make tea," Veda said, pulling items from the cabinet.

Cyra sagged into one of the chairs. Dez was okay. He had to be. He'd probably gone with the mining personnel to help with whatever had happened. Of course he did. That was so Dez. In a few minutes, he'd be knocking on the door.

Bodi's wings flittered rapidly. "Maybe he sent a message." She rushed back into the corridor, presumably headed for her station on the deck.

It was too soon for Dez to call. He'd be busy helping for a while. Cyra sipped her tea and told herself she was over-reacting.

"I'm going to check the scan." Rhysa left.

Blaize sat beside Cyra. Veda set cups on the table and took the seat on the other side of Cyra. The hot liquid settled Cyra enough to recall what she'd seen before the explosion. "I saw Varik. At least I'm pretty sure I did."

"What?" Blaize thumped her cup down, and a bit of hot liquid splashed over the edge. "What is that fork-tongued devil doing on Kolben? Did he follow us? Did he set the bomb? I wouldn't put it past him. There's no low he won't go to—"

Cyra interrupted. "If it was him, he got here before us. The only other ship was already on the tarmac before we landed."

"Wormhole?" Blaize's voice was low as if she was asking herself. "But how would he have known?" She left her seat. "I have to run another scan. That bastard has to have another tracker on this ship somewhere, and I'm going to find it and kill it since I can't kill him."

Veda swiped up the spill and cleaned Blaize's cup. "The dogs were unsupervised. They came up the ramp alone."

That meant Dez had led them off the ship and somehow lost control? Cyra stared unseeingly, sipping the tea. With every minute that passed, her confidence in Dez's safety winnowed away.

"Captain?" Bodi's voice brought Cyra back to the galley. "They're asking to speak with you."

Cyra set her cold tea down and went to Bodi. "On the comms?"

"Derrain is waiting for you outside."

"Right." Cyra blinked as she processed the words. "Dez?"

Bodi shook her head. Veda took Cyra's hand. "I'll go with you."

Cyra nodded and let Veda guide her out of her ship. The mining company contact sat in a sheltered vehicle. Cyra took the front passenger seat, and Veda sat behind her.

"We apprehended a suspect."

What did that have to do with Cyra and her crew? Unless it was Dez? But they couldn't think Dez would do something like this. "Who?"

"The name Jarn Ardkin sound familiar?"

Cyra shook her head.

"He's admitted to planting the bomb on your ship." The man steered away from the large office down a narrow road that had been recently scraped clean. He sped faster than such a narrow road warranted.

"The bomb didn't hurt my ship." Nothing made any sense.

"Your, um, crew member. Dez?"

Cyra grabbed the man's arm. "You know where Dez is?"

He swung the control hard in the opposite direction, bringing them back on the road.

Veda gripped Cyra's shoulders. "Don't kill us before we find Dez."

"Sorry. But—?"

Derrain rubbed the back of his neck. "Your man, he removed the bomb from your ship and tried to dispose of it. Crazy shit really. There was no way—"

"No." Cyra closed her eyes and wailed from deep in her soul. "Please no. Please don't tell me—"

"He's not dead. Not yet."

Cyra sucked in a ragged breath as tears streamed down her face. "Yet?"

"He was hurt pretty bad." Derrain pulled up in front of a long, low building with windows spaced symmetrically out from the double door that occupied the middle.

***

Pain radiated from every cell in Dez's body. He couldn't be dead. There was no way death would hurt like he did. He tried to open his eyes to see if he was alive, but even his eyelids hurt. He groaned involuntarily and could have screamed from the pain in his throat. Apparently, he'd tried to breathe fire recently. What happened? Had *The Treasure* crashed? Where was Cyra? He was breathing too fast but could do nothing to stop it.

"Dezmuhnd? Dezmuhnd, can you hear me? You need to calm down."

The man's voice wasn't telling him anything he didn't already know.

"Sedate him."

"No," he croaked despite the shards of pain that sliced through him. "Where's Cyra? What happened?"

"You don't remember?"

Dez shook his head a tiny amount, choosing to torture his aching muscles instead of testing his throat again. He must have been near death because he'd never felt so bad before in his life.

"Do you remember the bomb?"

There had been a bomb? The last thing he remembered was Cyra crying and turning him away from staying with her. A straw slipped between his lips, and he sucked the cool liquid down. Swallowing hurt like hell, but the moisture let him speak again. "Where am I?"

"Med center? On Kolben? Do you remember landing here?"

Cold. He recalled being cold. He had to open his eyes. His arms didn't move. One was lashed to a hard plane, where tubes rested against his skin.

"Try to stay still. You've been through a lot. You saved the mine and the space port from a bomb."

Dez took a moment to process what he'd been told. A mine. They must be at Kolben. A bomb. He wrinkled his brow at the man who must be a doctor of some sort.

"We had a ship land with an emergency mechanical failure, but we suspect it was a lie. I'm not sure why they would want to bomb us."

Fuck, if he was injured. What had happened to— "Cyra?"

"The captain of *The Treasure*?"

Dez nodded.

"She's fine. No one else was injured but you."

His mate was alive and uninjured. Dez passed out from relief and pain.

Cyra paused in the hallway, swallowing down the bile that had risen in her throat. Dez hadn't moved the entire time she'd been in his room. He didn't know she was there. She'd taken note of every single wound to his face, his chest, his arms. The gaping holes that crossed his tattoos. The arm that ended in a stump. She cupped her hands to her mouth to hold back the sobs as she folded in half.

Veda emerged a few minutes later. "Oh, Cyra. He's going to be okay. It will take time, but he will heal."

"He lost his hand." The hand that had cooked for her, caressed her, carried her through climax after climax.

"They have a very good prosthetics department here."

So they were good at saving people from horrific injuries. Ones that he would be at risk for after she left.

"But he won't be fitted for weeks at the soonest." Veda patted her arm.

"It was Varik, which means it was my fault."

"You can't know that. And even if it was, his actions aren't your fault."

"I want to speak to the man they caught. I want to know." Cyra pushed away from the wall to find Derrain.

Derrain was in the office building where Cyra had originally spoken to him. "Ardkin is being interrogated by the security officer. So far he hasn't said much."

The door Derrain led her to had a biometric lock. He held his palm to one sensor and looked into another small round sensor. With a heavy click, the lock released. He pushed open the metal slab but stopped Veda from entering. "I only have authorization for one, Doctor."

Veda took a step back. "If you don't return her to me—"

"Yes, ma'am." Derrain ushered Cyra into a long, narrow, empty space. White walls, white flooring, bright white lighting. The door clicked closed behind her. "This way."

Cyra followed Derrain through the hallway. They passed several dark offices that had a single window and door into the hallway. After they passed five, Derrain stopped. "He's in here. There's a glass wall. He won't be able to see you unless you go into the inner cell. But if you do, I'll have to scan you for any objects that could be used as a weapon."

Cyra bit back the question of whether that was for Ardkin's safety or hers. It was for his. "Fine."

She didn't recognize the man who was much younger than she'd expected. He was pale and blond. Muscular but lean. She couldn't see his eyes. He stood facing a side wall, his forehead resting against it. He arched back and banged his head. "Let me talk to him."

"I'll go in with you, ma'am," a deep, unfamiliar voice said.

Cyra jumped. She hadn't noticed the large figure in black sitting in a chair in the far corner.

"I'll wait for you out here." Derrain moved toward the chair the other man had vacated.

Cyra took a deep breath. The scan had been unnerving. Almost intimate and included being swabbed in various places for chemicals. She trailed the shadow man, the name she gave to the security officer since he hadn't offered one, past the glass wall that had slid back to provide a narrow opening. It closed behind her. If the Kolben Mining Company decided to keep her, there would be nothing she could do deep as she was into their lair, but she had to talk to the person who had hurt Dez.

"Jarn Ardkin, do you know who I am?"

Ardkin barely turned his head. With a squeak, he leaped backward. "Don't kill me."

"Do you know who I am?" Cyra used a stronger tone.

"You're the thief who stole Varik's ship."

Cyra explained how that wasn't true and who she was. "Do you know where Varik went?"

Jarn's blue eyes became watery. "He left?"

Cyra nodded.

"What about me?"

"What about you? You nearly killed my...a very special man." *Her mate* she'd been about to say. Because that was what Dez was to her. Her mate. And she'd been planning to leave him on this godforsaken planet like Varik had left Jarn. So what did that say about her?

"Varik told me no one was on the ship. I was supposed to place it and leave, but then I heard barking, and I panicked. I ran around the entire office building, trying to lose them. The bomb exploded before I could get back to the ship, and he left me." He stared at Cyra as if she would feel sorry for him.

"You don't feel bad about this at all, do you?" When he didn't respond, just blinked at her blankly, she turned on her heel. "Get me out of here," she told the shadow man.

"What will you do with him?" she asked Derrain as he drove her and Veda back to *The Treasure*.

"There will be a trial tomorrow. He's admitted his guilt, so it's simply a cursory procedure to get the documentation correct."

"He'll be punished?"

"He'll spend the rest of his life in the mines."

Good nearly came out of her mouth, except Dez was spending the rest of his life in those very same mines and he'd done nothing to deserve it.

Last-meal sucked. The crew was upset that Dez had been injured and would stay on the planet and the food was terrible. The fact that Jarn had been caught instead of Varik only added to the heavy remorse.

"Are we prepared to leave once the investigation is complete and we receive authorization?" Cyra asked.

"The fuel stores are full," Blaize told her with no excitement in her voice.

"I have a path back to Cassan charted. We're using a wormhole." Rhysa crossed her arms and glared at Cyra.

"Why?" Cyra didn't want to, but she didn't have a good reason besides it made her feel icky.

"We don't have any appointments to make. If we encounter a time cost, it will be irrelevant. The mining company uses this wormhole constantly. They haven't had any adverse results."

"Fine." Who cared if the experience made her feel horrible? She already did. It couldn't get worse. "Bodi, please arrange authorization to leave as scheduled."

"Yes, Captain."

They sat quietly for a few more moments, the air heavy with unsaid words. Cyra left the galley and went to her water chamber.

The chamber wasn't as restorative as she had hoped. Every time she let her mind drift, Dez filled her thoughts. The caress of the water reminded her of his hands on her body. Her lips tingled with the echoes of their last kiss. Her heart ached with an unexplainable pain. She would miss him deeply for a long time. She wasn't sure when she'd become so attached to him, but it had happened. She missed him more than she had ever missed Captain Auvi, and Dez wasn't dead. It was a shocking surprise. The water wasn't helping her. She got out quickly and hid in her quarters, hoping sleep would provide the escape she sought.

Cyra found no rest. Disturbing dreams that made no sense hijacked her sleep. She dreamed of Captain Auvi dying. But it wasn't Captain Auvi; it was Dez. He was in the captain's quarters, and she was the one who was putting a poisonous spider in the room with him. He was lying in her bed, dead. He didn't have the injuries from the bomb. But he was an unnatural blue-gray color, and his yellow eyes were open and cloudy, staring at nothing on the room's ceiling. She woke to the sounds of her screams.

CHAPTER 41

"You're awake." Cyra forced herself to smile, entering Dez's recovery room. He was ashy gray, and his eyes were dull. Tubes and wires had him so trussed up that she wasn't sure where to focus. Not on his missing hand. Tears pricked her eyes, but he shouldn't have to see her crying. "How are you feeling?"

"They are taking good care of me. I'll be fine." There was hardening in his jaw. "Why are you still here?"

Cyra stepped back, shocked by his tone. Dez had never spoken to her so coldly. "I...you...I wanted to thank you for saving the ship."

"No one was harmed? The ship is intact?" His eyes were almost as lifeless as in her nightmare.

"You were harmed." She ached to touch him, to run her hand along his bald head, to offer some kind of comfort, but she feared he would shut her out, exactly like she had done the night before they landed. Why had she let her emotions keep them apart when it was their last chance to be together? She would regret that forever.

"My injuries are not your concern any longer. You have completed your contract. And you have other deliveries to make."

She crossed her arms to keep from reaching for him. "What about when I next go to Din' Gale? What am I supposed to tell your family?"

"Tell them I found a good position and don't you dare tell them I'm injured."

Cyra glanced at where his hand used to be. There was no way she was that good a liar.

"Did you get a delivery contract from...what's his name?" Dez asked.

"Derrain?"

Dez nodded with a tiny movement. How could he ask her that? How could he talk about business as if he wasn't nearly killed? As if this wasn't the last time she might see him alive? Her heart ripped in her chest as if it was trying to free itself from her body so it wouldn't have to suffer this loss.

"I don't care about a contract. I care about you." Her eyes stung with the tears she couldn't let fall.

"I was only ever a contract. An item to be delivered. It's done. You should go."

"But—"

"Go, Captain. See to your crew and your contracts. I need to rest if I'm going to heal." Dez turned his head and closed his eyes.

She didn't move, staring at the man she'd fallen in love with. She'd spent all that time denying it, yet at that moment, she realized how stupid she'd been, how much time she'd wasted.

"Mr. Cuocua? I'm here to change your bandage." The med tech wheeled in a cart of supplies.

"Leave." Dez glared at her. "I don't want you here." He turned back to the tech, ignoring her.

She stumbled for the door, grateful he wouldn't see the tears that streamed down her cheeks as she left the room.

A few meters down the hall, two uniformed medics conferred over a portable comm screen. "Patient in room 6 isn't healing as expected."

"Isn't he Din' Galian?" the second tech asked, tapping her finger against the screen.

Cyra shifted closer.

"That's odd. We're seeing an elevated white count. Sure sign of infection. Are you sure he's unmated? Check his contract."

She scrolled again. "Broker's report states unmated. He should be halfway to healed, not getting worse."

"Let's run a full endocrine panel."

Cyra walked briskly past them as if she hadn't been eavesdropping. Unmated. Infection. Getting worse. The words ricocheted through her brain, tearing her apart and withering the shredded remains of her heart. Dez was dying because of her, and he didn't want her anymore. She didn't feel the cold as she exited the building and took the borrowed vehicle back to *The Treasure.*

"Cyr?" Veda met Cyra at the entrance to the cargo bay.

"Have the crates been loaded?" Not that she actually cared, but she was still the captain.

Veda's hands went to her hips. "Did you see Dez? Did you speak to him?"

"I did." The words were heavy, and Cyra barely got them out. "But I need to know if the cargo has been loaded."

"Where is he?"

"Who?"

"Dez." Veda gripped Cyra's upper arm. "What's wrong with you?"

"I saw him, okay? He kicked me out of the room and told me to leave. I have to check on the cargo. Get authorization to launch. There's nothing else I can do here." Fuck. Tears erupted again. "So let me do my job." She wrenched out of Veda's hold and ignored the gasp of her friend. In the far recesses of the cargo hold, she found the six crates of ore that were bound for Morgual. Close to Din' Gale. Where she could collect another load of produce and admit how she'd left Dez to die. Cyra slid down the wall and let all the tears flow. Tears she didn't deserve. Dez had been the one to sacrifice. Not her.

Princess whined in her crate. All alone. She'd lost her pack and her trainer. Cyra dragged herself over to the kennel and opened the door to comfort the puppy.

"Captain?" Rhysa's voice roused Cyra from where she'd fallen asleep against the cold metal floor of the cargo bay. Princess was curled up, asleep in her nest of blankets. Cyra's muscles protested against her effort to stand. "We have authorization to launch."

"I'll be right there."

Rhysa left without comment, thank goodness. Cyra stopped at her quarters and splashed her face with water. She dragged a comb through her hair and decided her uniform wasn't too wrinkled.

Rhysa raised *The Treasure* well above the flight lines in preparation to launch. Cyra let all her sadness and regret flow through her and placed her hands on the launch sensors.

Nothing happened.

The ship didn't even quiver.

Bodi glanced over, concern in her gaze.

"Ready when you are, Captain," Rhysa repeated.

Cyra channeled the memories of making love to Dez but found only more sadness and even shame. She'd let him go. Left him injured and alone. She tried getting angry with herself, at Varik for planting the bomb, even at Dez for sending her away. All she got was failure. "I can't do this. Set us down. Report mechanical issues."

"Captain?" Veda's voice broke through Cyra's frustrated thoughts.

"What?" she yelled at Veda and instantly regretted it. Her friend had done nothing to earn her ire. "I'm sorry, Veda. What do you need?"

"It's not what I need, Captain. It's what you need. As your medical officer, I'm concerned about your mental state."

"My mental state? What are you going to do? Lock me up and medicate me?"

"No. I'm going to issue you a prescription."

"What? You never recommend drugs."

"This isn't for drugs. It's a prescription for love, and you need to fill it. Or I will lock you up and file a mental report."

"Veda, that's ridiculous. 'A prescription for love' or you lock me up. Get serious."

"I'm completely serious. You need to go get Dez. Do whatever you have to do. Beg, cry, suck his cock. I don't really care. You are being an insane idiot to try to leave the planet without him. Even the ship knows better, and it's inanimate. The only one who doesn't acknowledge the truth is you. That, by definition, makes you insane."

Cyra looked around the deck at the rest of her crew. They were all focused on her, and no one breathed a word of dissent against Veda's diagnosis. "I can't deal with this right now. I'll be in my tank."

Cyra darted down the hallway, certain that the crew was figuring out how to commit mutiny. But they hadn't seen Dez's glare, heard him when he'd banished her, or felt the vacuum of space that existed between them. The water served to slow her heart and clear her head. It absorbed her tears without demanding answers or actions. She floated until she found peace. And with it came the answer. The only sane solution to an insane enigma.

She left the tank and went straight to her quarters. After several searches, she found the documents she required and completed them. With brief instructions to Veda as to what to do next, Cyra was free to return to Dez and beg his forgiveness, no matter how long it took.

CHAPTER 42

Cyra opened the door to Dez's recovery room and dropped her bag in the only chair. He'd gotten noticeably worse in the few hours since she'd last been in his room. His skin was peeling. Angry red wounds that should have been healing were opening up. His eyes were closed, and he'd made no acknowledgment that she had entered the room. He had never been unaware of her before. Something was terribly wrong. She softly walked to his bed and took his hand gently in hers. "Dez?"

He took a rasping deep breath. "What are you doing here?"

"What I should have done before. I can't leave you here alone."

"Why?"

"You know why." Tears pricked Cyra's eyes, and she blinked them back. "You knew long before I did. We're supposed to be together."

"It doesn't matter. If you don't want me, it will end the same way sometime in the future. I would rather just have it end now."

"Are you dying?"

"It doesn't matter." Dez shifted his gaze away from her.

"Of course it matters. Why aren't the doctors fixing you? They should be here. Giving you medicine and doing things. I thought you were healing."

"I was healing from the bomb blast. I'm dying because of mate sickness."

Veda's words came back to Cyra, but she had to hear it from him. "I'm making you sick?"

He shifted to face her again. She wasn't sure he would answer. But then he spoke with a sigh. "Once a Din' Gale male finds his mate, he needs to bond with her permanently, or he must be in her presence constantly. It was fine while we were on the ship because we were in reasonable proximity."

"Why didn't you tell me?" She grazed her fingers across his furrowed brow, seeing his pain and hating that she was the cause.

"Every time we talked about it, you insisted that we were temporary and you would be leaving me here. I did what I could to convince you we should be together, but ultimately, it's your decision."

"Veda was right. I'm an insane idiot. I didn't believe you would die. I didn't realize that I love you." She grazed her fingers down his sunken cheek.

"You love me?"

"Yes. I hurt so much, knowing I was never going to see you again. I couldn't channel any emotion to leave. I'm not supposed to go without you. I believe that, the crew believes it, and it seems even the ship knows better than me."

"You came for me because you couldn't take off?"

"No, I came for you because I love you. I couldn't take off because I was trying to leave the best thing that has ever happened to me. I'm sorry, Dez. I'm so sorry." She clutched his hand where it lay on the hospital bed. She wasn't looking at him, but she was sure he knew she was crying anyway. She hated crying, especially if someone was watching, but she couldn't help it.

"What do you want to do?" he asked her.

"I already did it. I transferred ownership of *The Treasure* to the crew. And you. They have to make deposits to your account here so that we have warm clothes and good food."

"We?"

"I'm staying. I'm your mate. You can't live without me, and I don't want to live without you."

He turned his hand and gripped her tighter. "You can't give up *The Treasure*. It's your dream, your future, your freedom. My captain—"

"Your queen."

"That too, but you can't. There's no way you can live on Kolben. They don't have water tanks. Your beautiful skin will suffer. And it's dangerous. I might not survive very long here. You've seen the statistics."

"My parents were very traditional. They clung to the NOAH traditions that were carried from Earth. Things like being wed to one person forever until death do you part. And I rejected them and all they wanted for me. But the teachings, the beliefs, don't disappear so easily. I don't care how long we have, Dez. I'm here with you. Until death do we part." Cyra bent and pressed her lips to his. Warmth, peace, and the sense of being home flowed through her. Sadness and regret no longer swamped her. He was her future and her dream for as long as it lasted.

"I love you, Cyra. I don't want this for you."

"I do. I want this because it's you, Dez. I don't want a life that doesn't have you in it. Even if it looks like the worst possible situation from the outside, it will be my heaven. I don't care what anyone else thinks. We belong together because *you* are my treasure, not the ship."

"My beautiful mate." Dez sighed and closed his eyes.

She lay her head next to his on the pillow, bent over his bed. She wouldn't leave the room. Not until he did. And then they would figure out what came next. His breathing deepened. She matched her breaths to his and settled into the rightness of being exactly where she was meant to be.

"Mr. Cuocua?"

Cyra jerked awake. Her back screamed at her. Two medics had entered the room, one with the rolling cart of scissors, bandages, gloves, and other supplies.

"We're here to change your bandage."

"I'm not leaving," Cyra said before Dez could kick her out.

"Yes, my queen."

"You're looking better," the medic with the comm screen commented, tapping away.

Cyra frowned and inspected Dez's skin. Not so ashy. His wounds were scabbed over. Even his eyes were brighter. "You're healing."

He tilted his head in acknowledgment. "For you."

She had no illusions that their life would be hard, but she didn't want him to feel bad about it. "Excuse me?" she addressed the medic. "How long will he have to stay here?"

"And you are?"

"His mate." Cyra puffed up her chest, proud to be mated to such an honorable male.

"So he *is* mated." The medic tapped faster on the comm screen. "I'll have to talk to the director." She rushed from the room. The other tech remained, cleaning the raw stump of his arm before bandaging it again. The loss of her ship was nothing compared to his sacrifice to save it and more importantly the crew. He was a true hero.

Veda burst through the door. "You can't do this."

"What are you doing here?" Cyra blocked Veda's view of

Dez's injuries even though Veda was her friend, a doctor, and had already seen his wounds. The instinct to protect him was too compelling to ignore.

"Do you know what she did?" Veda moved around Cyra to the end of Dez's bed, pushing the medic and her tray out of the way. "She gave up *The Treasure*. Transferred ownership. Well, guess what? We took a vote, and we aren't leaving without both of you."

"Veda, that's ridiculous."

"Excuse me." A stern man with dark-rimmed glasses and a shock of white hair came in the crowded room. "What is going on here?"

"Director." The medic shifted her cart. "I was just leaving. This woman..." The medic pointed at Veda. "...burst in uninvited."

"Everyone out." The director swung his arm out toward the door, nearly smacking Veda.

She ducked and left. The medic followed. Cyra tried to tug her hand free, but Dez didn't release her.

"She stays," Dez told the director.

"So it's true." The older man's eyes narrowed, and his frown didn't bode well for them. "Lying on the contact form has some serious consequences."

"I didn't lie. I discovered Captain Maejzur was my mate while traveling here."

"Well, you're useless to us now."

"I'll stay." Cyra wasn't sure what the consequences were that the director threatened, but Dez didn't deserve them.

"We don't have any facilities for married couples. As it is, the few Din' Gale and other tropical-planet workers have to share tight quarters within the entrance to the mine. It's the only place we can keep them warm enough overnight to be able to work."

Cyra glanced at Dez, hoping for reassurance or a solution.

"You were injured during the bombing," the director stated.

"Yes," Dez replied.

Cyra held her breath.

"Lost your hand."

Dez nodded.

"Prosthetics are expensive and, in these conditions, have limited viability. Meaning we have to replace them every few months. You're going to be far more trouble than you're worth."

Cyra gasped. How dare he? Dez squeezed her hand, and she clenched her jaw, settling for a good glare.

"The bomber was caught?"

Cyra refrained from rolling her eyes. The man was the damn director. He already knew the answer.

The director pressed his lips together, the tip of his tongue running in a line along the seam. His gaze traveled over Dez and then to Cyra. She scowled at him.

"Captain," the director addressed her. "Do you have medical facilities on board sufficient to care for this man?"

"Ye...Yes." What was he getting at?

"If we reject his contract, will you provide transport for him off Kolben and see to his medical needs?"

The man was running equations. Profit and loss. Dez was no longer a profit with his ongoing medical expenses and the need to house Cyra with him if he wanted Dez to live. And the man had the bomber instead. Ardkin. He would take Dez's place. Had probably already been tried by the local court and sentenced to a life of servitude.

"My captain?" Dez sounded nervous.

Shit. She'd been silent too long. "Of course, we'll provide transport and medical care."

The director tapped his screen several times. "I've terminated his contract and authorized his transfer to your ship effective immediately."

Before she could ask about the prosthetic or even respond, the man left. What the fuck had just happened? She faced Dez, and joy burst through her veins. "You're free."

"No." Dez shook his head. "I'm yours, my queen."

She pressed her lips to his. It was true; he was hers, but she was just as much his. Dez threaded his fingers through her hair, holding her to him. The kiss went on forever but was cut short when he gave a subtle tug. She lifted her head enough to meet his hot, golden gaze. "I love you."

"I love you too, Dez. Always."

"Aw. That's so sweet."

Cyra jerked up, ignoring the slight sting of her scalp as she freed herself from Dez's grip. Her crew stood in a semicircle around the end of Dez's bed. Rhysa fluttered her pink eyes and wore a sappy grin, totally fine with having interrupted the best kiss of Cyra's life.

"Is it true? Are they letting you go? You'll come back with us, right? I mean, I don't know exactly where back is. We have that load of ore to deliver to Morgual, but we really need to take a wormhole this time. I was telling Rhysa that we might be cutting it too close with the extra weight, but I know the captain hates ER bridges, so maybe we risk it. I don't even know what I'm talking about. I'm just so happy you don't have to stay here, Dez. Except you lost your hand, and that sucks, but I know a guy who had a similar injury and his prosthetic is totally integrated with skin sensation and everything. So once we make our fortune, we should be able to pitch in together to buy you the very best. In fact, we all agreed, since we all are owners now, that we shouldn't count profit until everyone on the team is taken care of, like the basic needs, and then we can divvy up any extra. And a hand is a pretty basic need—" Blaize paused to suck in a breath.

Veda put a hand on Blaize's shoulder. "We're so glad you're okay. I'll find out how soon we can get you released. You can stay in the med lab for as long as needed until you're healed. And we have plenty of supplies, thanks to your family."

"Thank you, Veda." Dez's deep voice resonated through Cyra. Her partners were as happy to have Dez back as she was or at least close to it. No one could be happier than her.

Bodi's wings fluttered. "I'm thrilled for you both. Now let's get the fuck off this ice hole of a planet."

CHAPTER 43

The next cycle, Cyra's team was in place to leave Kolben. Blaize monitored the systems and fuel from her station on the bridge. Rhysa had set their course for Cassan. Bodi chattered with the guys in the control tower. Veda had decided to join them for the launch and occupied the junior navigator chair. Soon, there would be more crew on *The Treasure*, but they were her team. The women who had made it possible for Cyra to realize her dream. And it was so much better than she had imagined. She didn't have to go it alone; she had support and love.

Veda had cleared Dez from remaining in the medical bay. After one planetary day and most of the night with Cyra by his side, his vitals were normal, and his wounds, aside from his hand, were more or less healed. Cyra had asked him to wait in their quarters with Princess to keep him company while she dealt with the launch. He might be cleared from staying in the med bay, but that didn't mean he would easily withstand the stress of a launch.

"Ready, Captain?" Rhysa asked.

Cyra nodded, hoping her plan would work.

"We're cleared to lift off," Bodi called out.

"Engines are go." Blaize's hands flew over the system controls.

The ship rumbled to life and lifted from the frozen launch pad. They would return with shipments from Arbotriz, but Cyra wouldn't miss the mining planet at all.

"Prepare for launch." Blaize glanced over her shoulder at Cyra.

Time to make the energy flow. Cyra rubbed her hands together and channeled all her joy. Her team, her ship, her mate. Life was more perfect than she could have imagined. Her heart swelled, and tears pricked her eyes, but she held them back. She funneled every bit of happiness she could into a roiling river of gratitude and elation.

A trace of a touch glided from her neck, slowly down her back to grip her hip. "My captain, my queen, I would like to assist you with the launch."

Her breath caught as he tugged her into his hard body, the heat of him melting her resistance. "How are you going to assist me, Dez?"

"Like this." He pressed his fingers between her legs, finding the perfect spot and rhythm even over her uniform. "And after we launch this ship, I'll strip you naked and make love to you."

He pressed his hard cock against her ass, and she closed her eyes, tilting her head back to rest against his shoulder. His fingers stroked her perfectly, heat building between her thighs. She moaned.

"And when you're ready, I'll mark you here." His tongue grazed her neck below her fluttering gills.

A wave of passionate energy surged through her body at the image of Dez's mating bite forever embedded in her skin like the tattoos he wore for her. She shivered with anticipation.

"Now, good girl." Dez's voice resonated through the

singular focus of the explosion erupting in her body. She slapped her hands on the launch panel. Awe and love rolled through her into *The Treasure*. They burst from the atmosphere in one smooth, powerful thrust.

"Yay!" her team cheered.

Dez released his hold and kissed her neck where his tongue had been moments before. "I'll see you shortly, my queen."

"Best launch ever." Rhysa grinned. "Nice show, too."

"I'll be in my quarters." Cyra ignored the heat creeping up her cheeks.

"Yes, Captain," Rhysa responded. "Do you want me to alert you when we're about to enter the ER bridge?"

"That won't be necessary. I trust you and Blaize will be able to handle it without me?"

"Of course. I just didn't want you to be surprised when you start experiencing the physical effects. I know you don't like it."

"I appreciate the warning, but I'm sure I'll be fine."

"Yes, Captain." Cyra caught the look that flashed between Rhysa and Blaize and chose to ignore it. Her only focus was being with Dez.

After leaving the bridge, she ran down the corridor to her mate. Lying naked across her bed in all his healthy glory, Dez casually stroked his cock. "I was wondering when you'd get here, my queen."

"Where's Princess?"

"Asleep in a bed in your bathroom." Dez's gaze went to the closed door.

"It looks like you started without me." Cyra toed off her shoes and opened her jumpsuit, still covering her body but exposing her between the open halves. She fisted her hands on her hips and tried for a disappointed glare that probably looked more like a heated request.

"No disrespect, my queen. I wanted to be ready for whatever you might *desire* of me." He pumped his hand again and wet his lips with his tongue.

Her core clenched with longing and anticipation. "You look ready enough, but I might need more assistance."

Dez sprang from the bed and was on his knees in front of her, his molten yellow eyes locked on hers. He was so gorgeous and built, and he worshipped her beyond anything she could ever deserve. She needed to give him something back. "I want to bond, Dez. Take me through the ritual. I don't want to wait one more second."

"Cyra," he growled up at her. "Are you sure? There is no rush as long as we are together."

"There is a rush. I wasted all the time we traveled to Kolben keeping you at a distance. I'm not letting one bit of doubt creep in to our relationship. I want to honor what we have, our love, by completing the ritual."

He stroked his hand up her leg to her hip.

She caressed his beautiful bald head. "Please, Dez."

"It's better if it happens during orgasm."

What wasn't? "That's never a problem for us. What do we do?"

"We must find our pleasure at the same time. As we come together, I will say the ancient words, and we will bite each other, marking our mate and sharing our blood." The hesitant look on his face squeezed her heart. She'd expected there would be blood based on the biting and his warning of it being primitive.

"What are the ancient words?"

"A prayer and a binding, in the old language. As the male I'm fusing my soul willingly to my mate and giving her every part of me." As if he hadn't already. He'd nearly died for her to give her the freedom to follow her dream. It would have been hollow without him.

"Do I say anything?"

"No, the taking of my blood is the act that confirms your willingness to be with me forever."

"I want forever with you, Dez, but I'm not sure how I can bite you hard enough to draw blood. I don't have teeth like you do."

"Trust the ritual will work."

Cyra gazed into Dez's eyes, and the connection she'd worked so hard to deny, the one she'd nearly lost—which, if she had, would have completely broken her—reverberated through every cell of her body and into her soul. "I trust you."

Dez rose and took Cyra's hand. His erection had sagged a bit during their serious conversation. She was sure he would fix that quickly. He led her toward the bed, and they worked together to slide the open jumpsuit off her arms and down her legs, leaving her as naked as he was. She leaned into him, his warm body pressed against hers, his hard cock against her belly. Their kiss spun on and on, twining them together. She gripped his shoulders, clinging to him so she didn't float away on the cloud of bliss he'd created.

"I want to lick your pussy until you overflow with need for me."

Cyra's body screamed yes, but as breathless as he'd left her, she couldn't form words. Instead, she sat on the edge of the bed, leaned back, and lifted each foot, placing it on the mattress. Opening her legs wide, she exposed her core completely to the sexy male who loved her.

He was on her in a moment, face buried between her thighs. His tongue lapped through her folds and teased her swollen clit. She shook with the need to come all over his face. He slid two fingers deep inside, beckoning her climax. Stars sparkled at the edges of her vision. She shook her head. It was too soon; they had to be together as one.

"I need you now."

"Yes, my queen." He shifted to plant one knee on the bed, under her thigh, and shifted her back. He lined up his hard cock and pressed the tip between her folds. A tease when she wanted him to fuck her.

"More," she demanded.

He slid inside, barely parting her, tantalizing her entrance and driving her crazy. She tried to move her hips to pull him in more fully, but he pulled back. "Put your hands over your head."

She did as he demanded, anything to get him deep inside her, where she craved him.

He gripped her wrists in his, pinning her in place, and slid in the barest amount more. If he wanted her to beg, she would from that moment to eternity. She'd beg for his cock, his cum, his love.

"Please, Dez. I need you inside me. Please."

"I'll give you everything you need, my queen." His small thrust wasn't enough. She shifted her hips. He pressed his body over hers, holding her down.

Cyra growled. She wrapped her legs around his hips and launched herself into a roll that resulted in Dez underneath her and his cock firmly shoved deep inside her pussy. Finally. She rode him, taking him hard and fast, her hands braced on his chest. He growled up at her. She glared at him, daring him to stop their pleasure. "You're mine."

"Always." He gripped her hip and met her thrust for thrust.

She fucked him harder and faster in response. His cock swelled, stretching her. Her thighs burned, but she couldn't stop. She was right on the edge and about to go over.

"Now, Dez. Say the prayer, now," she gritted out between her clenched teeth as she rode him. Her pussy contracted around him with aching need.

She didn't understand the words Dez chanted, but the sounds echoed through her louder than the rush of blood through her veins, more rhythmic than the slap of their flesh as they fought to become one.

He reached the end of the prayer and gripped the back of Cyra's neck, pulling her close. She bounced her hips, chasing the critical moment. His body stiffened, her pussy clenched around his cock, and she locked her gaze to his.

"Now, Cyra. We finish this now. I am yours forever, my love."

Dez opened his mouth and clamped onto the space between her neck and her shoulder just below her quivering gills. Cyra mirrored his action and bit. Her climax exploded through her, pulling her body in every direction and ripping Dez's orgasm from him. She broke the skin and brought his blood into her mouth. His bite didn't hurt as much as she'd expected. Instead, it sent her careening into a second wave of pleasure, and stars burst behind her eyelids. She forgot how to breathe as she exploded and coated her mate in her ecstasy.

Cyra didn't remember getting under the blankets on her bed or even lying in the correct direction to put her head on a pillow where it was now. Dez was beside her where he belonged. Where he would remain forever.

"Welcome back, my love." Dez brushed her hair back from her face.

"Was I gone?"

"I think we hit the wormhole as we were completing the ritual, and it overloaded you."

Cyra glanced around her quarters as if something would look different. "We already went through it?"

Dez nodded once his eyes locked on hers.

"We're having sex every time we travel through one of those."

"As you wish, my queen." He smiled at her.

She arched up to kiss his beautiful mouth. "Your mate."

"My love." He gazed right into her soul.

"That too." Always.

VARIK ROLLED AWAY from the blond. They were no Jarn. The novelty of the hybrid had been fun, but Varik missed his lover. What should have been a journey to take *The Treasure* back as its rightful owner and captain had only led to the loss of his dear boy, and the fucking gash, Cyra, still had his ship. *The Treasure* was his.

Knuckles rapped on the flimsy so-called door of the fuck-room. "Captain?"

"What?" Varik barked at Karnek. The escort shifted, putting their back to Varik.

"Ship's ready."

Varik hopped off the soiled mattress and yanked back the thin partition. "Repainted?"

Karnek grunted. "New title, too."

A spark of possibility arced through Varik. "What'd you name it?"

His man puffed up, exactly why Varik had let him name the ship. That and he didn't care what the name was since the only name that mattered was *The Treasure*.

"*Cain's Alibi.*"

"Excellent," Varik said, barely registering the new moniker. "What did the new title cost?"

Even braced for Karnek's answer, the number punched Varik in the gut. That cut a sizable chunk out of the funds Auvi had left him. "Are we fueled up?"

"Doing it now." Karnek tilted his head, clearly trying to see into the room.

Varik filled the opening. It was none of Karnek's business who Varik poked in his spare time. "Let me put on some clothes, and we can go."

"Sure we can't invite that one with us?" Karnek jutted his chin toward the room. "They'd please everyone based on what I heard."

Oh sure, invite the toy but tire of playing with it. Then Varik would have to be the one to shoot the fucker out the airlock.

"Overrated. We'll find new toys on the next stop."

"Good idea, Captain." Pointed yellow teeth filled the gap between Karnek's lips in what was probably meant to be a smile but only left Varik slightly sick.

Before Varik could close the panel, Karnek turned back. "Where are we headed next, Captain?"

"Cassan to secure more crew. Then we go in search of *The Treasure.*"

Karnek's cackling laugh faded as he stomped down the hallway.

***

Blaize dragged her hand across her neck under her tied-up hair. A bead of sweat trailed from her forehead down the side of her face. The engine room wasn't overly hot, but she'd been on edge since leaving Kolben. There was nothing she could pinpoint. After a perfect takeoff, their fuel-burn rate was within normal parameters. She'd checked every system report twice, inspected every manual gauge, and crawled through every crevice of the ship's heart she could reach. Nothing was wrong.

Except for the itchy sensation that wouldn't leave her alone. The dread that something was about to blow. Maybe it was her reaction to Dez removing a bomb from the outside of her engine and losing his hand. Perhaps it was the sensation that someone or something hadn't stopped watching her. The eerie foreboding had hit somewhere in the cargo bay and hadn't left her since.

It was probably too quiet. "I think I'll check out the stats on the rotating detonator. You know, the way it's designed on *The Treasure* is quite odd." She wasn't speaking to anyone, but her voice calmed her. "Emotional energy is transferred from the bridge apparatus through the converter, concentrated, and burst delivered right to the rotator, causing the spin needed to create the detonation. The RoDRE is technically pretty anti-quated technology, but whoever originally designed *The Treasure* was brilliant. The fuel savings is astronomical. Never having to burn fuel to punch out of the atmosphere is huge, especially with a ship this large. I'm kind of impressed Cyra could pull it off without Dez working her to climax on the bridge. I could die without seeing that. I mean, Dez and the captain are beautiful together, his dark striped skin and hers—deep blue nearly purple—with her striking green hair, I mean who wouldn't want to see them together. But not like that. I wouldn't be able to unsee his dick. I mean I like dicks, but his dick is taken."

Was that a snort? Did her engine snort? No way. Engines didn't breathe. Not like that.

Blaize spun around, searching for the source of the sound.

"Who's there? Show yourself."

Cifer clenched his hands into fists and bit his lip. Gods, she was phenomenal. That blazing red hair, nearly translucent skin, the lushest mouth he'd ever have the pleasure to kiss. Because he would absolutely kiss this brilliant, sexy woman before he made his way off the ship. But he couldn't show himself. Not yet. Not until they reached the station. If he did, he'd be out an airlock before he could finish selling an explanation.

If only he could find a way to keep her talking. He pressed himself into the wall panel letting his natural camouflage do the work of keeping his presence a secret. No more laughing. No matter how entertaining she was.

He had work to do and getting off Kolben had only been the first step. There was no room for error.

Remorse and regret washed through him. He'd let himself get stranded on that ice ball, and who could say what disasters awaited him on Cassan.

ACKNOWLEDGMENTS

First, last, and always, thank you to my husband for supporting my writing in every way. I love you!

Thank you to the Red Reines for everything you do.

Thank you to Brandi Doane McCann for another amazing cover and the fabulous series logo.

Thank you to Dayna Hart and Jenny Sims for the fantastic editing. Readers, please know that any errors you find while reading this book are mine. I'm incorrigible.

Thank you to my amazing beta readers who made this book infinitely better.

Thank you to Passionate Ink for providing a safe and educational forum for erotic authors.

And, most importantly, thank you to my readers who make it worth all the struggles to write!

ABOUT THE AUTHOR

Award-winning, best-selling author, Jordyn Kross, is an unapologetically naughty novelist who spent years honing her writing skills with tech manuals and marginal poetry before finding her passion for writing sexy, boundary-stretching happily-ever-afters.

When she's not writing, she's attempting to garden in the desert Southwest, hiking with her insane pound posse, and admiring that handsome man wandering around her house who continues to stay.

Jordyn enjoys saucy double entendres, pretending to be an extrovert, and is well-known for having no filter. And when she's not in social media jail, she can be found on Facebook, Instagram, and BookBub, or hiding in a dark cave peering out at the X file formerly knows as Twitter.